MISS
Matched

ALSO BY WENDY MILLION

When Stars Fall

MISS
Matched

WENDY MILLION

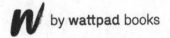

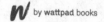

An imprint of Wattpad WEBTOON Book Group

Copyright© 2023 Wendy Million
All rights reserved.

Published in Canada by Wattpad WEBTOON Book Group,
a division of Wattpad WEBTOON Studios, Inc.

36 Wellington Street E., Suite 200, Toronto, ON M5E 1C7 Canada

www.wattpad.com

First W by Wattpad Books edition: June 2023
ISBN 978-1-99025-959-3 (Trade paper original)
ISBN 978-1-99025-960-9 (eBook edition)

Library and Archives Canada Cataloguing in Publication information is available upon request.

Printed and bound in Canada

1 3 5 7 9 10 8 6 4 2

Cover design and illustration by Lesley Worrell
Author Photo by Dianne Brandon Photography

For Jay-Jay, who taught me that a second (or third) chance can deliver the happiest of ever afters.

Chapter One

TAYLA

With the click of a button, my savings account hits zero. Shouldn't the moment be punctuated by something? A choir, maybe? Or a flock of doves zipping out of the computer in front of me? Or, since the whole office is decorated like a Valentine's Day commercial, maybe a herd of hearts? That much cash vacating my account should be celebrated or mourned. *Something* should happen.

"As soon as the money is deposited, Miss Murphy, we can get started," the client representative in front of me murmurs. "Wi-Fi must be slow today." He's staring intently at his screen.

Fingers of panic crawl up my throat, but I swallow them down. Words my dad used to say ping-pong around my head: *You know the good thing about money? You can always make more.* Except I spent five years making *this* money. If things had worked out the way I wanted, I would have gone on a vet exchange sometime within the past two years. Other ideas of what I could have used this money for play on repeat in my head, and the voices pointing out my folly sound a lot like a handful of skeptical friends and family members. A lower mortgage payment, less student debt, or state-of-the-art advancements for my vet clinic. Each would have been a more suitable use for this money, according to them.

Hell, I could have hired an out-of-work actor to pretend to be my husband for a very long time for the same amount of cash.

God, that might have been so much more value for my money. Why didn't that occur to me sooner?

Because you don't want just a husband, you want your happily ever after.

That's one of the taglines for this service, Soulmates Reunited: *Happily Ever After, Guaranteed.* And I've seen the results in person. Whatever magical algorithm they have going, it works—and after a string of failed starts with men from conventional dating apps, I'm done with things that don't work. No more men who say they're one thing and turn out to be another.

By coming here, I've taken my cue from my best friend, Ruby, who invested in finding her happily ever after with Soulmates Reunited. One trip here. One big fee. One magical meeting with Dean and Ruby was already planning her wedding.

As their frequent third wheel, I can tell they are disgustingly happy. The kind of happy I haven't been in a very long time. There's only so long you can be in the presence of that kind of contentment without having your own ache creep in. I want *that*. How do I get *that* again? So here I am. Sacrificing my bank account for a shot at lasting love.

"Are you staying in New York long?" Cade, the client representative, asks while we wait for my payment to clear.

"No. I'm headed back to Grand Rapids tonight. Well," I say with an uneasy laugh, "unless my match is here. He could be anywhere in the world, right?"

"That's right, but we do find pairings tend to happen geographically or culturally more often. Values and the way people are raised influence who we're attracted to as life partners."

"Right, yeah, makes sense." All of this was explained in a video call before I arrived in New York and sent my money down a virtual tunnel. Nothing I didn't already know.

The company has flooded the dating market with commercials, a podcast, and even a six-episode season of *Soulmates Reunited* on my favorite streaming service. I might have watched that series with a bottle of wine on a Saturday night more than once, thinking, *I want to feel that again.*

Everyone matched. Everyone married. Everyone happy. Soulmates Reunited is ubiquitous, and anyone who can afford to get serious about diving into the deep end of the dating pool seems to be coming here to do it. At some point, it started to feel like I was actively avoiding what was best for me, or at least that's what Ruby said after my last internet date gone wrong. I had the cash—why not spend it on the thing I wanted most?

Still, it's nice to be reassured I may not have to move to Australia to meet my match. Although my veterinary license could transfer—at least temporarily—to another country, which I know from applying to exchanges. Could I leave Michigan? Live somewhere else forever? I said yes on the company's application to get my appointment at the office, and now that's feeling a bit foolish. A cold sweat breaks out under my armpits.

"Okay," Cade says, "the payment cleared." He rises from his seat behind the giant desk and gestures to the hallway. "Your match awaits you at the end of our complex pairing algorithm."

"There's no way to get a top five, is there? Choice is good, isn't it?" My traitorous hand shakes when I stand at the threshold of the narrow, softly lit hallway. The walls are dotted with glowing screens. After a series of personality tests, the last pane will be the name of my soulmate. That's right. I've paid an exorbitant amount of money to enter an arranged marriage.

Well, not really. Whoever pops up on the screen can turn down the match. So there's that.

Not depressing at all.

"Just the one match," Cade reminds me without a trace of humor. "As you know, your life partner would have signed up for a matching service to even be in our

4

exclusive database. Whoever you're matched with is looking for a soulmate."

"They receive an automatic notification when we're
matched?" My voice quivers. "Is there any way to change
that?" Maybe give me a day or two to mull over their name,
stalk them on social media, build up some courage?

"If you choose not to pursue your match, you can join
the less than one percent of people who reject their pairing.
Either way, he'll be notified of his selection."

Hold on to Ruby, the little voice in my head reminds
me. Matched to Dean and married within six months of
meeting, using this service. In six months, I could be married to the love of my life. My savings, the fee, the risk
of humiliation—it will have all been worth it. Soulmates
Reunited has an uncanny ability to zero in on the person
meant for you. Everyone says so, including one person I
know personally and trust the most. Ruby called the process
magic. She'd never have met Dean otherwise. That's what
I need, a sprinkle of magic to bust me out of my six-year
dating funk.

With a deep breath, I step into the hallway and touch
the first screen. Before long, I'm deep into questions about
family background. The next screen covers the ways I like
to express love and have love shown to me. Each topic is
harder and forces me to think more critically about what I
want from a partner, from myself. The depth of the questions
surprises me, and I wonder whether I should have asked
more questions of the company. Are the men in the database filling out a questionnaire that's this detailed? It seems
unlikely, but how else are they matching so accurately?

The last screen before the reveal covers past relationships. The first question stops me short.

How did your last long-term relationship end?

Abruptly. I scan the options. Not one of them. *In a blur of missed signals?* Not there either. Instead I select *badly* and *dramatically.* In truth, the situation was more embarrassing than anything. The night we broke up, I thought he was going to propose. Could I have been any more clueless? Even six years later, the memory shoots a spike of anxiety down my spine.

The next question causes me to choke back a laugh.

What has prevented you from forming a lasting relationship?

Using my finger, I scroll through the options. The instructions say I can pick more than one. What's most accurate? My gaze strays to the same one over and over. Probably the most honest. I tap the word before I lose my nerve. *Fear.* Being blindsided tends to do that. While I was planning our future in my head, he was crafting our demise. The way he broke up with me was so confusing it made me wonder if I ever knew him at all.

The rest of the questions pass by in a blur as I comment on dating preferences and give my response to multiple dating scenarios. Finding the right answer in fiction is easy. Real life is much messier. How does a computer program account for that?

At the final screen, a big silver button is lit up in the middle. *Process Results.* My heart kicks, and I stare at the words. Of course I want a result. I paid a lot of money for this moment. Why am I so nervous about hitting that button?

'Cause once you do, you might actually have to pursue a guy, pursue happiness.

No more burying myself in work and Tinder dates. After I press this button, I'll have the name of the person I'm supposed to be with. Amazing, right?

"Cade," I call, and even I can recognize I'm stalling. "So, I just hit this button?"

He appears at the end of the hallway, framed by the light behind him. "Yes, Miss Murphy. The program will take a few minutes to run, so you can sit in the armchair at the end of the hall. The screen will alert you when your match has been made."

He explained the sequence to me before I paid. The woman who called me also took me through the process, and the TV show was quite detailed. Does he realize I'm just nervous?

"Okay, great." I nod, and, before I lose my nerve, I tap the button.

Across the screen, a bar appears, and numbers run along the top with the words *Comparing your unique profile with 5,679,459 others.*

"Hey," I call to Cade again, "there are only five million people in your database?" I was led to believe there were a lot more.

He slides his hands into his pockets, and the hint of a smile tugs at his lips. "That just means there are five million people who share at least twenty data points with you. Anyone else in the database would never be a good match."

"Oh," I say. "Okay." I sink into the chair across from the monitor and stare as the numbers on the screen decrease every few seconds. When the number is less than one hundred, I close my eyes as first names streak across the screen. Why does this feel like a gamble? It's supposed to be a sure thing.

"Tayla Murphy, we have found your match." The automated voice is surprisingly smooth and soothing.

I crack open an eye. All I can see is my name. I frown and move closer to the screen. Ah, I have to hit the *See Result* button. Goose bumps form along my arms, and I shake out my hands.

Just press the button. Read the name. See what happens.

With a quick poke, I hit the green arrow.

Tayla Murphy, you have been matched with Simon Buchannan.

I stare at the name in silence for a beat. "You've got to be fucking kidding me," I mutter.

"Everything okay?" Cade calls down the hall.

I roll my eyes. "Yeah, it's just . . . I know someone who has the same name as my match. Not the same person, I'm sure. What are the chances?" An uneasy laugh escapes.

Cade wanders down and peers at the screen. "I'll send their contact details to your phone. You get the city or town they live in and an email address."

I smooth my fingers across my brow. Of all the names to turn up on the screen, it had to be that one. Never mind. I'm sure this Simon Buchannan is nothing like the one I know. If I let a name throw me off, I might as well have stood around burning my money instead of using it for this. It's only a name.

"Just sent the details," Cade says.

"Great, thanks." I open my email and tap on the Soulmates Reunited message, eager to put this new Simon in place of the old one. Maybe he'll be from England or Australia after all? I scan the top of the message, which thanks me for choosing Soulmates Reunited, but when I get to Simon's contact details, my heart stutters to a stop, and a chill streaks across my chest. "Uh, Cade," I call, "I think there's been some mistake."

"Oh?" He's at the end of the hallway again.

This Simon Buchannan lives in Grand Rapids just like *my* Simon Buchannan. "Yes, I know who this is. There's no way we're a match."

Cade chuckles. "Sometimes people are surprised by who they're a good fit for. I know when my wife's name came up on the screen, I was not expecting her."

"No," I say. "No, you don't understand." The panic I swallowed earlier is creeping up my throat again. All my money, wasted.

"Let me see." Cade takes my phone and scrolls through the details. "Ah, he's from your city. That's great news."

"No, no, it's not." I let out a frustrated noise and cradle my head in my hands. When I look up, my expression must finally clue Cade in to my distress because the smile drops off his face. "I've already dated *this* Simon Buchannan. He left me for another woman."

There it is. The ugly truth.

My soulmate already decided I wasn't his.

Chapter Two

SIMON

I'm covered in vomit. When the drunk chick from triage turns pale and covers her mouth, I grab the nearest plastic bin and shove it into her hands. What a fucking day. I check the clock near the nurses' station before I draw the curtain around her bed. Five more minutes of this dumpster fire shift and I can get the fuck out of here. Aaron wanted to meet for a beer, but I'll have to text him that I'll be late. No way I can go like this.

Drunk Chick heaves again, and this time, she mostly hits the bin.

"This is so embarrassing," she cries, tears streaming down her face. "Why did I have to get a hot male nurse when I'm so, so drunk?"

"It's true," I say with a wry grin, "we're a rare breed. Also, you're drunk. So it's possible I'm not as hot as you think." How she can comment on my attractiveness when I'm covered in a half-eaten kebab and probably smell like shit thanks to the guy behind curtain number two is a mystery. She's probably seeing two of me anyway.

"God, your eyes are so green. Are they contacts?"

"They're real." My hands are braced on her bed rail, and I glance over my shoulder for the doctor.

"Are you single, Simon? Do you want my number?" She gives me a hopeful look, which is almost comical with the mascara running down her face.

"You know, it's tempting." I pretend to ponder the request. "Unfortunately, I have a girlfriend." That's a lie, but there's no need to make Drunk Chick feel any worse than she already does. Before she puked on me the first time, she told me she went on a bender because her boyfriend broke up with her on their anniversary.

I have been that shitty boyfriend, so when the contents of her stomach rushed out, dousing my scrubs, I wasn't even mad. Probably my ex-girlfriends would pay money to watch me being vomited on over and over. At least one of them would. If I'd known it was coming, I could have recorded it for them. Oh, who am I kidding? If I'd known it was coming, I'd have moved out of the way. No one would willingly smell this much like tequila and despair.

Joan Watkins, a middle-aged female doctor, throws back the curtain, focused on a chart. Anticipation stirs in my chest. I've worked with her before, and she's great with a lot of things, but she has an unusual quirk for someone in the medical field. I watch as Joan's nose twitches, and a line appears between her brows. "Is that—" Joan looks up and sees me, and her face pales. "Vomit?"

I'm practically gleeful when I admit, "It is." I hold out my shirt and shake my head in mock remorse. "Puked all over me."

Joan covers her mouth with the back of her hand, stifling a gag. "I'll have to get—"

"Yeah," I say with a smile. "Sure. Don't worry about it." Joan ducks out, and I hold back a laugh.

"Jesus, Buchannan," Wendy, one of the other nurses in the ER tonight, says as she pokes her head through the curtain. "You coulda warned Dr. Watkins."

"Where's the fun in that? I've never actually seen her lose it."

"Well, now she's losing it in the bathroom toilet." She sighs and comes in to survey the situation. "Severely intoxicated?"

"Bad breakup." I start to cross my arms and then remember the puke.

Drunk Chick groans. "I didn't see it coming." The last word is a slur before she begins to snore.

"Your shift is over, right?" Wendy glances at the clock.

I follow her gaze and realize my shift finished a few minutes ago. "Yeah, but I think I might stick around until she's been dealt with."

"You've got a soft spot for a lonely heart."

Even in sleep, the girl's expression is sad. Where are her friends? No one should be alone when they feel this shitty. There's something about her, though the hair color isn't dark enough, and the shape of her face isn't quite the same, that reminds me of someone I once knew. An ache spreads across my chest. If time travel is ever invented, I'm going back to that restaurant when I agreed our relationship was over and punching myself in the face.

"Don't tell anyone about that soft spot." I smirk. "Wouldn't want to give up all my toxic masculinity credits."

Wendy scoffs as she slips out through the curtain, and I sink into the chair beside Drunk Chick's bed. Aaron and I will have to reschedule that beer.

"I thought you were busy saving some damsel in distress," Aaron says as he flags down the bartender. I take the bar-stool beside him as he orders our drinks.

"Managed to track down her mom from her phone. Once the mom arrived, I left her to sleep it off." I pass the bartender some money for our beers.

"So, what's new, man? I feel like I never see you any-more. What are you working? Eighty hours a week?"

"Something like that," I admit, taking a gulp of my beer. Even when work is literally piles of vomit, my job is my life.

"You still sworn off women since you and Mandy broke up?" Aaron picks at the coaster under his pint.

"Yep," I say. I have zero desire to talk about Mandy. How can I get romantic relationships so wrong so often?

"Did you get Noah's email about his bachelor party in a couple months?"

"I haven't checked my personal email in a while." When

was the last time? With texting and chat apps, who really uses email anymore? My work account is the only one I check regularly. "I work, run with Rex, and I crash. Repeat until the end of time."

"Well, he sent all the details—hotels, flights, how many drinks we're all allowed to have."

"How far up his ass he wants the pole. Did he ask for lube as a present?" I take my phone out of my pocket and open my mail app. A flood of emails downloads, clogging my inbox. "Ah, shit. I have like five hundred junk emails to wade through here. What did he call it?"

"I think the title had the word *set* in it for some reason. All set? Get set?"

I type *set* into the search box, and sure enough, there's Noah's email. But the one under it causes my heart to skip and then race. "You gotta be fucking kidding me."

"What?" Aaron leans over to peer at my phone.

"Fucking Soulmates Reunited sent me another email." I toss my phone on the bar, my jaw rigid with annoyance.

"Another one? I thought you blocked them."

"I'm not opening it. How many women can they tell me I'm perfect for?" The first time I heard from them, I bought their spiel. They weren't even famous then. *Data-driven soulmate selection.* Who wouldn't want a relationship guarantee? A lot of people bought into it, apparently, if you go by how huge they've become. Fancy language for a scam targeting women and unsuspecting men. No matter what their ads and that stupid fucking TV show claim, they *do* get it wrong. A lot.

"You still considering a lawsuit?"

"Been busy with work. The one lawyer I consulted said I might have a case eventually. I'd love to take them down, but I need a sure thing, you know? A guns-blazing sure thing. They're giant now." Soulmates Reunited might have ruined my life, but they didn't defraud me personally. "These women pay so much money, and they don't even realize it's lies dressed up as the truth."

"You told the girls the truth, didn't you?"

I wince. "Yeah, I did. It's probably best if I stop meeting with them. The last girl cried for like an hour because she'd taken out a loan, and the company has a no-refund policy even if your match rejects you." Even the word *rejects* makes me cringe because I wasn't rejecting *her* but more so the process. If something sounds too good to be true, that's probably a clue.

"Give me your phone," Aaron says, tipping his chin at where it rests on the bar.

"Why?"

"I'm going to email them back and tell them to stop contacting you. At some point, this becomes harassment."

"It's been a handful of emails in six years. The last one was almost two years ago. Not exactly harassment." I asked the lawyer about that too. These emails don't qualify, but if I had more proof of what they did to me six years ago, I might have a case. Shredding the paper trail in a fit of rage and despair wasn't my smartest move. At the time, I just wanted all of it gone. Tracing the phone calls was a dead end, and when I showed the lawyer the emails I did have, he said they could be interpreted multiple ways and weren't definitive proof. They covered their harassment tracks. I've been saving their emails, even though every single one fucks with my head.

"Fraud then, whatever. What they're doing isn't right. And that initial email seriously fucked you up." He raises his eyebrows and takes a long drink.

That it did. Though the email wasn't the only thing fucking me up. I pass him my phone. "I've got a folder. Just stick it in there. Don't delete the evidence. Someday, I might have enough to take them down."

Beside me, Aaron goes eerily still.

"You reading Noah's email again?" I ask as I take a swig of my beer. "Some extra horrific detail tacked on at the end?"

"Uh, no."

"What is it? Did you accidently put a virus on my phone?" I swivel in my chair to face him. "I thought these devices were bulletproof, literally."

A muscle twitches in Aaron's jaw, and then he meets my gaze. "The, uh, match they sent you." He clears his throat. "You know her."

I rear back and then snatch my phone from his hand. "I know her?" The question dies on my lips when I see *Tayla Murphy* in bold at the center of the email. "Oh, shit." I *know* her.

"*Oh, shit* is right. We've come full circle." He clenches his fist.

I check the date on the email. A week ago. "Oh God. She probably thinks I'm ignoring the match." Annoyance flares in me that I even know the company's shitty process. Why haven't they learned to leave me alone? Their tactics don't

MISS MATCHED

work on me. I'm personally demolishing their *less than one percent* claim. Of course, that's probably bullshit too.

"She hasn't contacted you either, so maybe she's ignoring the match."

I rub my forehead, trying to gather my thoughts. I haven't seen Tayla in five years. Aaron isn't wrong—this email is like coming full circle.

"What should I do?" I ask.

"Meet her and tell her she's been scammed. Offer to help her go after these assholes. This is your chance to nail them. Being matched with you must give *her* a case, at least."

Aaron's plan is the sensible one. The chance to truly take down Soulmates Reunited has never been so close. There's almost nothing that would make me happier than exposing their seedy underbelly. There's only one thing these last six years that I've wanted more than revealing their deceit. "Yeah, I could tell her they're a fraud, or . . ."

"Or you could meet with her for funsies? Come on, Si. You were like one step removed from jilting her at the altar. You're not coming back from that."

He makes our breakup sound terrible, and it *was*, but I never proposed. We never moved in together. But that isn't to say she didn't expect those things. *Rightfully* expect those things. Tayla deserved better than my fucked-up confusion, but I'm not that guy anymore.

I reread the generic soulmate sales pitch at the top of the email. Three other times I've glossed over similar paragraphs with a sense of foreboding. This time, it's not dread churning in my stomach. "She thinks we're soulmates."

"I can guarantee you Tayla Murphy is smart enough to realize you are not, in fact, soulmates."

"She went there. She paid the money. Whatever is going on with her, she wants to believe *this* is possible." Excitement courses through me. Take down Soulmates Reunited or get another shot with Tayla? That's a no-brainer.

"Okay," Aaron says, holding up a hand in my direction. "Let's say you meet her, and you manage to convince her, by some miracle, that you're meant to be together. What happens when Soulmates Reunited's house of cards comes tumbling down? It's only a matter of time before one of the people who pay all this money and don't get the result they want has the guts to speak up."

In six years, no one has bothered to complain, or at least not loudly enough to deter other people from flushing their money down the toilet. Instead, the company has only gathered more steam. More testimonies. More people who are starting to believe that *this* is the route you take when you want to get serious. Just the other day at the hospital, one of the male doctors I work with was lamenting the fact that Soulmates Reunited only takes women as clients since they're statistically "more reliable" in their desire for marriage. Statistically. You can make up statistics about anything. In this case, the doctor referred to some bullshit about *The Bachelorette* having more successful relationships come out of the process. Seems implausible the company would cite that show as a legitimate source, but whatever. Their marketing strategy is obviously working for them. Men are now coveting a match.

When I told him I'd been matched more than once, he

shrugged it off as though it didn't matter and wondered how he could get his match to see whether it truly works, even as I was telling him it doesn't. People believe what they want to believe. Or what they're told to believe. The company's propaganda machine is finely honed.

If Tayla believes this, she's not going to want to hear it's bullshit.

"I like my odds."

"Going into a relationship on the back of a deception is a bad idea." Aaron scratches his stubbled cheek.

"The company is the one deceiving her." My explanation is weak, and I don't even try to hide it. "Look, if I tell her, I never get my second chance. You said it yourself, I fucked up last time. Huge. This is fate stepping in."

"Almost like you're soulmates." Aaron's tone is wry. "I just want to be on record about what a terrible idea this is."

At this point, he could show me a video of this plan blowing up in my face and I'd probably still be on board. In the back of my closet is a box, and in that box are mementos of Tayla Murphy, including a tiny velvet box, the one I clutched in my hand in the bathroom of the restaurant, right before I went out and we broke up. This is my chance to set things right. Why wouldn't I take it?

Chapter Three

TAYLA

I might be out an exorbitant amount of money, but I still dodged a bullet. I've been back in Grand Rapids for a week, and Simon Buchannan hasn't contacted me. Weirdly, that thought is the only thing that soothes me when I stare at my empty savings account and realize all my careful planning was for nothing. Maybe I should take this as a sign I'm not meant to be romantically happy. If the deluxe, high-tech matching algorithm can only give me the one person on the planet I can't stand the sight of, well, perhaps I'm meant to be single forever.

That hasn't stopped me from exchanging a flurry of emails and phone calls with Soulmates Reunited protesting my match. The least they can do is give me a second option or refund my money.

After I've finished giving Mrs. DeRosen's thirteen-year-old cat a checkup, I go to the lobby of the veterinary clinic I share with one other doctor. Sandy is already gone from the front desk, and Mike, my practice partner, is only working a half day. It's just after twelve thirty, and Ruby should be here with lunch any minute. Her dental office is closed on Thursdays, so it's our life catch-up day.

My phone pings with an email to my personal account. Since the only one I've been emailing back and forth with is Soulmates Reunited, I click on my inbox. As I scan the email, relief floods my system. They aren't offering either of the solutions I want, but it's more than I was going to get.

"Ladies who lunch," Ruby says as she bursts through the glass door and strikes a pose, a take-out bag clutched in her hand. Her long black braids swirl like serpents around her shoulders.

The paper bag is from the gluten-free, dairy-free, nut-free restaurant down the street. The sign on their window has so many "free from" items on their list that Mike and I joke the company makes their sandwiches out of air. "What'd you get?"

"All plant-based items, don't worry," Ruby says as she follows me back to my office.

I'm not a vegetarian, and neither is Ruby, but every time we eat at the office, she seems to believe she can't eat meat.

"So, no word from your match yet? God, that must be so frustrating."

"Uh, no." At first, I was too embarrassed to admit I'd been matched with an ex—and not just any ex, but my worst one. Now, it's too late to come clean to anyone. Besides, it's pretty clear Simon isn't going to contact me, which is exactly what I want for several reasons now. "The company just emailed me, actually." I try to act casual, as though I haven't been frantically negotiating with Soulmates Reunited for a week. "If the guy doesn't respond to my email through Soulmates Reunited's app in the next month, I can get half my money back."

"Honestly, that's sort of great. The potential for lost money was my biggest worry when I went. The company plays it off like an investment in your future. And it was, for me." She takes all the salads out of the bag and lays them on the empty desk. "Glass half full? You can put that money back into your account for when you get an exchange placement. You're still on that list, right?" Ruby plucks up the salad she wants and pops off the top. "I'm still pissed for you. God, the process worked so well for me. Granted, I didn't tell anyone I was doing it. It was all so new and untested, and it was so much money." She laughs. "Then Dean's name was on the screen. When I saw him, it was just like . . ." She fans herself. "We went for coffee and spent the next week living out of each other's pockets." She sighs and gets a dreamy expression on her face. "Like, we both just *knew*. The craziest thing. I *so* wanted that for you."

I have heard this story a bazillion times, and I lived it. Up close. That initial week she spent basically living with him, I worried she'd been kidnapped. Then, once I did see her, the change was obvious. I'd never seen her so loved up over a man.

"Some people get lucky, and some people don't." Except I haven't been lucky in any area lately. The vet exchange I signed up for—and planned to use my savings for—stalled. No one in any of my countries of choice was looking for a match to Grand Rapids, Michigan, and I got tired of waiting. I couldn't force someone to choose me for an exchange, so I opted to change my life in a different way. No one would choose me, so I'd choose someone. That isn't working out either.

I read the labels on the salads. Ugh. She has the worst taste. Even lunch isn't a win for me today.

"I'm still on the exchange waiting list, but I'm not holding my breath on that one. Two years on the list and not even an expression of interest. But I did email them today to ask if it might move things along if I'm more flexible in where I'd go." If that comes through, I'll need the money I just spent on stupid Simon to cover the exchange costs. Flights, transporting my stuff, storing the rest of my things, going on adventures—all of it would be expensive. Since I'm now living paycheck to paycheck for a while, I wouldn't be able to afford it, even if they offered something tomorrow.

"Hopefully your soulmate pulls his head out of his ass and shows up for you. Dean was skeptical when Soulmates Reunited contacted him, you know. And look where we are." She tosses out her hands, a bite of salad on the end of her fork. "Unlike back then, everyone knows about Soulmates Reunited now. It's flourishing."

Except I don't want my match to see the email or contact me, so I make a noncommittal noise and select the best of the worst salad options.

"Do you want me to ask Dean if he's met any single profs at the college this semester?" Ruby hands me a fork and settles into the chair across from me, gazing at the wall of college textbooks above my desk.

How do I put this tactfully? They set me up at a Christmas party with one of Dean's colleagues. While there are probably lots of women who swoon over a man who can recite poetry and who reads literary criticism for fun, that's not me. Give me a man who likes getting his hands dirty any day of the week. "Um, you know, I have to wait a month for the guy to contact me. So it's probably better if I sit tight."

"If you change your mind, just ask." Ruby tucks a piece of lettuce into her mouth. "I'm so disappointed for you, and I want to do something."

"Maybe I should focus on the life goal that doesn't have anything to do with being married and having kids." I stab my salad. That thought has been going around my head from the second I left Soulmates Reunited's head office. Being matched with Simon was a kick in the teeth. Focus on work. Fuck love.

"Oh, Tayla." She makes an exasperated noise. "You're thirty-one. You've got at least ten years before you need to think about altering that goal."

"Maybe I should freeze my eggs. Or forget finding a guy altogether and just opt for a donor," I muse. "I have a friend who did that. Do you remember? She seems happy. She also said she thought that going to Soulmates Reunited was a waste of money. I should have listened."

Ruby wags her fork. "If you go the donor route, I want in on those profiles. I've got good genetic instincts."

"Good genetic instincts? What does that even mean?" I laugh.

"It means having a baby, even with an anonymous daddy, is a big deal. You need a second set of eyes on that shit."

"Are you and Dean going to try to have a kid soon?"

Ruby sighs and pushes her empty salad container across my desk. "You know Dean's parents adopted him from that orphanage in Tanzania when they were there doing missionary work, right?

"Yeah. You two still donating to that place?"

"We are." She takes a deep breath. "Before we have kids, he wants to go back to Tanzania for a few months and give back to the community. Meet some of his extended family."

"That's amazing." That's what I need—some sort of lofty goal to give my life meaning beyond love and my career. "What about your dental practice?"

"I'd have to hire someone to fill in temporarily. I think it'll be fine. A lot of organization. But this matters to him a lot, so it matters to me."

I take a deep breath. Have I ever had that kind of support from a partner? Ruby and Dean really are #Goals. Why couldn't the stupid algorithm have turned up a not-Dean Dean?

"Let's figure out something to take your mind off the wait for the guy—or half your money back." Ruby takes the jug of sweet tea out of my mini fridge and pours some into two mugs. "I know at the time you thought you were too busy with your vet practice to be distracted by dating, but remember the hot guy who came and asked you to help him turn rescue dogs into therapy dogs?"

"Right." I toggle the mouse beside my desktop computer. "That was a while ago. What was his organization called again?" The search engine pops open, and I close my eyes, trying to picture the business card he handed me. "Ugh, I can't remember."

"Ask Sandy, your vet tech. I bet she'll remember or can find out for you. Don't they have like a network or something for shelter dogs?" Ruby tidies up the rest of our lunch.

"Sandy is a good idea. I'll definitely ask her." I rub my face and then look at Ruby. "This isn't me burying myself in more work, is it?"

"No," Ruby says with a slash of her hand. "You'll be out in the community meeting people with a hot guy by your side, not in here waiting for your future husband to bring in his dog for a checkup."

"Valid." I chuckle. "Hasn't been the best strategy, huh?" I lean back in my chair and take the proffered mug of sweet tea.

The bell chimes in my office to let me know someone's entered the front door. "Shit. I forgot to lock it."

"Maybe it's Sandy or Mike coming back from lunch?"

"Mike only worked a half day today. He's got an appointment. And I love Sandy, but she's never back early from lunch." I open my office door and wander down the hall past the two examination rooms. Probably just someone a little overeager for their 2:00 p.m. appointment. When I come out of the hallway, it takes a moment for my brain to react. A chill streaks across my back, followed by a rush of warmth. "Simon?" I whisper.

His hair isn't the messy length it once was; instead, his brown locks have been tamed by a crew cut. But his eyes are just as striking, the kind of color that stops a person short in the middle of a conversation when they realize just how intense the green is. I used to tease him that he wasn't good-looking, he was beautiful. Why couldn't he have put on fifty pounds or been one of those people who don't age well?

He waggles his phone. "I got your email from Soulmates Reunited. So . . ." He tugs lightly on the leash for his German shepherd, Rex, who was sniffing the reception desk but now sits and looks at me expectantly. "I guess we're soulmates after all?"

From behind me, Ruby gasps, and her mug clatters to the floor, smashing into a thousand pieces. "Holy. Shit. You were matched with Simon? *Fucking* Simon?"

"Yeah," I say, unable to tear my gaze from him. "Fucking Simon."

Chapter Four

SIMON

What sort of greeting did I expect? Not a good one, which is why I brought Rex. Play to my strengths. But to realize I've been nicknamed *Fucking Simon*, as though I'm some sort of plague, is over the top, even for Ruby and Tayla.

"Nice to see you again, Ruby." I tuck my phone into my pocket and gesture to Rex, who is in danger of achieving liftoff with his wagging tail. "Can I let him loose?"

Tayla's brown eyes, which widened from shock when she saw me and transformed to granite when she realized Ruby heard me, have now softened into oozing milk chocolate as she gazes at my dog. Seven years ago, she helped me pick him out of his litter.

"Aw, Rexie. At least I'm happy to see *you*." She crouches

on the ground, her dark ponytail swinging onto her shoulder, and Rex bounces his front paws in excitement but doesn't leave my side. When I drop the leash, he bounds toward her, slurping her face as she laughs. "Aw, look at you." He sits in front of her, preening. She takes one of his paws in her hand and stares into his eyes. If it's possible for a dog to have the look of love, he's got it. "Has dickhead Simon been looking after you okay?"

"Actually," I say, undeterred. She's got a right to be angry. As long as she talks to me, I'll let her call me a dickhead for years. "I have documentation that proves I am, in fact, Soulmate Simon. Might be the alliteration throwing you off."

"Yes," Tayla says, sarcasm dripping from her voice. "The alliteration is the problem. It wouldn't be that whenever I look at you, I see a giant dick where your head should be."

I pretend to think about her comment as I shove both hands into my pockets. "You know, I always suspected you had a penis fetish, but this visualization work you're doing is next level."

Her cheeks turn pink, and her jaw tightens. Rex whines and nudges her hand. "To be clear, the penis I am picturing in place of your head is neither yours nor is it attractive."

"So, what's I'm hearing is that you think *my* penis is attractive? Well, this conversation has taken quite a—"

"Stop!" Ruby holds up both of her hands, her eyes closed. "Please, it's not scientifically possible to scrub my brain of memories yet." She cracks open one narrowed eye. "Is it?"

"It is not," I confirm.

"Great," Ruby huffs. "Here's the recap." She points at me. "You're a douche. You're not her match." She swirls her hand around as though she's erasing me from the room. "There was some kind of mistake at the company. We're working with them to find out how a glitch this awful could have happened so we can get Tayla the *right* match."

"A glitch?" I frown. That might explain the other emails I received over the last few years. The company is making pretty expensive mistakes if that's the case.

Except Ruby was surprised to see me. Shattered a mug of something all over the floor. If Ruby already knew about me, no need for the shock and awe. Something isn't adding up.

"You didn't email me back, did you?" Tayla stiffens, but she's still stroking Rex.

"Why does that matter?" Does that even matter? None of the other women asked me that question. Of course, I did email them back just to meet and explain I was *not* their soulmate, and as far as I was concerned, the company was a fraud. Emailing Tayla wasn't necessary. She'd planned to open this office with Mike after veterinary school, and she was almost done the setup when we broke up. Tracking her down was a breeze . . . and opened a floodgate of suppressed memories. I've tried so hard not to think about her, about how stupid I was.

"No reason." Tayla frowns and shrugs.

Evasive. Easy enough to force her hand. I whip out my phone and open my mail app. "I can email you back right now if it's that important to you."

"No!" She shakes her head, the ponytail almost whipping her in the face. "No, no, nope. We're good. No need."

I narrow my eyes. "It's probably best to close the loop-holes, what with the glitch. I wouldn't want anyone to think I wasn't contacted." I might not have seen her for a while, but she hasn't gotten any better at bluffing.

"Please," she says, walking over to me, Rex trailing her. She places her hand over mine, and my body instinctually inches closer as though she's a flicker of heat in the dead of winter. Warmth spreads across my torso and down to my groin. "Please don't."

"Why not?" I murmur. Her husky voice strikes a chord in my heart. An old, long-dead instinct awakens.

Protect her.

Stupid caveman instincts. Tayla's no damsel in distress. One of my favorite things about her was that she was more likely to be the one doing the saving.

She swallows, and slowly she lifts her gaze to mine. Time stops. I forgot how light her eyes are up close, almost golden, as though someone poured honey over the brown, muting the color. She's searching my gaze too, and then she bites her lip, and my focus shifts down to the way her teeth snag on the fullness. Does she still kiss the same? Soft, subtle lips that parted on a satisfied sigh, as though kissing me was the solution to every problem.

"Why can't I email you back?" My voice is rough with desire.

She takes a beat to answer. "If you don't email me back, they'll return half my money."

"You get money back?" I rock back on my heels a fraction. Must be a new policy, otherwise I fucked over those other women by being polite enough to respond. A muscle in my jaw jumps at the thought. What a shitty system. Anything but silence rewards the scam artists.

"Just half."

"How long do you have to wait for a response?"

She hesitates and glances over her shoulder at Ruby before admitting, "A month."

I rub my chin and stretch my hand down my throat. "What if the match wasn't a glitch?"

"It was a glitch." Her voice is stronger this time, more certain. "And I have plans for that returned money."

The doorbell chimes, and the door behind me opens. Rex sits on his haunches and pants. Must be another animal. Reluctantly, I turn to look.

"Oh, Dr. Murphy, I'm sorry. Did I come too early?"

Tayla glances at the clock over my head. "Right on time," she says to the elderly woman carrying her purse-size poodle. "You can go into the first door on your right. I'm just finishing up here."

The door chimes again, and a tall, larger-framed blond woman in scrubs walks in. "Sorry I'm late, Tay. Got caught in traffic."

Tayla's face stays deceptively neutral. She used to have a thing about people being late. Has that changed?

"No problem, Sandy. Mrs. Henhawk just went into room one. I have a question for you later about a guy I want to *connect* with. I think you know him."

So obvious. Even her tone of voice screams, *See, see? I don't need you for a soulmate. I have options.* I cock my head and give Rex a whistle. He scampers to my side, and I stoop to pick up his leash.

"I know a cue when I hear it. I'll reply to your email, and we can arrange for a time to hang out. Let you get your money's worth outta this."

Fury sparks in Tayla's eyes when the full force of her attention swings back. "Don't you dare. I'm serious, Si. Don't you even open that email ever again."

"I tell you what," I say, because I'm sure they're lying about the glitch and about re-matching Tayla with someone else. "You meet me at Arnold's near the hospital Saturday for lunch. If you've got proof from the company that they made a mistake, that they don't think we're soulmates, I'll pretend like I never tracked you down. Unless you've got something from them that I can see right now?"

Tayla flushes, but her jaw is set. If there was a glitch, and the company was working on it, whether I responded wouldn't matter. But if they refused to give her a second match, then I've got her over a barrel.

"I'll print it off for you. You'll have a visual any time you're tempted to think this might have been real. Because it's not. It's not real."

"I can wait, if you want to print it now." One of the things I used to love about Tayla was how she never gave up. She's got no proof, but the more I back her into a corner, the harder she'll dig in.

"We've been talking to them on the phone," she says, but she slides a giveaway glance at Ruby. "Saturday. Noon. Arnold's." Tayla rises to her full height, which barely reaches my shoulder. "I'll bring the proof. Then we can pretend this meeting never happened."

"It's a date," I say with a wink. "Nice to see you again,

Ruby." I offer her a little wave, but she glares in response. "Oh, and Sandy? Traffic? Really? It's a residential area with zero traffic issues. You gotta get a better excuse. Maybe a glitch of some sort? It's a really popular lie . . . er, excuse right now. Or so I hear." I open the door and walk out whistling while Rex prances at my side.

Chapter Five

TAYLA

The door clicks shut, and I stare after him. His tangy cologne permeates the air. The scent hit me like a Mack truck when I got close to him. Did he use the same one on purpose, or has he really not changed it since we split?

Once the last whiff of him is gone, I shake my head, and the spell is broken. I whirl on Sandy and Ruby. "Oh my God. Did I just agree to forge documents? Did he accuse me of lying?"

Ruby lets out a derisive laugh. "That's not even the worst part. You agreed to go on a lunch date with him." She sucks in a deep breath. "He's good. I don't remember him being that smooth."

"Definitely more confident." I raise my finger. "But I can

handle him." Can't I? God, I hope so. I grab the dustpan and broom for the broken cup.

"He's kind of a dick," Sandy says from behind the desk. "But in a hot way. Why was he calling himself your soulmate?"

"That's *Simon*," Ruby says.

"That's *Fucking* Simon?" Sandy chokes out.

I wince at how crass his nickname sounds. Every other time someone said it, a zip of pride would go through me. Seeing him again has left a sour taste in my mouth. Maybe I should finally drop the eff bomb from his name? I dump the remnants of the cup in the garbage.

"Oh my Lord," Sandy groans. "That's why you went to New York? You paid for Soulmates Reunited, and they gave you *him*?"

"Uh, yep. That's the summary." I return the broom and dustpan to the small cleaning closet. "I gotta get in to Mrs. Henhawk before she thinks I've forgotten her. Sandy, can you track down that guy who came here a while ago who wanted to turn rescue dogs into service dogs? Do you remember him?"

"Hard to forget. I'm sure I've got his card around here somewhere. He was such a flirt. I thought for sure you'd ask for his card at some point."

"We're at that point." I flick my ponytail. "And you," I say, pointing at Ruby, "learn how to forge documents while I'm at work today, okay?"

"I kinda have to. I'm the one who talked you into doing the stupidly expensive exclusive matching algorithm madness."

"Data science, Ruby. *Data science.* How could a computer get it so wrong? I'm supposed to be able to trust science." Not all science is good science. Clearly, Soulmates Reunited isn't as advanced as they think because there's no way Simon Buchannan is my soulmate. It's just not possible.

♥

Saturday morning, I examine the letter Ruby printed off her computer and compare it to the email Simon would have received. "You did a good job with the logo."

Ruby lets out a relieved breath. "Took me all friggin' day. Photoshop and I don't get along. Dean tried to help, but he just made it worse."

"Hey!" Dean calls from the kitchen.

"I love you, but you know it's true." Ruby shrugs. "He's not going to look at it that closely. He can't want to be matched with you any more than you want to be matched with him."

Her voice lacks conviction, and I don't believe her. There was something about his appearance on Thursday that gave me the opposite impression. When we stood close together, when I touched his hand, desire swirled in my stomach, threatening to flood the rest of my body. How can I hate him and still find him attractive?

"He could have just ignored the emails. Or not shown up. Or opened his email and said, 'Oh, hey, Tayla Murphy, been there, done that, no need to do *that* again,' but instead he tracked me down."

"That seems impressive to you? That he tracked you

down? Do not make him into a hero. He's no Captain America."

"Ohh, Chris Evans." The face isn't right for Simon, but the build is very similar.

"He's not even a Chris Evans level of human being. I'm sure Chris never arranged an incredibly romantic night at a restaurant, then broke up with his girlfriend, and *then* let the waiter pour champagne as though they'd gotten engaged."

"Don't remind me," I groan. "I had nightmares so real I woke up sick to my stomach for months afterward."

"I know. You were often sleeping on my couch, remember?"

"Why did you break up?" Dean appears in the doorway, a plate with a sandwich in his hand.

I take a deep breath and let it out slowly. "Irony of ironies, he came back to the dinner table after being in the bathroom for like twenty minutes and told me we weren't a good long-term match, and he couldn't do it anymore." I throw out my hands. "Now we're soulmates."

"That's fucked up." Dean takes a bite of his sandwich and chews.

I sink into the couch with the forged letter from Ruby in my hand. "We don't even know each other anymore. We can't be soulmates." A silly thing to say since I was willing to meet a complete stranger and buy into the idea. Simon and I have history. Complicated, messy, unresolved history. At one time, I did think he was the one. If he'd asked me to marry him that night, I would have said yes. No hesitation. I drop the paper on the couch and put my head in my hands.

"I remember you telling me when you were dating that

you thought he was the one for you." Ruby says the words quietly, like she's afraid to voice them.

"I was just thinking about that too." I shake my head and stare at her. "But while I was thinking that, he was having doubts. Doubts big enough to sink us. He can't show up six years later, email or not, and pretend that didn't happen."

"Maybe he's got regrets," Dean reasons. "He's not married yet, is he?"

"For all I know, he's been married and divorced six times. Or maybe he's considering cheating on his wife. He had someone else all set up for himself when he dumped me." My mind latches onto this mythical wife, clueless like me, sitting at home thinking their relationship is #lifegoals when it's really *Iceberg, right ahead*. I check the time and snatch the letter off the couch with one hand and grab my purse with the other. "I gotta go or I'll be late. Get this over with and put him back in the rearview mirror."

"I hear you," Ruby says, following me to her front door. "I wouldn't even order any food. Give him the letter and peace out."

"And maybe a quick kick to the balls on my way to the exit." I manage a smile.

"That's why you and my wife are best friends. She'd go for the parting sack shot too." Dean chuckles behind me.

"Damn right," Ruby says. "I'm glad you realize it." She winks at him and holds the door for me.

"Wish me luck?"

"You don't need luck, Tay. If all else fails, lay on the guilt. Tell him he owes you one."

In my car, instead of starting the engine, I grip the

steering wheel and stare into space. Last night, I dug Simon's shoebox out of the back of my closet. I fiddled with the lid, but I didn't let myself open it. Ruby and I symbolically burned concert tickets and love notes in a drunken rage one night six years ago. But in the box were things I couldn't bear to look at, much less burn. After seeing him again, the temptation to go down memory lane was strong.

Life isn't about going backward. With a determined huff, I shoved the box under my shoe rack and vowed to junk it all after I got rid of Simon for good.

I glance at the letter on the passenger seat. This madness ends today. He owes me.

Chapter Six

SIMON

I get to the restaurant before her. This morning I went for a run with Rex to clear my head, and I've been buzzing ever since. I know what I have to do, but my insides are twisting and writhing in protest. There's a good chance she'll hate me more after our conversation today.

Using the company that helped ruin us last time to bring us back together this time is wrong. There's no doubt about it. Six years ago, when they contacted me out of the blue because some woman named Jada was my "ideal soulmate" who was "guaranteed to last a lifetime," I couldn't think straight. My head and my heart went to war for too many reasons. Most of my insecurities or hesitations were bullshit, but they led me down roads I never should have traveled.

Or maybe I did need to travel them. I don't fucking know anymore.

It's been a long time since I've let myself think about the destruction they and I wreaked on my life.

Since that disastrous first match, I've been convinced the company is bogus and their soulmates claim is a complete scam. They take advantage of people's desperation to find love, to have certainty, and I hope to prove it someday. Take them down.

But no matter how I examine Soulmates Reunited's manipulation then or now, my choices are limited: give up pursuing them or use the situation to my advantage. Prove the company is a fraud or get Tayla back. Right or wrong, I'm staying the course. I'm tired of having regret as a constant companion.

She breezes in the door of the diner, her midnight hair lifting on a draft when another customer comes in behind her. A half smile lights her face when he speaks to her. She says something in return, and my heart constricts. Jealousy at this point is stupid, but there it is. He gets a smile, but as soon as she spots me—three, two, one, and her smile disappears. Hitching her purse higher onto her shoulder, she strides to the table. A single sheet of paper flutters in her hand.

When she gets to me, she slides the letter across the surface of the table. "Satisfied?"

I'll be damned. She took the time to forge a letter. Or she forced Ruby to do it. The logo is close, but it's not crisp and clear. Photoshop or a screenshot off the internet, maybe. I lean across the table and tug the metal chair along the floor so she can slide onto it. "Lunch?" I suggest, easing back into my seat. "It'll take me a minute to read this over." Or gather myself for battle, because given her posture and my determination, we're going to be trading blows.

Tayla purses her lips and then sets her handbag on the table before perching on the chair across from me. "I'm not eating lunch with you."

"Sure you are." I pretend to scan the letter. Might as well jump right in. "This isn't a real letter from the company."

"Yes, it is."

"Show me the original email." I sit back and cross my arms. "Or attachment or whatever."

"They sent it by real mail." She must realize how quickly that would have needed to happen, and she flushes. "Express."

"Not a single crease in this paper." I lift the perfectly flat piece of paper.

Her gaze darts around the room. "They sent it in a nine-by-twelve manila envelope. The paper didn't need to be folded."

"Did they send you a check with it?"

She frowns and places her purse on her lap, hugging it to her stomach. "Why would they send a check? I told you I get half back if you don't respond."

"Yeah, but if the *real* problem was that I wasn't your soulmate, they'd either refund you the money or run the test again, right? Or maybe they'd have contacted me to clarify the situation? So many people are watching for these soulmate emails now. 'Whoops. We fucked up. Sorry.' Or something. Whether I email you back or not shouldn't matter. If there was a glitch, I can respond to your email right now, here, at the table. *They* made a mistake. Right?" I hold my phone up with a copy of Soulmates Reunited's email on display. It's my lock screen picture. I might be an asshole.

Her mouth forms an O as realization dawns on her face.

Then I take a chance. "The letter is good, but Ruby didn't quite get the logo right. It's not crisp enough."

"You're an asshole." The words barely make it past her lips.

No point denying that. I'll take that blow and land one of my own. "We're soulmates, Tay."

She barks out a laugh. "Oh? When did that realization hit you? Sitting on the shitter? Or was it when you got the email from Soulmates Reunited? Or at some equally random point in the *six years* since we've seen each other?"

"Five years. I came to see you, to talk to you—"

"And I slammed the door in your face, which is what I'm trying to do now too."

"You opened this door."

"I didn't know going to New York to a famously successful soulmate matching company would invite you back into my life. Obviously, if I were psychic, I wouldn't have bothered. Of course, if I were psychic, I wouldn't have said yes to that first date with you eight years ago."

"Harsh, Tay." Despite how we ended, she can't mean that.

"Harsh? Do you even remember the night you broke up with me? The waiter served us fucking champagne while I bawled my eyes out. He thought they were happy tears. The candles and the wine, the flowers, the private room—all of that to break up with me? Do you know how long it took me to get over that, over you?" She snaps her mouth closed as though she's said too much. "It doesn't matter. But you owe me this, Simon. I can't get all my money back. Their system is obviously broken or flawed or something, but my best chance at getting anything out of this experience is if you pretend like we didn't talk. I have things I want to do with my life, and none of them involve you."

I clear my throat and gather my courage. Listening to how badly I hurt her is like being stabbed with tiny knives all over my body. The way things went down that night is why it took me so long to turn up on her doorstep to try to make things right.

"I can't begin to tell you how sorry I am, Tayla. There's no excuse for what I did." The sequence of events leading up to that night and what came after tipped my world sideways. My choices back then are my deepest shame.

"I'm over it," she says with a dismissive hand. "I want to close the door between us once and for all."

Her hand rests on the edge of the table, and on instinct I grab it, lacing our fingers like I used to do. Her startled gaze flies to mine. Her hands are small. Tiny bones like a bird. We're staring at each other, and I wonder if the yearning also runs through her. The distance across the table doesn't seem so great anymore. Her hand has softened in mine, and her brown eyes have gone from startled to confused and are shifting into something else.

Say it, Simon. Now or never.

"I won't respond to the email if you give me the month to make things up to you."

Her eyes widen, and she yanks her hand out of mine. "You think you can make it up to me?" Her tone brims with disbelief. "You can't."

"You must believe in this scheme, or you wouldn't have gone. You wouldn't have spent all that money knowing you could end up getting none of it back." I will her to make eye contact with me, but she won't. "Out of all the people in their database, they matched us."

"They made a mistake." She crosses her arms and slouches in her seat.

"But what if they didn't?" When she finally looks at me, I almost wish she hadn't. Her eyes are glossy with tears. My stupid, traitorous heart squeezes in response, and I want to grab her hand again.

"We already did this. For whatever reason, you didn't think we were right for each other."

"I was young and stupid." That much is true. "This can be our second chance." There's so much more I could say, but none of it will help me win her in this moment.

"You really hurt me, Simon." Her voice is thick with tears. "I can't just forget what happened."

"I'm not asking you to forget. I'm not suggesting a clean slate. I know I've got my work cut out for me. Every single activity we do together, I'll plan. I'll pay. If there's a sacrifice that needs to be made, I'll make it. The only thing you'll be out is a little bit of time." *And, God help me, your heart.* "At the end of the month, the email will have gone unanswered, and you'll get half your money back. If we truly aren't right for each other, I'll even try to help you get all your money back." At least three other women I know and have access to were also deceived by Soulmates Reunited. The lawyer might have said I don't have much of a case personally, but if I have to seek out those women to see if collectively they can find some justice, then I will. Present a united front.

"All of it? How would you do that? I signed a contract."

She's close. She wants me to convince her. Can I tip the scales? I meet her gaze, and she doesn't look away. "I give you my word. If you give me a chance, and it turns out we're a terrible match, even now, I'll do everything in my power to help you get your money back." I take a deep breath because I'm about to be stupid. "Fuck it. I'll even cover the other half. If we're no good together anymore, I'll make up the difference. Half from them, the other half from me." Which would be my down payment to finally get out of an apartment and into a house. But I don't intend to fail. I won't.

She snags her lip with her teeth, searching my face. "I'm only willing to see you once a week."

"Four times a week." Will she barter? If my money is on the line too, once a week won't get me anywhere. Four dates are nothing. Not enough for a second chance. When we went to Morocco together, she bartered like a boss. That's actually not good news for me right now.

"Two lunches." A hint of a smile touches her lips.

"One day of the weekend, two evenings, and a lunch."

She shakes her head, leaning forward, and a hint of her perfume drifts toward me. I want to drown in it. "That's still four. One evening and two lunches." She taps the table. "That's my final offer."

First rule of negotiating—be willing to walk away if the deal isn't good. She wants her money back for something, even if it's just so she doesn't feel so foolish having spent it to get me.

I take my wallet out of my pocket and drop some bills on the table to pay for my coffee. The waitress never came back after Tayla arrived. Arnold's always did have shitty service, but I picked here because I haven't been since Tayla and I broke up. "That's fine," I say, rising from my seat. "I'll send you a quick email from the car to arrange—"

"When we don't get back together, you'll cover the other half of the money? I get it all back?"

I freeze, sensing victory of a sort. "I will."

"Fine," she grits out, all hint of amusement gone. "You can have Sunday, one lunch, one evening."

"You drive a hard bargain." I hold out my hand.

Reluctantly, she rises and slides her palm against mine. Our gazes lock, and the determination in hers tells me it's going to be an uphill battle to win her back. She's always been stubborn. No problem. My endurance is going to surprise her. I grin, and she scowls.

"Tomorrow. I'll pick you up just after lunch."

"What?" She shakes her head. "No, we'll start next weekend."

I rub my thumb along her palm since we're still holding hands. Goose bumps rise on her arms. "Four weeks. We've already lost one. So that's three. I'm not cutting it to two. We start tomorrow." At this rate, I'll need every minute to win her over and keep my money.

She tugs her hand from mine and tucks her hair behind

her ears. "Fine. Tomorrow. You remember where I live?"

I drove past it a few times the year after we split, but with her one-car garage, I could never be sure whether she still lived there or if she was home. "You're in the same little house?" Her parents bought it when she started college, and she was supposed to rent from them once she was working full-time. She told me it was a starter house—there were bigger things to come.

Her purse is on the chair, and she picks it up, sliding it over her shoulder. "Same place. It's all the space I've ever needed."

A stark reminder that my choice altered the course of her life. We were house hunting in the months leading up to my abandoned proposal. We nitpicked every place we saw and were never able to agree enough to make an offer on something. All the plans we made stretch over us like a plastic bag, smothering. It wasn't just the proposal I abandoned that night.

Before I can ask for her number, she heads for the exit without a backward glance.

Chapter Seven

TAYLA

I sink into Ruby's couch in a daze. "I agreed to date him. For three weeks."

"What?" Ruby rushes out of the kitchen, a tea towel in her hand. After letting me in the house, Dean disappeared upstairs. Must have read the expression on my face. That man can take a hint—unlike the man I left at the diner.

"He didn't believe the letter?"

"Not one letter of it." I slouch deeper into the cushions. His smugness made me want to punch him in the face. Mostly. The flare of desire when he laced our fingers together and stared into my eyes was a fluke. Like a muscle memory or a reflex. Same with the heat that pooled in my core when his thumb grazed my palm. My body may react, but my mind isn't fooled. He's a hot mess. Literally.

Ruby winces. "So, if that didn't work, did you lay on the guilt? Nice and thick?"

"I tried." Not hard enough. How could I ever make him understand the depth of sadness, anger, and humiliation I felt? I started to tell him, and then I couldn't bear the sympathetic expression on his face. He didn't care enough then, and I don't need his sympathy now. He may be the reason I'm not married to someone else, but that isn't because he's my soulmate.

Ruby sits beside me on the couch folding the tea towel. "How'd you get from a guilt trip to three weeks of dating?"

"The simple answer? Blackmail."

She doesn't miss a beat. "He threatened to email them if you didn't agree to date him?"

"To give him a second chance, yeah." I twirl my finger in my hair and sigh. "He offered to make up the other half of the money too. He wasn't a total shit." Which actually annoys me. No part of me should be softening. He *did* say he'd email them if I didn't agree, which would leave me with nothing. "I can put up with seeing his face for three weeks if I can get all my money back." That would give me some added flexibility with the exchange program. Maybe I can get something I want? A detour, but not a dead end.

"Fucking Simon," Ruby mutters. "Getting all your money back would be an okay result. Not what you wanted, but . . . you don't seem mad."

"I was mad at Arnold's. Now I'm just numb. You know how sometimes you just want to be able to hit fast-forward on your life? That's me right now." I mime hitting a button on an invisible remote. "Boom. Three weeks, done. My life is back to normal. No more Simon. All my money back."

"What's he getting out of this?" Ruby's brow furrows.

I scoff. "Easing his conscience, maybe? I didn't ask. I don't care."

Ruby braces her back in the corner of the couch and stares at me. "This isn't about him feeling bad. If he wanted to ease his conscience, he'd let you get half your money back with no hassle. Or contact Soulmates Reunited and ask for them to rerun the algorithm for you. Get you a real match."

We stare at each other, and while we might both be coming to the same conclusion, I can't make myself say it.

"He wants you back. Regret is running through Simon Buchannan like a wildfire, and he wants you to play firefighter."

"I'm not doing any role-playing with him." I cross my arms. The moment when our fingers slid against each other and our gazes locked flickers in my memory again. My body warms. "He left me, Ruby."

"At the time, everyone agreed it made no sense." She tosses the folded tea towel on the coffee table. "Maybe there was something else going on. I never bought that Jada was the reason."

"Oh, was that her name?"

"You know that was her name. We practically stalked her. God, that was so unhealthy. Why did I let you do that?"

"Let me do it? You were driving the getaway car." I lay my head against the back of the couch and stare at the ceiling. "We were twenty-five. What else were we gonna do when he wouldn't talk to me, and he started dating some other woman out of the blue?"

"Then when he *did* come talk to you . . ."

"A year later. I wasn't slicing that wound open for him no matter what he had to say." I had another gaping hole in my heart already. "I don't regret shutting the door in his face." The roses he brought me got caught in the slamming door, and petals littered my floor for days. Just seeing him again was enough to send me into a tailspin. Not anymore. I've seen him twice now, and I'm still flying straight. Whatever hold he had on me is gone.

"He sees an open door now," Ruby muses.

"A mirage." I glance toward the kitchen. "You got any wine? I need a drink. Also, I didn't eat because Arnold's is the worst and Simon is . . . worser."

"Red or white?" Ruby chuckles and heads to the kitchen.

"As long as it's wet, I'll drink it."

"So, when do these dates start?"

"Tomorrow."

"I'll grab both bottles."

"Excellent decision." Unlike all the ones I've made in the last few weeks—plus, a hangover might make tomorrow easier to bear.

When I open the door to Simon the next afternoon, I've braced myself for a terrible, uncomfortable day. All morning, dread swished around my stomach like the remnants of yesterday's wine.

With my hand braced against the doorframe, I take in his

appearance. Scruffy face, button-down shirt with a stripe that perfectly matches his green eyes, worn jeans, Vans on his feet. He's made an effort, and a twinge of anger flickers because he looks like a model I'd screenshot to stare at in my free time. Why couldn't he show up covered in vomit or have contracted chicken pox overnight and have spots all over his face?

"Is this okay? I don't know what we're doing." I glance down at my leggings and oversize sweatshirt.

"It's perfect." His hands are in his pockets. "I'll drive."

I give him a wry look. "I assumed." Grabbing my purse, I close my door and lock it before following him to his sports car. "Nice car."

"I still have the same shitty apartment." He gives me a sheepish grin. "Spent my money on the car."

"Cars depreciate. Houses usually don't. Seems like a waste of money." I'm prickly like a porcupine as I slide into the buttery leather of the passenger seat.

His lips twitch when he gets into the car and faces me. "We all seem to waste money on something."

I narrow my eyes at the dig. "Touché." With crossed arms, I stare out the window as my residential neighborhood morphs into a more industrial area. "You're not taking me to an abandoned warehouse to murder me, are you?"

"Murder's not on today's agenda." His gaze is full of amusement when he sneaks a glance in my direction.

The longer we drive, the more I can't ignore the stench of his cologne. Why is smell the biggest driver of memory? He's coated himself in the same scent he used to wear— again—and it's causing my stomach to churn with anxiety.

"You haven't changed your cologne in six years?" The words are out of my mouth before I can stop them.

"It was on sale last week. I was feeling nostalgic. Must be a sign." He makes a left-hand turn into an industrial plaza. "I have a couple different brands I rotate through."

"What days is this one in rotation?"

"So far Thursdays and Sundays."

"We'll have to schedule our dates on other days then."

"You used to love this smell."

"Tastes change." I stare at him, willing my jab to land. The truth is the cologne he's wearing is tied up in all these good memories, but also one really terrible one that coats everything. The smell makes me want to either curl into him or gag, and I'm not sure which one is going to win out.

He winces. The car comes to a stop, but I don't look at wherever we've parked. Hurting him shouldn't make me feel good, but his wounded expression causes a zing of satisfaction. In his seat, he turns to examine me.

"Do you still have your stack of ceramic plates?"

His question surprises me, and I narrow my eyes. "Of course. I'm not going to throw those out. Someday my children will have to bury me with them." When I was a kid, my mom took me to make a birthday plate at a pottery place, and then I started going on my own to make plates whenever something important or significant happened. Most of the time, the experience of painting out my emotions is cathartic.

"Well, in honor of meeting your soulmate," he says, gesturing to the building ahead of us, "we should add a couple plates to the pile." A hint of a smile touches his lips.

I follow his chin nod and read the sign above the build-ing: PARSON'S POTTERY. At first, I'm too stunned to respond, but when the clouds of disbelief clear, I have an idea of what will go on this plate. "You want me to make a plate to celebrate . . . you?"

His shoulders lift a fraction of an inch. "Me, us, new beginnings." His lips twitch. "Soulmates reunited."

Ideas percolate as I stare at the sign for the store. "You're making one too?"

"Why not? I'm not much of an artist, but I'm sure I can figure something out."

"All right," I say, opening my door. "You asked for it."

Chapter Eight

SIMON

It doesn't take long for me to figure out why there was such a twinkle in her eyes when she picked a plate and selected her paints. While we've been talking about our jobs—a safe subject—she's been constructing what, I'm pretty sure, is a replica of me on the plate. He's dressed like me right down to my Vans, and she keeps examining me as though I'm her model. Obviously, I can't be sure since his head doesn't quite match mine.

Starting at his shoulders, a shrunken, flaccid penis takes the place of a normal head. Every time I look at it, I have to smother a laugh. The woman in charge came over early on and was impressed with Tayla's artistic skills. Just now she came around and stared at the plate for a moment, her head cocked. Then she examined me, took in the masterpiece immortalized on the ceramic, and turned bright red.

Tayla glanced over her shoulder and gave her an impish smile. "He's a dick, so . . ."

"Right, yes, I can . . . see that." She wandered away without another word and hasn't returned.

At the top of the plate, Tayla's written *Soulmate Simon* in a swirling, beautiful cursive that belies the eyesore below. "You know," I say, tipping the end of my brush toward the dick head, "someday our children may wonder why you've got a picture of my most prized possession on a plate. Also, they may question where you put my actual head."

"It's up your ass. Makes it hard to see." A hint of a smile tugs at the edges of her mouth. "You think this is *your* penis?" She purses her lips and pretends to assess it. "I can't really remember. Is that what yours looks like?" She bats her eyes.

Our gazes lock, and her smile slips a fraction. "If you need a reminder, I'm happy to oblige." Is it too soon for those comments? Probably. But when an opening presents itself, it's hard to ignore. I reach for the top button of my pants.

Her eyes widen a fraction. "Oh no!" She crosses her arms over her face.

"No? You sure?" I try and fail to suppress my amusement.

"Quite sure," she says, straightening her back and dipping her brush into the pale pink. "How's your sister?"

"Married to a decent guy. One kid. Second on the way." I pick up my brush and examine the colors. In contrast to hers, mine has *Soulmate Tayla* scrawled across the top.

When she started her plate with the swirly *Soulmate Simon* in such careful, neat letters, I got sucked in and thought we were making progress. Turns out, not so much. Although I suppose she didn't label it *Fucking Simon*, so that's something. I'll count it as a win.

Since I can't draw, my creation is a colorful list of all the things I loved about her when we dated. Some of them, like her sense of humor, clearly still apply, but others are a leap of faith. Whether they're true now or not, they were, and the plate can celebrate the good parts of our past together. What I'm determined to make is our future. "Your brother?"

She sighs. "A manager at McDonald's. No house. Not married. No kids. Not even a serious girlfriend."

"He's happy?" Her brother, Damon, is a free spirit, and his motto is work to live and not live to work. Over the years I wondered whether he'd outgrown his stance. I guess not. "Still traveling the world?"

"Yeah." She rinses her brush in the bowl of water. "He's saving up for an Eastern European trip next. To me, his lifestyle seems ridiculous, but Mom and I have given up trying to talk him into something else."

"What about your dad?" One of the things I loved about her was her close connection to her family. When we met, I thought we shared that.

She bites her lip and paints for a few minutes in silence. When it seems like she's not going to answer, I set down my brush and swivel on my chair to face her. Maybe Damon's lack of career aspirations has driven a wedge into the family? When we were dating, they tried to talk him into becoming a flight attendant like her mother.

Her brush hovers over the paints, and she takes a shaky breath. "He died five years ago."

A lead ball drops into my stomach. "Holy shit, Tay. Jesus. I'm so sorry. I had no idea."

She shakes her head and dips her brush into the paint with determination, still focused on the plate. "It's okay." She surveys her drawing, and her shoulders fall. "I mean, it's not okay. It wasn't okay then. It's not okay now. We miss him all the time. All the *freaking* time."

My hand itches to reach out, and I fight it for as long as I can. I'm not sure she even wants me to touch her, but the instinct to comfort runs deep. Finally, I glide my hand along the top of her head, smoothing her hair, and then down her narrow back. When she glances at me with tears in her eyes, my heart cracks in two. I stand up and tug her into my arms, and her paintbrush clatters to the table. She comes willingly, her arms thrown over my shoulders, and I squeeze her tight. "I'm so sorry I wasn't there. So sorry."

Her face presses into my chest, and her tears dampen my shirt. She hugs me in return, her shoulders shaking. I run my hands along her back in soothing patterns. His loss must have been awful for her, for her family. She sniffs and eases away, using the heels of her hands to brush at her tears. The green paint leaves streaks across her cheeks.

"Just a sec," I say, focusing on the paint instead of on the tightness in my chest. Her father was funny and kind. The loss, though not mine, makes my throat close up. With a paper towel, I wipe her face, and when I see it's not coming off, I dip the edge in water and try again. "Paint," I murmur.

"I'm such a mess." Her voice catches.

We make eye contact, and I can't look away. The sadness and uncertainty in the brown depths intensifies the ache inside me, the desire to make it better somehow, even if that's impossible. "You've never been a mess a day in your life, Tay. Gorgeous, funny, clever . . ." I gesture to my plate, filled with all the things I think she is. "So many things, but not a mess."

"I'm not looking at your plate." She holds my gaze with a touch of defiance.

"Why not?"

"Because then I'll feel bad I spent my time drawing you as a literal dickhead when you were thinking up nice things about me."

A laugh escapes, and without thinking, I kiss her cheek. Her breath catches, and when I pull back, I frame her face with my hands. "For the record, I think your Soulmate Simon plate is hilarious. My favorite part?" I grin. "When the saleslady wasn't sure if she should be embarrassed or offended for me. That's one ugly dick."

"I called on all my artistic talents," she says, a half smile breaking the melancholy.

"It shows."

"I'm sorry about crying all over you." She takes a shaky breath. "I don't know—I don't know why I did that. I haven't cried like that about him in a long time."

"Grief is weird like that." At the hospital, I've seen the gamut of emotions in people when it comes to a serious diagnosis or a discussion about end-of-life options. Closed off, wide open, and every variation in between.

"Sometimes it feels like he's on a trip somewhere. Except I can't see him or talk to him. But I don't—it doesn't really feel like he's gone." She steps back from me and slides onto her stool. "But then other times it's like . . . like this weight that never leaves."

"Have you been coping okay?" I pick up my paintbrush and dab it into the paint. "I know it's been five years, but grief isn't linear."

"Most of the time I am, and then like right now when you asked about him, his loss will just hit me full force. He's not out in the world somewhere. He's not really anywhere."

We grow quiet for a minute, painting in silence. I add the word *loved* to her plate. She glances over, a crease forming in her forehead.

"'Loved'?"

"Yeah," I say, a whisper of a smile tugging at my lips. "When we first started dating, after I met your family, I thought part of the reason you carried yourself with so much confidence was because you knew you were loved. There was never any doubt you were loved."

She shoves my shoulder, and another tear slips down her cheek. "You're going to make me cry again. No more crying." Her voice is thick with tears.

"We can talk about the dick in place of my head again if you want." I point to her plate with the tip of my brush. "That seems to cheer you up."

"It's true," she says, laughing through her tears. "I may have to break down and get one of those metal holder things for my wall and hang this plate in a place of honor."

"Ohh, a place of honor? I'm moving up in the world." I do a fist pump.

"Well, your dick head is, at least." She grins.

"Gotta start somewhere." I put the finishing touches on my plate and peer at hers. "You done?"

She brushes one more coat over the top and turns her creation from side to side, examining it. "Yeah, I think so."

"What do we do now?"

"We leave them here, and they put them in the kiln. We come back to collect them when they call."

I chuckle as I grab her plate and take both to the kiln racks near the exit.

"What's so funny?" She follows me.

"I'm just wondering how many more people are going to ponder why Soulmate Simon is such a dickhead."

She looks up at me, her eyes alight with amusement. "The eternal question."

Being with her today has been a revelation. I've had regrets since the minute I walked out of that restaurant, but as the years passed, part of me wondered if I was adding a shiny gloss to my memories, giving our relationship a perfection it had never achieved.

When we get to the car, I'm torn between driving her home and offering to cook her dinner. I'm working the night shift, and I should really get some sleep. But all we've got is three weeks. If I haven't convinced her to stick with me after that, we're done forever. I've been lucky to get a second chance; third chances don't exist.

"Have dinner with me? I'll cook." I turn on the ignition and let it sit idling while I wait for her response.

She slouches in her seat and pinches her lips between her fingers. She shoots me a sideways look. "What are you cooking?"

"A few years ago, I took a Thai cooking course. I make a mean pad Thai, if you're willing to take a chance."

"I'm more of a red curry girl, actually."

"If you agree to come, I'll make it happen."

"When do you work?"

"I start at eight, so it'll have to be an early dinner."

"Don't you want a nap or something before you go in?"

I was already working when we split up, so maybe she remembers how much I used to need a nap to get through night shifts. Six years later and I'm much better at surviving on less. "Sleep or hang out with you? The choice is easy."

She fiddles with a ring on her index finger and doesn't look at me. "I don't understand why you're trying so hard."

Such a simple answer in some ways. "Because I've compared every other woman I've dated to you, and none of them have measured up."

"That would be a really great line if I actually believed you." She meets my gaze, and her jaw is set.

I rub my face and debate how honest I should get at this point. "I used to drive past your house. But I could never figure out if you were home. Then—then I did come, and you slammed the door in my face." The bouquet of flowers I brought was crushed in the door.

She scoffs. "When you showed up at my door, I thought you were there for a different reason. My father's funeral was the day before. It's stupid, but I spent the whole process thinking you'd magically turn up, know I needed you.

When I opened the door, you started saying how sorry you were that you broke up with me. Nothing about my dad. I just lost it. You had no idea what was going on in my life. We weren't connected anymore. I had no emotional room for you. None."

"That explains the look of disbelief on your face when I started talking." I stare at my hands clenched around the steering wheel. How could I have fucked up so badly so many times? "I never came back because I thought, based on your expression, we were a lost cause. I'd burned it down, and there was nothing to rebuild."

"I don't know what's left, Simon. Maybe nothing good." She digs a hand into her thick hair, lifting it up and letting it fall.

After today, I'm sure the foundation of our relationship is still there, solid as ever. I might have burned down the house, but the footings held firm. "So," I say, raising my eyebrows. "Dinner?"

Chapter Nine

TAYLA

All the reasons I should say no are clear. After crying on his shoulder earlier and having him say one or two absolutely perfect things, my heart isn't cooperating with my head. A good line shouldn't turn me to mush. But sitting next to him at the pottery place, having him go along with my dickhead nonsense, the tightness of his hug, and even now when he's looking at me so earnestly, so intently, as though he actually means all the soulmate malarkey he's been spewing since Thursday, my resolve is slowly eroding.

"I think I'd like to just go home." Because as much as my outside has softened, there's still a tight ball inside of me filled with anger and confusion. Having him storm back into my life doesn't change what's passed between us.

He catches my gaze, and we hold eye contact for a beat, but he breaks it first. "If that's what you want—"

"I don't understand what your goal is here, Simon." The industrial warehouses around us are stark and impersonal and maybe more suited to this conversation than sitting cozied up together on stools, a penis plate in front of us. "But you can't snap your fingers and make things right between us. Whether you were there for it or not, there's a lot of water between us. There's no bridge."

"My goal is the same as yours." He grabs my hand and laces our fingers together, but I can't look at him again because tears are welling in my eyes. "I already know I didn't do the right thing six years ago, for so many reasons, but something has brought us back together again."

"A faulty computer system." I sniff and lift my gaze to the roof of the car, willing my hand to stop tingling from his touch, for my eyes to suck back the tears so they don't fall.

"Maybe." I can hear the smile in his voice. "Or maybe the computer system actually got it right this time."

My heart aches at his words. What's driving him? Guilt over how he broke up with me? Loneliness? Though I can't imagine Simon having a hard time getting women to swipe right. He's gorgeous with an outdoor ruggedness not many men possess. I used to love that he was as comfortable in a suit as he was in sweats around a campfire.

I never needed an algorithm to tell me we were good together. I felt it in my bones. For me, our connection was almost instant, and it flared so big and bright that everyone who came after him didn't compare. At one point, Ruby accused me of self-sabotaging by picking men who were the opposite of Simon. Maybe I did. None of them lasted more than a few months before we broke up. No hard feelings, just not right for each other.

I went into this Soulmates Reunited experience with an open heart, determined to be different, but matching with Simon has closed my heart right back up. Old wounds run deep.

"Can you take me home now?" Thankfully, my tears vanished without falling, so when I shift to look at him, my expression is impassive.

"I can't tempt you?" He releases my hand to put the car in Drive.

My fingers long to seek his warmth again. Could he tempt me? He already is, and that is a problem. "No." I focus on the scenery whizzing by. "I don't think you can."

Since we've had a cancellation, I'm holed up in my office, the door slightly ajar, researching vet exchange opportunities the organization sent me to broaden my selection. If I'm willing to go remote and rural, they think I might be able to get a match within the year. The most likely match, they said, is with a farm of some sort. Exciting and terrifying. When I left college, I was hoping to work with large animals eventually. I might need the money from Simon and the Soulmates Reunited refund to hire extra hands if I want to experience running a farm and still have an adventure I'll remember forever—find a work-life balance somewhere else that I can't seem to manage here in Michigan.

"You busy?" Sandy asks from the doorway.

"Not really," I admit and turn off my monitor. Both Sandy and Mike know I applied for an exchange two years ago, but we haven't spoken about it since. I'm sure if I told either of them I was considering adding remote veterinarian farms to my options, they'd tell me to give my head a shake.

"I have the business card you asked for. The guy who wanted your help to turn shelter dogs into therapy dogs?"

"Oh, right." With everything that has happened with Simon, I completely forgot. She passes the card to me, and I stare at the name. *Luis Gomez*. Fitting for the dark, smoldering man who tried to charm me and Sandy a few months ago. "Do you think he still needs help?"

A slow smile spreads across Sandy's face. "Only one way to find out." She leans against the doorframe. "How was lunch with Simon?"

"It ended with me agreeing to see him three times a week for the next three weeks." I sigh and set the card on the desk.

"Holy shit." Sandy laughs. "That escalated quickly."

I massage my fingertips into my temple, unsure how much I want to tell her. We're friends, but I'm conscious of my role as one of her bosses too. "I think I'll call Luis. Give me something else to focus on."

"Just how are you going to squeeze him in?" Sandy's brow furrows.

"I don't know," I admit. "But I think I need to make some changes in my life. Why not start here? Maybe he doesn't even need or want my help anymore."

"Is it your help you want to offer," Sandy asks, waggling her eyebrows, "or something else?" The bell for the front door chimes, and Sandy dashes off to meet our customer.

With five minutes before my next appointment, I pick up my phone and dial Luis's number before I lose my nerve. Someone who is interested in animals and helping people is exactly my type of person. When the call goes to voicemail, I leave a detailed message with the best times to call me back. Satisfied I've put the wheels in motion to make a change, I head to my next appointment.

"Dr. Murphy," the client, Elaine, exclaims as soon as I've entered the examination room. "I have great news. My son and his girlfriend just broke up."

"That's great news?" I gesture for her to put her puggle on the counter. As I run my hands along his round body, I'm already second-guessing my phone call to Luis.

"Yes! I've thought forever you'd be perfect for my son."

I chuckle. "He might have something to say about that." Sandy brings in the vaccines and places them on the counter behind me. Picking up the first one, I squeeze the skin on Hero's rump and inject the serum.

Elaine massages Hero's neck, and he licks her cheek. "He doesn't know what he wants," Elaine mutters. "That's his problem. I know what's good for him."

If I were even interested in meeting her son, that'd be a huge red flag. "I'm not convinced that's how parenting works." Given how round Hero the puggle is, Elaine might be a little too involved in the wrong way in several lives.

"Should be," Elaine huffs. "He's thirty-five. At what point is he going to grow up and pick a woman who is well suited to him instead of these college girls with air in their heads?"

I swallow my reply. College girls with air in their heads? Does she realize that's almost an oxymoron? "Well, I'm flattered you think highly of me," I say, inferring her meaning, "but I'm seeing someone right now." Although I'd prefer not to be, and I'm not treating my commitment to Simon as exclusive.

"I'll admit," Elaine says, "I spent a lot of years telling my son not to settle down too early. Experience the world and all that. I didn't think he'd take my advice quite so much to heart."

I bite back my smile. "That's the thing about advice." I select the next needle and squeeze the skin on Hero's other side. "You can never be sure how it'll be interpreted." There have been a few times during my career when I've had to relearn that lesson. No two people are built the same, and sometimes a message that seems simple is understood in the wrong way.

"Do you listen to your parents?" Elaine takes a biscuit out of the jar on the counter and passes it to Hero.

"Sure." My father's advice to work for myself once I was done veterinary school has turned out well. My brother, even though his life is nothing like mine, also took advice from my parents when planning his trips abroad. My mom's extensive travel knowledge as a flight attendant has been invaluable to him. "But I like to think I follow my gut too, and that I have enough faith in myself to know what's right for me."

Most of the time. My dates with Simon rise to the surface.

Being around him again probably isn't what's best for my mental health, but it's necessary for my bank account. The money will fund the more remote veterinarian exchanges. Tough choices have to be made.

"You can't make someone love you." When I realize what I've said, I amend it. "Or even like you. People feel what they feel, and sometimes there is no explanation for it."

Elaine waves her hand while she clips Hero back onto his leash, and I type some updates into the computer. "You're right. Maybe my son's reluctance to settle down has to do with his lack of a father figure."

Okay, then. We're not going to make any headway in this conversation. "Well, it's been great catching up with you, Elaine." I usher her out of my examination room so Sandy can wipe it down and I can move on to my next client. "You may want to lay off the biscuits for Hero for a while. His heavy stature can lead to health complications the older he gets."

Elaine sets Hero onto the floor, and he waddles toward the exit. When she follows behind him, they are two ducks in a row.

"She already paid?" I whisper to Sandy.

"When she came in," Sandy says. "How was that? She's always a wild card."

"Tried to set me up with her recently single son."

"Never rains but it pours. Soon you'll have three men on the go." Sandy winks. "Room two is ready for you."

Chapter Ten

SIMON

It's weird to admit, but dressed in her scrubs, meeting me at the front door to her practice, Tayla is straight out of my best memories. After we split, I dreamed about her for months—dreams so real I would wake disoriented, sure I hadn't turned my life upside down.

"I brought your favorite fish and chips." I hold up the insulated bag.

"That's really far from here." A small crease forms between her brows before she turns and heads down the hallway.

"Hence the bag." I follow her to her office.

While I unpack everything, she watches me, clearly wary. As I would have expected, her desk is free of clutter, and her textbooks are organized in neat, alphabetical rows on the shelf above.

"You woke up early, drove there, put the food in an insulated bag, and then came here?"

"It's not a big deal." I pass her the Styrofoam container with her portion in it. She said there wasn't a bridge between us for all that murky water to flow under. I intend to build it brick by brick, so strong that nothing can blow it up. If that means driving across town to do something for her I know she wouldn't do for herself, that's what I'll do.

"I haven't been there in a long time." Her brown eyes are full of curiosity. "Did you sleep?"

Being on nights this week would normally mean I'd be passed out at home for six to eight hours with Rex curled up next to me. "A bit." I dump the ketchup and utensils on the desk. "I'll go back to bed when I leave here. Go for a run with Rex before my shift."

"We didn't have to do lunch," she hedges, opening her container and sitting in one of the steel-armed chairs.

I chuckle and pop a fry into my mouth. "Oh yes, we did." I wink. "Gotta eat, right? Why not together?"

She narrows her eyes as she cuts into a piece of crispy fish with her fork. "Well, then you didn't have to go to the other side of the city to get this. We could have eaten from the restaurant just down there." She points to her right in the direction of the health food shop.

"Oh yeah? You're into eating that sort of thing now? I always find the salads from that chain are weird combinations, bordering on disgusting." I dip a piece of fish in ketchup. "What's your favorite meal there? I've got two other Tuesday lunches."

She sucks her teeth and purses her lips. "Okay, truthfully, it's my least favorite place to eat. But it's convenient."

"Convenience sometimes has to trump taste." I grab another fry. "What's your favorite place to eat now?"

"I don't go out much." She keeps focused on her food. "I work a lot, so it's just as easy to grab something at home."

We eat in silence for a minute before I break it. "I've been burying myself in work a lot lately too. It's easier, I guess, than having to think about *why* work is easier." My reusable water bottle is on the desk, and I pop off the top. "While I'm being run ragged by emergency room patients, there's not a lot of time for thoughtful introspection."

Up until now, that's been how I've liked it. Any time a girlfriend complained I worked too much, it wouldn't be long until we broke up. When Tayla and I were together, I wanted a work-life balance because being with her was better than anything else. Why did I ever think that feeling might fade? This past week, she's been all I can think about. I've already rearranged shifts so I can meet our three-dates-a-week commitment. And I won't let anyone dump extra work on me.

"Thoughtful introspection," Tayla muses. "You did a lot of that before you worked so much?"

I pause with a bite halfway to my mouth, and I lower my fork to my container. Our gazes connect, and a heaviness settles between us. "Not enough," I say, my voice a rasp. "Not about the right things."

She breaks eye contact, reaches for the fridge beside

her, and withdraws some sweet tea with a shaky hand. "I'm surprised you work so much with Rex. That's one of the reasons I don't have a pet of my own. No time."

"I have a dog walker who comes at least once a day. I go for a run with him every day too. Sometimes I drop him off at the doggy daycare near the hospital." Tayla and I planned to raise him together. When that fell apart, I realized pretty quickly I had to find ways to take care of him, give him a good life, even if it wasn't the life we expected.

As though she's read my mind, she grows quiet before saying, "I'm glad he's gotten the care he deserves."

"Tayla, I—" The doorbell sounds.

"Sorry," she says, dropping her lunch on the desk. "You'd think I'd learn to lock the door at lunch. Mike and Sandy are both out."

She hustles out of the office before I have a chance to say anything else. What was I going to say? I can't keep circling back to the past. I have to figure out a way to move us forward. After I've taken a few more bites, I begin to worry that Tayla isn't returning. She doesn't have any clients until one thirty, and it's just one now. With a frown, I head down the hall and hear two voices talking in the front entrance. Tayla's is light and comforting, and the other is a deep, masculine voice whose flirty tone sets me on edge.

"Saturday, then?" The guy, who is barely taller than Tayla, passes her a piece of paper. "It's a date?"

"How could I say no?" Her grin is filled with genuine amusement.

"That's what I like to hear," the guy says. His dark hair glints under the lights.

"Hey, Tay," I say, stepping out into the customer waiting area. "Everything good?"

"Yeah, fine." She flushes and half turns toward me.

"I'm Luis." Deep-voice guy extends his hand in my direction.

Before I can stop myself, I slide my hand into his. "Soulmate Simon."

Luis gives Tayla a confused glance and then raises an eyebrow. "Is that some kind of band?"

"Not a band, no." I smother my grin, trying to seem as serious as possible. "Tayla's nickname for me. I think it's cute. Some guys might think it's nauseating, but I'm just glad she's so sure about us, you know?"

Tayla gasps and smacks me in the arm. "That's *not* true."

Luis's gaze travels between the two of us while I give a shrug of *what can you do* and Tayla practically vibrates with anger.

"I don't know why he said that. It's not true." She subtly edges Luis toward the exit.

"Pumpkin, I don't know why you're so embarrassed to admit our love. When we're alone—"

She whirls on me, her finger raised. "No."

Luis's confusion is apparent, but he doesn't question me or Tayla on our behavior. "Saturday? We're good?"

"Yes," she snaps out. "Yes," she says again, softer this time. "Sorry about him." She tosses a thumb in my direction. "He's poorly trained."

"Hopefully we won't have the same problem with the dogs we pick out." His shoulder grazes hers at the door.

"I have faith in our dog selection skills." She smiles

at him and holds the door. Over her shoulder, our gazes connect. "I was really hoping to hook up with you—and your charity." She focuses on him again. "It's so great that you're giving back to the community in such a meaningful way."

"I'm trying," he says. "See you Saturday."

As soon as he's gone, Tayla closes the door with deliberate slowness. It's only then I realize my attempt to foil her flirtation might have been ill-advised. Impulsiveness is definitely a weakness in my character.

"You are such an asshole," she grits out. "Why would you say those things to him?"

"Probably for the same reason you slid in that 'hook up' comment at the end."

"I didn't mean anything by that." She crosses her arms.

"Bullshit." I laugh. "Are you seriously seeing other people in the next three weeks when you're supposed to be giving me a chance?"

"Did you seriously think I wouldn't? I gave you a chance six years ago—two years' worth of chances. You didn't say I had to give you my *exclusive* attention."

"Fine. We're exclusive for the next three weeks. I thought it was implied, but if I have to spell it out—"

"That's not how contracts work, Si. We have a deal." She wags her finger at me. "Nothing was said about us *only* seeing each other for the next three weeks. Three dates a week for three weeks. That's the deal. Nothing more. Nothing less."

I stride back to her office, and my brain ticks through this loophole that will probably sink me. She was so at ease with him, not wound tight as though one of us might detonate at any point. I toss a fry into my mouth and pace her office. She comes to the door and watches me.

"Need a run?" She crosses her arms and leans her shoulder into the doorway.

Whenever we got into a fight when we were dating, I went for a run. Cleared my head, got my feet back on the ground, and usually ended up agreeing with her. "Might help, yeah," I admit.

"So, we're just going to eat lunch like we didn't get in a fight?" Lips pursed, she takes her food and sits down again.

"Seems like. We gotta eat." I pop a piece of fish into my mouth but don't sit down. "I went across the city to get this." We eat in silence for a minute. "You still run?"

"Not like you." She picks at her fries and then cuts off another piece of fish. "I try to do a five-K race once in a while." A laugh escapes her. "You're going to find this funny, maybe. But I've really gotten into the ninja warrior courses. Not seriously, obviously. But I like the challenge."

"Isn't it hard when you're so short?" I eye her petite figure.

She throws a fry at me. "Hey, now. I'm no weakling."

"I didn't say that. Just that—I've watched that show— height is an advantage."

"You'd probably be good at it," she admits.

I scoop the fry off the floor and toss it into the garbage can by the door. A tentative plan is forming in my mind for Sunday. Assuming she doesn't completely ditch me after her superdate with Luis on Saturday. Now I just have to figure out Thursday's dinner date.

The doorbell rings again, and Tayla closes her container of food and slides it into the mini fridge where she got the sweet tea earlier. "Duty calls. You can finish eating before you go if you want."

I stare at her desk before sweeping up my container to leave. More sleep and a run might help clear my head. Although our conversation eased back into something resembling normal, my gut is still clenched, brimming with frustration. I told her I wouldn't ignore the past, but I can't help feeling like I'm not making enough headway. *Rebuild it, Simon.*

Chapter Eleven

TAYLA

We're seated on the patio overlooking the water. It's not an ocean view or even a Great Lakes view, but there's something soothing about a large body of water. A long-dead instinct, perhaps? Access to water is the difference between life and death for many species. I take in a deep, steadying breath and glance at Simon.

"Good choice?" He smirks.

"I cannot complain." A midsummer breeze blows across the lake, lifting the tips of my hair. As far as settings go, Simon nailed this one. We talked about coming to Reeds Lake while we were dating but never seemed to get around to it. I did come here for walks a few times in the intervening time, but I've never eaten at this restaurant.

It's picturesque and gorgeous and exactly right. A sigh of contentment escapes me. I might not understand why Simon is so insistent on making amends, but this date is a nice perk. "I hope the food is good. Have you been here before?"

"Nope. I've run the trails around here quite a bit, and I always looked at this place, but I could never seem to find the time to actually eat here." He hasn't opened his menu; instead, he's staring out across the lake.

It gives me a chance to examine his face. Was his jaw always that chiseled? The baby fat from his midtwenties is gone, replaced with a sharper outline. He's going to be one of those men who look better and better as they age. No sign of hair loss. No beer paunch. There's probably still the faintest outline of a six-pack under his T-shirt. A memory surfaces of my fingertips tracing those lines as his muscles contracted. So many lazy Sundays where fingers turned to lips and tongues and . . .

I shake my head. *Get your mind out of the gutter, Tayla.* "How are you parents?" I ask.

"My parents?" The question seems to surprise him. "They're . . . good. My dad lives in Florida now. My mom still lives not far from my apartment."

"Your parents always had such a great marriage. I'm surprised your dad loves Florida enough to be there without your mom." I open the menu and start to read through the selections.

Simon clears his throat. "Actually, he's in Florida for precisely that reason—to be away from my mom. Not that she minds all that much now."

"What? I don't understand." I glance up from reading the steak choices.

"They're divorced."

"Divorced?" My voice rises in surprise. "You're kidding me."

"My dad left her and went to a monastery in France. And before you ask, no, he did not speak French at the time."

"A monastery in France?" When Simon and I were dating, we often held up the marriages of our parents as something to aspire to. His parents were so close they finished each other's thoughts. "That's wild."

"I went to visit him. I wasn't in a good place, and being there helped him, so I thought, why not?" Simon scratches the back of his neck and opens his menu.

Had that been during the time I stalked him from afar? "After you and Jada broke up?"

"What?" His head jerks up as though I've fired a shot.

A flush creeps up my neck. Shit. Why did I say that? "I just assumed . . ."

"No. Not even. It was after you slammed the door in my face, crushing my lovely bouquet of flowers. Of course, now, knowing the whole situation, I'm the one who feels like an asshole . . . again." He flips the page on his menu and waits a beat before pinning me with his gaze. "How'd you know about Jada?"

The blush has migrated from my neck into my face. The heat is scorching. Just how red am I? "Social media, I think? I mean, probably?" Certainly not obsessive stalking habits by me and Ruby. "I can't really remember."

"Anyway," he says with a dismissive wave of his hand,

"that kicked off the travel bug for me for a while. Went to a bunch of monasteries while I was over there."

"You liked it that much?"

"I had a lot of thinking to do, and being there was exactly the right place to do it."

"So, getting away from all this for a while was helpful?" The vets abroad exchange program jumps to mind. "I've been planning to do something similar."

"A nunnery?" Simon closes his menu and picks up his drink. "Wouldn't have pegged you for the sort." His eyes are twinkling with a teasing light.

"Not a nunnery." A hint of a smile tugs at the corners of my lips. "There's a vets abroad program where you do a straight practice swap with a vet from another country."

He swallows and holds my gaze for a moment. Surprise and regret flicker in the green depths of his eyes for a moment. "Where are you thinking about going?"

"I'm in the process of expanding my choices to see if I can get a match." The thought stirs my excitement.

He takes a deep breath. "You should definitely do it. Travel is good for the soul. Anyone who got you as an exchange partner would leave their practice in good hands."

We make eye contact, and my heart thuds in response. Goose bumps rise across my arms, and I'm tempted to take his hand, which is resting on top of the tablecloth. We were a PDA couple when we were together. Affection flowed between us as naturally as air.

Flustered, I knock my glass, tipping it across the table. "Oh no." Jumping up, I mop at the mess on the table, and

Simon uses his own napkin and then borrows some off the table next to us. A waitress appears out of nowhere.

"Just water?" she asks, plucking up anything that could be damaged in the flood.

"Yes." I glance at her. "Sorry."

"It's not a problem. I'll get someone to remake the table. Why don't you move over there?" She points to a table two down from us.

"I took the napkins from that table." Simon points behind us.

"I'll replace them. Nothing to worry about." She smiles at us both as she gathers everything. "Did you know what you wanted?"

I order the steak, and Simon follows suit.

He plucks up his drink, and his free hand grazes the small of my back as we walk over to the table she suggested. Heat spreads from his palm, a wildfire across my back, blazing to my core with a desire so strong I almost stumble. I long to turn in his arms, have him duck his head, his lips capturing mine. What would it be like to kiss him again? To feel the sweep of his tongue?

Once we're settled, an awkward silence descends before Simon says, "Do you have anything else going on on Sunday?"

Relieved for the change of subject, I offer a smile. "Besides our date?"

"Yeah. I was hoping I might get you for the whole day. I have big plans. I don't work, so I don't have to rush off or have a nap. I could cook dinner?"

The whole day? Dinner? Big plans? Anticipation zips

through me, but unease follows behind. These dates have been fun so far, but if he keeps being this good, I'm going to get sucked in deeper than I want. "Will I like it?"

"I think you'll love it. Honest assessment. Not just inflating my ego." He surveys me over the rim of his glass before taking a sip.

"Your ego probably doesn't need much help."

"Tends to rise on its own." His lips twitch.

"Is this still your ego?" I narrow my eyes.

"Of course." He feigns confusion. "What else would we be talking about?" Then, as though it's suddenly occurred to him, he leans across the table. "Unless . . . unless we've pivoted back to talking about my dick?" he stage-whispers. "I knew you had a penis fetish."

"You're ridiculous." I make a duck face trying to hold in my laughter.

We fall into an easy chatter about the running races Simon has tackled the last few years. "I'm gunning for Boston. I made the qualifying time one year and then screwed up my knee, so I couldn't go."

"Twenty-six miles of running is my worst nightmare."

"You can pace me on your bike."

"You're running that fast now?"

"Depends on how fast you're biking." He grins. "Spent a lot of time the last few years running and working."

"Doesn't leave much time for anything else."

"You're not alone in that thought." His expression darkens.

Not that I'm one to talk. I have my veterinary practice and then I do work for various shelters and volunteer for emergency hours all over Grand Rapids. No hour is too early or late for someone to call me. In fact, next Thursday night I'm on call.

His work-life balance was good with me. Of course, we used to spend Sundays mapping out our schedules for weeks in advance to make sure we'd see enough of each other. Our priority was each other . . . until it wasn't.

"How was your steak?" He nods to my empty plate.

"Excellent. This cabbage side dish might have beat the steak, though." I point to the purple mark on the plate where the cabbage was.

"I'll have to see if I can find a recipe for it online." He takes out his credit card and passes it to the waitress.

Simon checks his phone for the time. "I've got about thirty minutes before I need to drive you home. Walk with me?" He holds out his hand for me to take as we head for the exit.

The sign for the path is to our right, and I only hesitate a moment before sliding my hand into his. Is this a good idea? Not even remotely. We're not a couple. I don't want to be a couple.

"What are you thinking about?" Simon asks, his gait matching mine.

"It's so pretty here."

"That's not what you were thinking about." He chuckles. "But I'm gonna let that slide. Your face was far too serious for pretty thoughts."

"What was your last serious relationship?" I ask on impulse. Maybe if I figure out why he came to my veterinary clinic when he got the email instead of ignoring it, I can loosen up. He broke up with me. He knows we're not a good match, so his behavior is baffling.

"Her name was Mandy. We dated a couple months. Ended a while ago." His jaw tightens a fraction.

"Why'd you break up?" A few days ago, I would have said I didn't want to know any of this, but now I'm not so sure. Can I figure out anything about our breakup from his other relationships?

"I'm a workaholic. That's according to her . . . and a few others."

We walk in silence for a few moments while I process his answer. So strange for him to go from good at prioritizing relationships that matter to putting work first. "You were never like that with me."

"I know," he says, sliding me a sideways look. He stops walking, and his hands loop around my waist in a comfortable embrace.

The closeness of our bodies stirs the long-dormant embers of desire. He's not wearing the same cologne tonight. It's woodsy rather than the tangy scent he used to wear. Even without the memories attached to the other smell, this one suits him more. We're facing each other, and he smooths my hair, looping a strand around his finger.

"Why?" I whisper. The air around us is heavy with things unsaid and a building desire I wish I could ignore.

"Spending time with you was easy. A joy. Something I wanted more than I wanted anything else." His eyes lock with mine. "I've never felt that way about another woman."

My breath catches. I want his words to be true, for the sentiment to be real. Apart from one attempt, he's never reached out to me, checked up on me, asked for another chance. How do you feel that way about someone and *not* act?

"I resigned myself to never having a chance to get you back." He smooths my flyaway hair when it gets caught by the breeze, tucking it behind my ears.

Will he kiss me? Do I want him to kiss me? Time hangs suspended, and I remember how in sync we used to be, as though we'd kissed a thousand times before our lips ever skimmed across each other. On our third date, he said he felt like he'd known me for years, not days. We joked that we'd been together in another life. All these memories I haven't allowed myself to access. To remember them, to dwell on them, was madness.

When I gaze into his green eyes now, the same familiarity settles over us, and I long to wrap myself in the comforting sensation. My heart thunders in my ears, a reminder that underneath the residual affection is something primal, a well of passion to drown in. Even if I would never say it out loud, I want *him*, *crave* the connection. If *this* is still between us—so alive, so rich, so solid—how did we ever fall apart?

"On your right!" a biker calls, whizzing past us, the wind from his bike swirling my hair around my face.

The spell snaps with the sudden whip of my hair. I step away from Simon and roll my shoulders, the weight of our past dropping off. None of this is real. He's manufacturing a bond. I agreed to these nine dates for money. That's all. The simmering chemistry between us can't addle my brain. "We should get going," I say without checking the time.

"Yeah" He shoves his hands into the pockets of his jeans and takes a deep, steadying breath. "I guess we should."

Chapter Twelve

SIMON

Sleep, something I used to drop into without any effort, has eluded me lately. Longer runs, pushing myself to exhaustion, haven't helped. Last night, memories of Tayla clicked through my mind, teeth on a ratchet, each remembrance tightening my gut.

As a result, when I drive into Aaron's high-end car dealership on Saturday morning, I'm on my third coffee, and I've brought one for him as well.

"Here with a coffee on a Saturday. Your bargain with Tayla giving you trouble?" He takes a sip and settles into the leather chair behind his desk.

I chuckle and take a gulp of my drink. Aaron has lived through the fallout of every breakup I've had since high school. The one with Tayla was the worst by miles. "I took her to Reeds Lake on Thursday for dinner."

"Sparing no expense." He whistles and taps a pen on his desk. "Even with you opening your wallet, I still cannot believe she agreed to your plan. I hope you've started a shrine to some sort of god, because that's a miracle if I ever saw one."

"Tayla would probably like a shrine, right? Who wouldn't want that level of devotion?" Some women find obsession hot. Tayla is not one of them.

"Would not recommend the shrine." Aaron sighs. "Whenever you come in here full of avoidance, you're not ready to get to the heart of things."

He's not wrong. I sink deeper into the plush chair across from him. Aaron's theory is that customers spend more money when they're surrounded by opulence. Everything in his office is high-end and incredibly comfortable. My theory is that if he can afford this nice furniture, he can also afford to give people a deal. Our friendship means I've never asked for one, and even when he's offered, I haven't often accepted.

"We're going to be a while, aren't we?" He tips his chair forward and stands. "I've got a group of animal shelter people coming here to use the parking lot later today. Come help me set up."

He reads me well. I want company, but I don't want to talk. I grab my coffee off his desk and follow him. "What's the deal?"

"I gotta move some cars to make space for their cages and fenced areas at the front." He plucks keys out of a lockbox on the way to the lot.

"They're doing adoptions or . . . ?"

"Adoptions. They sell some merchandise too. Take donations. We sponsor them. One of our community outreach things." He shrugs and passes me three sets of keys. "Those ones can be moved to the back over there." He points toward the rear of the building where there's a strip of gravel rather than asphalt.

"Got it." I pocket the keys and head for the sports cars on display along the road. I slip my coffee into a cup holder and set to work. As I move a vehicle and walk back to get another, I try to gather my wits. Thoughts of Tayla are a constant undercurrent, a deep underground stream I'm not sure I can tap around Aaron without causing a geyser of emotions.

When we're finished, we stand together watching the traffic stream by on the main road. "I was an idiot six years ago."

"You were, yeah." Aaron grimaces. "We both know that. I might even have told you at the time."

"You did." Part of me knew I wasn't making the best choice, but I couldn't seem to get a handle on my warring emotions.

"Part of my charm as a best friend? Unwavering honesty." He laughs.

"I should have called *you* that night." I drain the last of my coffee.

"Yeah, not much I could do the next day after you blew up your life."

"I was so stupid."

"You should have told Tayla what was happening

instead of trying to keep it from her." He gives me a meaningful look. "It wasn't Soulmates Reunited matching you out of the blue or even the pressure they put on you that sank you . . . or the never-ending house search or even your dad's midlife crisis. It was you."

I rub my face. There's his damn honesty again. "Yeah, I came to terms with that. I wanted to be ready, but I wasn't, which is why I went to her house to explain."

"Have you told her? Talked about what went wrong? Trying to rebuild a relationship with her isn't right if you aren't going to give her all the information."

"Makes me look like an asshole." If I tell her the complete truth before she at least likes me again, she's not going to stick around.

"Because *you* were an asshole. A confused one who eventually got help. Just own it." He gives me a quick jab to my ribs. "Everything going on last time isn't happening this time."

It's true. The tornado of events leading up to the botched proposal aren't factors now, and I spent a lot of time meditating in monasteries and speaking to their counselors over how quickly I was swept away by uncertainty. I was weak when I needed to be strong, and I'm not making that mistake again. More than ever, I understand what I've lost.

Thursday night on the path, my gaze locked with Tayla's, and an overwhelming sense of rightness seeped into my bones. From the minute she stepped out of her little house on our first date, it felt like I could take a full breath for the first time in my life. How did I lose sight of that when it mattered most?

When she shut the door on me five years ago, I thought giving up was the respectful thing to do. She couldn't stand the sight of me. I'd watched my mom fight for a lost cause, and it only drew my father's scorn.

But now, knowing the circumstances in her life at the time, I wish, more than anything, I had gone back one more time after I got help. Where would we be? Would she have been able to forgive me then? Can she forgive me now?

"I don't think I can own everything yet." I fiddle with my empty cup. "At least not to her."

"The longer you wait, man, the closer you'll be to fucking up again." He takes my cup. "That's the shelter coming now in that cargo van. I'll throw these out and be right back."

As the van drives into the lot, I pretend to be an air traffic controller, and the woman in the driver's seat, who looks about my age, laughs as she steers into the parking spot I selected. "Very clever," she says, climbing out of the vehicle.

"Need a hand?" I grin and shove my hands into my pockets.

"I'd never say no to that," she says. The woman and her middle-aged partner from the passenger seat walk around to the back of the van. As soon as the back doors are open, I take out fencing and let them direct me through their setup. Aaron returns and, after watching for a minute, pitches in even though he's in a suit.

Another van arrives with the puppies, kittens, and older dogs. Once they're all set up in their various pens or cages, Aaron tips his head at the puppies. "You're not tempted?"

94

"To take one or to get in the pen?" Truthfully, I've been itching to climb into the enclosure with the mutts. They look like a Labrador or German shepherd cross, and I can't help remembering Rex as a pup.

"Both." Aaron grins. "I'm even tempted."

When he says it, he's not looking at the puppies, he's checking out Denise, the young blond who joked with me earlier. "No ring," I say, following his gaze.

"Not exactly a true marker for availability."

"Want me to ask her if she's single?"

"And risk her thinking you're going to ask her out? Uh, no. I suspect you're more her type anyway. She's been sliding glances in your direction."

As though sensing our scrutiny, Denise approaches. "Did you want to hold a puppy?" Her hands are on her slim hips.

"I kinda want to climb in there and roll around with them," I admit.

She laughs. "Might as well do that before we get busy or there's too much poop and pee." She shudders.

No need for a second invitation. I climb into the pen, and two of the ten puppies come over, their butts causing the rest of their bodies to wiggle. While I pick each one up to examine them, Aaron strikes up a conversation with Denise.

A puppy haze descends, and I don't realize how many people have started to mill around. When I get my favorite puppy comfortable enough to relax on her back like a baby, I'm pleased I remembered the handling Tayla taught me. I glance up, and there at the edge of the fencing, light brown eyes tender with affection and amusement, is Tayla. My heart kicks at the sight of her. Her jeans and fitted T-shirt aren't as fancy as the dress she wore the other night, but it doesn't stop me from wanting to climb out of the puppy enclosure, sweep her into my arms, and feel her sigh of contentment against my lips.

"I can't believe they let you in there," Tayla says, but her eyes are lit with amusement. "Who'd you have to bribe?"

"I used up my charm quotient for the day." I grin. "Are you finally giving in to the call of the puppy?" I gesture to the little one in my arms. "I've got a good candidate right here." Would she take a puppy with her if she moved to another country? Another reason I've been twisted in knots. If I do manage to win her around, would I be holding her back? Or would she go even if I couldn't follow? Neither of those options sits well with me.

She shakes her head, a hint of a smile playing on her lips. "She is a good one to let you hold her like a baby."

"Think we should take that one?" the man at her side asks.

My body tenses when I realize the man beside Tayla is Luis, the guy from the vet clinic when I was there for lunch. A flare of annoyance bursts to life. Is she spending the day with him? Are they picking out a puppy together?

"What do you think, Si?" She examines me thoughtfully. "We're picking out rescue dogs to be trained as therapy dogs."

Relief douses my annoyance. They're not really puppy shopping together, and she's asking my opinion. A burst of pride rips through me that she values my opinion. "Well," I say, setting the pup down, "I've already taught her to sit." As soon as she's out of my arms, she tries to crawl back in. Tayla laughs at my efforts to keep her out of my lap to show off the hard work I've done this last half hour. "She *was* sitting."

"Are *you* interested in her?" she asks me, her gaze intense.

I examine the puppy, and the desire to snatch her up and take her home spreads across my chest. She would be a great therapy dog. Her focus, temperament, and joy in human companionship would be assets. "No," I say with a shake of my head. "Better not."

"I think we've got our first candidate," she says to Luis. "We should take her."

Luis's gaze travels between me and Tayla for a moment, a hint of a frown marring his forehead. What's he thinking? Finally, he nods and heads over to intercept Denise, who is busy trying to upsell a woman adopting a cat.

"I didn't realize you'd be here," Tayla says as the pup collapses in my lap with a sigh.

I stroke the dog and tip my head toward Aaron. "This is Aaron's dealership. I just stopped in to have a chat and then . . . well . . ." I gaze into my lap. "Who can resist puppies?"

"Aaron owns this dealership?" She glances around, surprise clear on her face.

When we were together, Aaron had just started selling cars. For him to own his own dealership now means exactly what she thinks. He's done extremely well for himself. Perhaps there *is* something to his expensive furniture theory. "For about a year now."

"Explains your fancy car."

"Gotta support your friends." Our gazes connect, and she's searching me, looking for something. What, though? "You're still driving the same car. Maybe it's time for an upgrade?"

"I'm loyal in a different way, I suppose." She crosses her arms and scuffs her feet. "Don't need the fanciest model, just one that's reliable and comfortable."

Is that a dig at me?

"I filled in all the paperwork," Luis says, drawing level with Tayla outside the fenced pen. "They'll call us tomorrow if we're approved."

"Great," Tayla says, but she stays focused on me and the pup. The longing on her face causes an ache to bloom across my chest.

"Seems she's a bit in love with you," Luis says with a chuckle.

Tayla's attention snaps to him, a protest on her lips, but she closes her mouth and follows Luis's gaze to my lap. Warmth spreads across my chest. She thought he was talking about her?

"Maybe," I say, a hint of a smile tugging at the edges of my mouth. Tayla's gaze connects with mine, a flush in her cheeks. "I might be a little bit in love with her too."

Chapter Thirteen

TAYLA

Simon has abs. Rock-hard, clearly defined, delicious-looking abs. How do I know? I've been staring at them all day. He must have gained an ab for every year we were apart. The man has an inhuman amount of energy. After a five-mile run, he drove us to the ninja warrior gym I belong to.

"I think you should try it," Simon says, eyeing the salmon ladder.

We've already done all the obstacles I'm good at. Having him trail me around the gym has been a pleasant surprise. He's been thoughtful in his approach to the harder obstacles and willing to laugh at himself when he fails. I suppose it's only fair I return the favor. "I can only get three rungs. Ever."

"I'm betting on four today." His gaze slides down my body.

"Oh yeah? I've magically become stronger overnight?" I laugh and shake my head. "I was here yesterday." Even still, I can't help my answering grin. I hate him and I love him for nailing every date so far. Our unexpected encounter yesterday caused my insides to melt like gooey marshmallows, and today isn't helping that sensation. "You're not allowed to give me a hand." I point a finger in his direction as I stand in front of the obstacle. The bar lies across a set of angled rungs, and I have to pull my body up, lifting the bar into the next rung in midair. My abs ache just looking at it.

"I will keep my hands to myself." His lips twitch.

I stretch to reach the bar, and then I pull up in a quick movement, drawing my knees up to my chest. I make one, two, three rungs, and I can't get the bar out of its slot again. With a frustrated noise, I drop.

He stares at the bar, his expression pensive. "Can I try?"

"If you can reach the bar."

He lifts his arms, and with a little hop, he's on the bar. *Show-off.* He doesn't even need to lower it. Without saying anything, he lets go, examines the bar again, and jumps with a wider grip. Simon pulls up, drawing his knees into his chest over and over until he reaches the top. "Now what?" he calls down.

"Ratchet back down or drop down and we can use a special stick to retrieve the bar." Although I never get far enough to worry about it, there are plenty of people who make this obstacle look easy when I'm here working out.

"I'm thinking that five-mile run wasn't such a hot idea

now." He drops down gracefully and shakes out his arms. "You could get at least one more rung, maybe two."

I eye him skeptically as I pass him the retrieval stick. We replace the bar, and when I reach up and grip it, Simon hesitates a second before saying, "I think if you put your hands just a little wider, you'd get a better angle."

He's been good about every pointer I've given him throughout the course, so without comment, I inch my hands farther apart. "Like this?"

"Yeah." He comes around behind me. "Permission to give you a hand?" His tone is teasing, but he won't touch me unless I agree. At least that aspect of him hasn't changed.

"Just one?" My lips quirk up.

"If you'll let me do two, I'll definitely use both." One hand comes to rest on my hip, and I'm keenly aware of the pad of each finger on top of the thin material of my T-shirt. A shiver of pleasure rolls over my body.

"I'm not sure I like you suggesting I'm a handful." *Oh no.* Even my voice sounds turned on.

"Two handfuls." His voice is rough, laced with the same desire that's hit me. "Perfection."

Against my will, my body heats. While we lay in bed, he used to cup my breasts in his hands—*the perfect handful*, he'd say as he ran his thumb across the nipple. At the memory, my nipples pucker. I close my eyes and will myself to focus. "What were you going to show me?" Is that squeaky voice mine?

He clears his throat. "When you bring your knees up . . ." he says, cupping my hips and my ass to assist me in a faster hinge motion. Of course he has to touch me now when I'm so turned on I could burst. "Try to do it quicker."

"Says the guy with the six-pack abs," I mutter.

He chuckles softly. "You're better than you think." His hands trail along my legs a little longer than necessary before he steps back. Once the warmth is gone, I want to call him back. With his hands on his hips, he takes a deep breath. "All right. We're going for five."

"You said four."

"Aim high, Tay. Aim high."

After a deep breath, I hitch up the first rung, and as I'm climbing one, two, three rungs up, Simon cheers me on. "Come on, Tay. Bring those legs up. Make those abs scream."

Something in me is dying to scream, but it isn't my abs. I hitch up to four, and I lower my legs, prepared to quit. That's a new record for me.

"Don't give up on me," Simon says, peering around the post so he can see me hanging. "One more."

"I don't think I can."

"You haven't tried. What's the worst that happens?"

I lose my grip on the rail and fall to the plush mats below. Not the first time, but I've never been so conscious of some-one watching me. Letting out a deep breath, I tighten my grip on the bar and bring my knees up to my chest. I make the fifth rung and let out a gleeful laugh. Without thinking, I try for a sixth, but my arms have decided they're done, and my brain doesn't get the signal fast enough. The bar only makes it onto one slot, and I cry out as I drop backward.

Long, muscular arms circle me in a bear hug before I hit the mat, and we tumble back together. My *oof* of surprise is followed by his groan. "You're heavier than you look." He loosens his grip on my waist.

I roll over, still pressed against him, and straddle his waist. "Are you okay?" He's got all his limbs, and nothing seems to be thrust out in a weird angle. No breaks or obvious damage. When I get to his face, there's a hint of a smirk. His hands rest lightly on my hips, and the warmth from before returns, swirling around my core like a serpent. How many times have I looked down at him like this? The ache inside me builds, taunting me to grind against him, lower my lips to his. Forget where we are and just let go. Why does he have to be so freaking attractive?

"I've been in worse positions." His smirk widens to a grin.

I smack his chest and climb off him, cursing him and my traitorous body for remembering all too well how good we used to be together. Just like his approach to the ninja course, in the bedroom Simon was eager to please, to excel. If I wasn't satisfied, neither was he. A rare man. The kind you want to hang on to. Too bad I couldn't.

"I think we should go," I say, grabbing my towel and water bottle off the ground. "I should probably get home."

He's slower to get up and stays in a crouch position for a few breaths before rising. "You said we could spend the whole day together, Tay."

All these mixed-up, muddled emotions where he's concerned need to go away. "It's already four o'clock." I nod to the clock above the door. "I need a shower, and I'm tired."

He runs a hand through the short strands on the top of his head, and they stick up at odd angles. "You can shower at my place. No more feats of strength, I promise." Our gazes meet, and his is full of frustration and pleading. "Let me cook you dinner."

I break eye contact and take a long drink from my water bottle. I *am* hungry, but I'm starting to realize too much time with Simon will break my heart . . . again. His motivation for pursuing me is baffling, or maybe it's just that I don't believe the reasons he's given me. "Dinner," I agree. "But then I'm going home."

Simon showered first, and then while I took a long, hot one, he started dinner. The rice is bubbling on the stove, and he leans against the counter in his small kitchen. Rex is lying on a dog bed in the main room; his initial excitement over seeing me again has mostly subsided. It's the same apartment, but it doesn't look anything like the one I spent time in years ago.

"The landlord let you make all these renovations? He paid for them?" I eye the white backsplash and grey cupboards. The countertop is a white-and-grey quartz. Neutral. Tasteful. So well-done.

"Once I showed him a few other side projects I'd done, he realized I wasn't a complete idiot. My sister does interior design, so that was helpful too."

I run my hand along the wood and pop open one of the doors. "You made these from scratch?"

His lips twitch. "Yes. Took me a couple years to get the whole kitchen done. You're really *this* surprised? I made stuff all the time."

That's true. Any spare moment Simon had between me, running, and working, he spent doing odd projects in his parents' garage with his dad. Everything he made impressed me. Stools. End tables. Children's chairs or train sets. "Do you still sell some of your stuff?"

"The odd thing. My sister puts in requests for her kid, soon to be kids, most of the time." He turns down the bubbling water. "I take a lot of extra shifts at work, so I don't have as much free time."

"You're such a contradiction," I muse, invading his privacy by peering into more of his cupboards under the guise of inspecting his craftsmanship. They look professional. Can't fault him. I wish he had these skills when we were together. My kitchen needs an update.

"A contradiction?" He raises his eyebrows and crosses his arms.

I peek at his biceps, remembering how they looped around my waist. Another surge of desire pools in my belly. "You fly to Europe for all these meditation opportunities. Deep thinking or whatever that is. But at home, you bury yourself in work."

"I find my job rewarding." He shrugs. "Didn't you say you've been burying yourself in work too?"

"Yeah," I say. "But that's because . . ." The words die on my lips. I can't tell him the rest. *Because I was afraid of making a connection like the one we had.* To love someone to the depth I loved Simon has been impossible.

"Because?" Simon prompts, trying to catch my gaze.

I laugh, but it sounds false to my ears. "Because I find my job rewarding too."

He sighs, but instead of pressing me, he checks the chicken in the oven and stirs the sauce on the stove. "That why you're doing the rescue dog thing? How many did you and Luis pick out?"

"Two," I admit, grateful for the change in subject, for the tightness in my chest dissipating. "We're going to see how we get along with them and then go from there."

"He's training them?" When the timer beeps, he removes the pan from the stove and places it on the heating pads.

"I'm taking the pup you liked," I admit. "I pick her up Tuesday."

Simon's eyes light up. "What time?"

"After work. Probably around five thirty."

"I'm not done work on Tuesday until five." He scans my face. "Can I—can we switch lunch to dinner? I'll bring it with me. I'd love to see her again."

I bite my lip. The thought of having Simon in my little house is appealing and appalling. His apartment used to be run-down, but it's always been spacious. My house, in comparison, is cramped quarters. Our original plan was for me to take a longer lunch and eat at the hospital cafeteria with him. Nothing remotely intimate about that setting. Dinner at mine would be a whole different scenario.

"You can think about it over dinner." Simon plates our food.

We slide onto seats side by side at the island. His shoulder brushes mine as he cuts into his food. We eat dinner, mostly in silence. Everything he cooked is delicious.

"Tell me your best memory from the last six years," Simon says as he takes my empty plate.

I tap my lip as I search through various travels and events during our time apart. "Backpacking through Australia for two weeks with my brother."

"Why?" he asks, loading the dishwasher and filling the sink for the items too big to fit.

"I can do those," I say, rising to stand beside him at the sink.

He scans my face, and my breath catches in my throat. There's such intensity and hunger in his eyes, as though, like me, thoughts of us in this apartment have taken over. So many times we worked after dinner, shoulder to shoulder, doing dishes. Other times, the dishes were ignored, a different sort of dessert on the agenda. One time, the sink overflowed on the floor while we made love on the island. When we emerged from the orgasmic haze, we laughed while we cleaned up the mess, surprised we'd become so lost in each other.

Now, he ignores the bubbles sprouting in the sink, his gaze fixed on mine. His hand lifts hesitantly before smoothing down the back of my hair. "I've missed you, Tay."

Instead of questioning him, I mute the voice of reason in my head. My body is switched on, yearning for him, for the surge of electricity. Will he taste like chicken and rice or like the minty gum he chewed all day?

His fingers graze my cheekbone, and warmth swirls out from my core, making my insides tingle. "Are you gonna kiss me, Si?" My voice is husky.

"Do you want me to?" The low tone of his words sends a vibration right to my center.

"Yes," I whisper because lying isn't an option. He's

hands and eyes and lips, and I want to devour him whole.

Without hesitation, he slides his hands into my loose hair and tugs me against him, dipping down to capture my lips, seeking, testing, and then diving in. A sigh escapes me, and I clutch his biceps for a moment to keep from sinking into the ground. He hits the handle on the tap with one hand and then lifts me onto the counter in a smooth motion, his lips barely leaving mine. My body is on fire, but my brain is starting to perk up, niggling thoughts invading the desire-filled haze. I kiss him harder, trying to convince myself the questions rising to the surface don't matter. My fingers tug at strands of his hair because as much as I want him, there's a part of me still confused and hurting.

What am I doing?

Chapter Fourteen

SIMON

She tastes like peach lip balm. When she sighed, the sound I remember so well, my dick rose in response. I've missed her. I've missed this fire blazing between us. I press closer to the heat, deepening the kiss. She said yes, and I'm not letting this opportunity go. We fit together. I was such a fool to let other people's doubts become mine.

When she pulls back, I try to follow, desperate to remind her we're good for each other. Her fingers tugging on my hair are almost painful. *Hurt me if you need to, Tayla. I'll take it.*

"Stop!" She gasps out the word as though it's been torn from her.

I wrench my mouth from hers and take a step back. My chest is heaving, and I'm relieved hers is too. When our gazes connect, her eyes are heavy with desire. I brace my hands on the counter on either side of her, but it takes a moment before I can speak. "Are you okay?"

"No. I want to go home. I want to leave." She brushes my arm aside and hops off the counter, grabbing her workout bag and keys from behind the couch.

"Tay," I call, almost jogging after her through the apartment. "Tay. Wait." When she won't look at me, I grab her elbow and spin her around. "What's wrong?"

"What's wrong?" She scoffs as though the question is ludicrous. "God, Simon, how can you be so clueless?" Her finger stabs my chest. "You said if we did this, if I agreed to do this, you weren't going to pretend the past didn't happen. But you are. *We are*." She drops her hand. "And I—I can't do that. I won't do that. You broke my fucking heart." Tears pool in her eyes. "I don't know why you left me. I've never understood why you did it."

I rub my face and cup a hand over my mouth. Christ. I can't tell her now. How can I? "I'll tell you. We can—we can talk about it."

"When? When are you going to explain to me why you didn't love me enough?" A tear slips down her cheek.

Holy fuck. My chest tightens, squeezing so hard I wonder if my heart is in an actual vise. "That's what you think?"

"You broke up with me, and within a week you were dating Jada. Two years together, and seven days later, you've got a new girlfriend. What did you expect me to think?"

"I didn't—I didn't expect you to think anything. We were—we weren't really dating."

Jada's flurry of social media posts comes to mind, but I

untagged myself in those, and that was months after Tayla and I broke up. Months, not weeks. Maybe it just felt like weeks to Tayla given the circumstances, or maybe Jada was there earlier and more than I remember. I try really hard not to think about it.

Tayla cocks her head, a mixture of hurt and anger coating her face. "Are you trying to spare my feelings? It's too late for that." Her voice is thick with unshed tears. "I just want the truth."

She makes it sound so simple. The reasons for my change of heart are what she wants, and I'm not ready to give her those. She won't honor our deal if she realizes Soulmates Reunited is a fraud. "Why did you go to Soulmates Reunited?"

She rolls her eyes. "Seems obvious, doesn't it? I was doing a shitty job of picking a partner." She purses her lips. "You're not going to tell me the truth?"

"I will. I told you I will, and I will. Not tonight. I can't tonight."

"Your truth has a timeline? Nice, Simon. Doesn't sound shady at all." She grabs the door handle. "Take me home."

Once we're in the car, an uneasy silence envelops us. We're not far from her place when I take a deep breath. Jada is a complication I didn't see coming. Last time Tayla brought her up, I was surprised, and when she didn't push, I didn't elaborate.

"Have you ever been pressured into doing something you didn't want to do?" We're turning down Tayla's street. She's quiet as I inch past each house, willing her to answer, wishing I said something sooner.

"Probably everyone has at some point." Tayla bites her lip and glances in my direction. "Maybe a cookie when they aren't hungry or maybe something bigger. I'm a vet. I work with shelters and rescues. We have perfectly healthy animals that come into the clinic that owners or shelters want to euthanize."

Not the direction I was anticipating the conversation going. She's talking to me again, so that's a win. "What do you do?"

"I didn't go to vet school to kill animals." She rubs her forehead, and the car crawls up the driveway to her house. "I went to save them. To care for them. The reality, sometimes, is that I can't save them all. So, yeah, I've been in situations where I've been torn in two." Our gazes meet in the burgeoning darkness. "Is that what happened, Si? To us?"

"A lot of things happened in the weeks leading up to our breakup." I put the car in Park and clench the steering wheel. "Aaron is right. I should have told you about all of it then. I don't know if it would have made a difference—that's the truth. Looking back now, I think I was an absolute idiot. But I don't know if I was *ready* to marry you. I wanted to. I didn't want to fuck up, and I felt like no matter what choice I made, I was going to fuck up."

"I don't understand." Tayla searches my face.

"I want you to know, from the bottom of my heart," I say, taking her hand in mine and lacing our fingers, "I wanted to marry you. I realized what I had with you. I wasn't ready for it then. I am now. There was never something missing with you. There was something missing *in me*." When our gazes meet, there are tears glistening in her eyes again. "I wish I'd had the words and the courage to tell you that then."

"So do I," she says, her voice catching on a sob.

The unrelenting tightness in my chest won't go away. I just want to hold her, but while my sports car is great for many things, cuddling is not one of them. I climb out and walk around to her side. Opening her door, I offer my hand. She stands up and takes it and then wraps her arms around my shoulders, rising onto her toes. I duck down so she can bury her face in my neck, and I breathe her in.

Maybe I won't need to tell her everything. Maybe this will be enough—for her to know what happened had less to do with her and so much more to do with me.

Once she slammed the door in my face, I never stopped thinking about her, but I thought what had broken between us couldn't be fixed. Turns out I might have been wrong about that too.

"I don't know why I'm so upset about this," she says, drawing back from me and wiping the tears on her cheeks. "I shouldn't be so upset about this."

Hope builds in my chest. Someone who was over me wouldn't still be shedding tears six years later. She's got at least some residual feelings. Her reaction also means I hurt her deeply, and while I suspected my abrupt departure did some damage, I never knew for sure. "I hurt you, and you care. There's no shame in that for you." For me, on the other hand . . .

"I just—" she chokes out. "I never understood why you would do that to me." She sniffs. "I had a really good time today. I've had a really good time on all our dates." Confusion lingers in her glassy eyes. "Which has just fucked with my head even more. We *were* good together, weren't we? I didn't imagine that?"

"Why do you think I came, Tay? When I got that email? I wanted a chance to make things right between us." I take a deep breath. "I wasn't the guy you were hoping for when you went there. I get it. But I want to be worthy of you. I'm going to be worthy of you."

"Did you cheat on me with Jada?" she whispers in a rush.

"No!" I rear back as though she's hit me. "No. God, no. I never cheated on you. I've never cheated on anyone." My list of bad qualities is easy to access. They've been thrown in my face quite a few times. "I'm commitment-shy. I work too much. Emotionally distant sometimes. Far too attached to my dog." I give a wry smile. "How is that even a thing?"

"Certainly not a negative on my list." She stares up at me, searching my face. "I don't know how to trust you again."

Her sadness causes the vise in my chest to rotate, squeezing harder. "I've got two more weeks to convince you it's possible to trust me, even if we're not there yet."

She rises onto her toes and kisses my cheek. "I loved you so hard, Si. So friggin' hard." Her gaze brims with sorrow. "I don't know if I can do it again." Her hand trails down my arm as she heads for her front door.

I'm tempted to snatch her back, to kiss her, to try to remind her this feeling is worth any heartbreak. Whether she wants to believe it or not, there's still *enough* between us. The foundation is there. First I'll build the bridge, and then, brick by brick, I'm rebuilding the home we had with each other. I don't care about the money or the stupid soul-mate service. I just want her.

Chapter Fifteen

TAYLA

Ruby is on speakerphone, and I've drunk three glasses of wine while filling out this amendment to my exchange application. My conversation with Simon sent me spinning, and I've landed on the vet exchange site.

"This is a good idea, right?" I ask as I enter my practice details into the website. "I'm not running away *from* something; I'm running *to* something. That's the difference."

"If you say so," Ruby says, the sounds of drilling and various dental instruments in the background. Her office is open extra-late one day a week to compensate for her Thursdays off. "Maybe you should save it at the end instead of submitting? Give yourself these weeks before making a life-altering decision. A remote practice might not be so fun."

"I'm tired of waiting." I tip back my glass, red wine slipping down my throat. "I should have done this instead of going to Soulmates Reunited."

"Look, I'm not going to disagree the matching software was weird for you." She takes an audible breath. "But you wouldn't be in a tailspin like this if you didn't still care about him a bit. You realize that, right?"

"Yeah, of course. For me, he's still . . ." I'm not admitting he's the closest thing to perfect out loud. I can't even believe I'm thinking it. Might as well jump off a cliff instead. I shake my head and sigh. "He freely admitted last night he's commitment-shy and emotionally distant. Hello, huge, flaming red flags, nice to see you again." I resume my pounding on the keyboard.

"He admitted that?" Something clatters in the background. "That's pretty self-aware."

"Sure, if he believes it. Or maybe enough women told him he's like that, so he knows that's how he comes across." The cynic in me is out in full force, fueled by almost a full bottle of wine.

"Did *you* think those things about him? Before the night you broke up?"

"No." My reply is quick, instinctual. I pour another glass of wine. The truth is more complicated. Should I have seen him in that light? Probably. Last night I lay in bed going over every conversation I could remember from our relationship. He never brought up moving in together, marriage, any of it. Not once did he contradict me or suggest we slow down, but he didn't initiate those talks. I did. Whether or not my memory is playing tricks on me, I can't stop thinking about the question Simon asked as he drove me home. "Do you think I put pressure on Simon to marry me?"

There's a long pause on the other end of the phone. "Is that what you think?"

I hate when she goes into therapist mode. She's a dentist. She should just answer my question.

"Yeah," I admit. "Maybe I did." Every time I recall one of our conversations, though, I don't see my behavior as pressuring him so much as working off the assumption an engagement would happen. He never gave me any reason to believe it wouldn't. I rub my forehead and check the clock. A hangover at work isn't cool at my age. "I should go."

I gulp down the rest of my glass and hit Submit on the amendment. Shortened timeline. Longer exchanges. Last-minute cancellations. Remote locations. I agreed to it all. Everything I was picky about two years ago when I first applied is now a green light.

"Dinner tomorrow night?" Ruby suggests.

"Can't," I say, sliding deeper into the couch. "New puppy for that shelter therapy program . . . and Simon is bringing dinner here."

"He's getting a second dinner? Isn't it supposed to be lunch?"

"The puppy weakened me."

"Sure. It was the puppy. Call me if you need to decompress. Doesn't matter what time."

My heart expands at her words. She's never once let me down. "I will."

♥

When he arrives, I'm not ready. Not ready for the way he takes up space in my little house; not ready for the way the rescue puppy, dubbed Pixie, greets him; not ready for the thrumming tune of my heart, straining against my chest, desperate for more. More of what?

Something inside me awoke when he kissed me on Sunday, and I can't seem to knock it out. That woodsy smell is back, and when he brushes past me to take the Indian food to the kitchen, the puppy and I trail after him. He's freshly showered, and in worn jeans and a green T-shirt the color of his eyes, he looks and smells like the dreams I've been having since Sunday night. My subconscious has latched onto Simon, and my libido has no problem piling on the sexual frustration in person. Why does he have to have this effect on me?

Having sex with him would send the wrong message. I don't know if I can trust him, if I can let myself drown in love again. How can you love the person who broke your heart?

"Do you still like Indian? I should have asked." He unpacks the boxes, and I observe him from the kitchen doorway. The puppy keeps trying to climb his leg. When her tail wags, her whole body shakes. She is the embodiment of me.

"Never say no to a bit of spice."

"Only a bit?" His lips quirk up, and when he glances at me, there's a wicked glint in the green depths.

"I can handle any heat level. You like it hot, right?" I may need to turn on the ceiling fan if this conversation keeps up.

"If the sweat isn't pouring off us, we're not doing it right." The partial smile spreads into a grin.

The memory of his body rubbing against mine, his breath hot in my ear, is enough to make my insides squirm with need. "Sweaty, huh?" I murmur.

"Slick with it." His gaze doesn't leave mine, intent, challenging, daring me to go further.

I pretend to mop my forehead. "I'm already a little wet just thinking about it." It's not my forehead that's damp.

"Come pick your dish," he says, gesturing to the food he's laid out. "Then tell me how you want it."

Any way you'll give it to me. Those aren't words I can say when I won't follow through. Instead, I sidle up to him, ignoring the puppy collapsed at his feet, defeated. When I'm close enough to touch, his hand grazes my hip.

"What do you think?" His voice is husky. "What are you in the mood for?"

He's so close the heat of his body warms me, and I'm so aware of his physical presence, I'm not reading the containers so much as staring at them. Every fiber of me wants to turn and drag him to me. "What's the hottest dish here?"

He steps forward, and his chest grazes my back as he reaches around me to point to a container. "This one." He keeps his arm around me, his chest pressed against me. "Is that what you want? To be on fire?"

I chuckle, and it has this turned-on, breathless quality I don't expect. "No reason to get burned."

"If you want to play it safe," he says, his breath a whisper against my neck, sending a shock wave of desire rippling down my spine, "the korma is mild, sweet, creamy."

How are those words so erotic? "What do you suggest?" My voice is that of a phone sex operator, and I don't even care.

"Life on the edge," he says.

His arms are braced on either side of me. He's got me boxed in, but I like it. If I lean back, I'm sure I'll feel his erection against my ass. There's no way he's not as turned on as I am. Our breathing is ragged, charged with anticipation.

Then I turn in his arms, and we're kissing. Or maybe we're devouring each other. My brain is switched off, and my body is switched on. He sweeps the dishes to the side of the counter and lifts me onto it, pushing between my legs, deepening the kiss. We're frantic. Hands everywhere. Mouths and tongues tangling on instinct.

I dig my fingers into his hair, and I can't get close enough. I wrap my legs around his waist, and he tugs me to the edge of the counter so I'm balanced, my pelvis and his groin connected, grinding together as though we can both get off this way. Can we? God, I think I can.

His hand slips up my shirt, and he's cupping my breast, his thumb skimming the nipple through the thin fabric of my lacy bra. We break the kiss, and my shirt is up, my bra down, and his mouth covers my breast, his tongue swirling around the tip before his teeth graze against it. Another jolt of desire zings to my core. My breath catches in my throat, and I want the spiral of lust to go on forever.

"Don't stop," I groan when he backs off.

He's not leaving, though—he's readjusting his hands to take me off the counter. My legs clamp on to his waist as we head to the couch. It's a short walk, and I can't stop staring at him. Am I really going to do this? Before any doubt can take hold, he's easing me down to the couch, and our lips connect again. All rational thought flees as every single one of my brain cells is consumed by noticing all the places our bodies are united, the way his lips and hands explore my body. His erection presses against my core through our clothes, and if he keeps going, I'm sure I'll come.

"Fuck, Tay." His voice is a harsh whisper against my neck as we grind against each other.

I'm so close I could scream. When I turn my head on a gasp of pleasure, Pixie appears, her front paws on the edge of the couch. She licks my cheek and then tries to jump onto my head.

Simon shoos her away with his hand, but her interruption stalls my flight over the cliff. I freeze underneath him. The puppy tries again to climb on top of us, and Si gently pushes her away.

What am I doing?

My core aches with unspent desire. "Si," I murmur, and he goes still.

"Too much spice?" His voice is strained. Pixie sits beside the couch staring at us, her head cocked.

I search his face while he gazes at the dog for a moment. When his focus comes back to me, we stare at each other in silence. I shift under him to straighten my clothes, and he closes his eyes and grits his teeth.

"A little hotter than I expected," I admit, my voice still breathy.

He sits back on the couch and rubs his face. "I'm gonna

need a minute." He squints at me. "I didn't read that wrong, though, did I?"

I shake my head and set my feet on the floor. Pixie comes over and puts her paws on my leg, her tail whipping from side to side. "I was right there with you. I promise." I give him a wry smile. "Sexual chemistry was never a problem with us." The intense desire that was surging in me a few minutes ago is still bubbling under the surface, threatening to burst forth again. I should probably avoid touching him for the rest of the night.

He mirrors my pose and rubs the back of his neck. "We never had many problems at all."

I bark out a laugh as I get up and head for the kitchen. "Except two really big ones. I put pressure on you to get married, and you couldn't tell me the truth."

Chapter Sixteen

SIMON

I stare after her, unable to move from the couch. Apparently, I'm not going to be able to get away with owning the underlying issue without revealing the causes. I drag a hand through my hair. I can't get up yet or I'd be following her. If I tried to walk now, I'd look like a cowboy who rode a horse over rough land for hours. No one needs to see that. Even now, when I should be answering Tayla or refuting what she's just said, the majority of my brain is still lodged in my jeans, straining for release.

"You're not going to deny it?" she calls from the kitchen.

"If the right head was in charge, this conversation would be easier," I mutter.

She laughs and brings me a full plate of food. After she

sets the dish on the coffee table, she plants a kiss on my forehead. "Want me to call you Blue for the rest of the night?"

"Blue?" I ask with a smirk, dragging her into my lap. "Because I'm sad?"

She wiggles against my dick, and her gaze connects with mine. "Is that what I feel? Sadness?"

"You like teasing me?" I tuck stray strands of her hair behind her ears. The right head hasn't kicked into gear yet. All I can think about is kissing her, laying her back on the couch again, carting her off to her bedroom—whatever she'll let me do. I cradle her face between my hands, and the air around us electrifies.

"Screw it," she mutters, and she leans forward, capturing my lips with hers again.

Then she's straddling me, her hands in my hair, grinding against me, and the world could explode around us right now and I wouldn't give a shit.

A clatter sounds from behind Tayla, and I groan. Fucking Pixie cockblocking me again. An explosion I can ignore, but a puppy knocking my dinner off the table is a different matter. Tayla breaks the kiss and glances over her shoulder. "Oh Lord," she says, jumping off my lap to pick up the plate.

Heaving myself off the couch, I risk walking like a cowboy to help clean up the mess. I snatch Pixie off the floor, searching for the pup's bed. "You have a place for her?"

"The crate's in my en suite bathroom," Tayla calls over her shoulder as she scrubs the floor clean of Indian food.

"I'll take her outside first," I say, grabbing the leash

hanging by the front door. "I was looking forward to seeing you, buddy," I tell the dog as I lead her outside. "But I gotta tell you, you're not doing me any favors tonight."

Pixie wanders the grass for a while before doing her business, and after smothering her with praise, I take her back into the house.

Tayla has replaced my plate and added hers to the coffee table. She glances at me, her cheeks flushed. The glassy, turned-on look in her eyes gives me a moment of pause in the doorway with the dog cradled in my arms. Does she *want* to do this? I thought we decided we *weren't* doing this, but that look in her eyes says something else entirely.

"Want me to put her in the crate?" I offer.

"Yeah," she says, her voice husky again.

I unhook the leash and take the puppy toward the en suite. Once I've latched the crate, I turn to head back and catch a noise in the bedroom. Tayla's at the door, blocking me from returning to the main room.

"Are you really hungry?" She bites her lip.

My last chance to be a gentleman. Tell her I'm starving, that I don't want to eat cold Indian food. Aaron's voice whispers in my ear that going down this route with her when she doesn't have all the information is wrong. Fuck it. She's gorgeous and horny, and I'm so hard I'm going to last approximately two-point-five seconds. If she wants me, I'm not saying no. Not a chance. I don't care whether a better man would hold off. That's not me tonight. Maybe it's never been me.

"I work a microwave like a pro."

That's all the invitation she needs. When she closes the

distance between us, I sweep her into a kiss, rotating her toward the edge of the bed.

"This doesn't mean," she says between kisses, "that we're back together."

"It's just chemistry." I tug off her top and unsnap her bra. "Really fucking great chemistry." I draw her jeans down her legs while she unbuckles my belt.

"Yeah," she breathes out. "Science."

We shed our clothes in a flurry of rushed movements, and then we're naked on the bed, a torrent of lips, hands, and tongues. When I cup her ass and flick my tongue against her clit, she gasps and grinds against my mouth.

"God, Si. I'm so turned on I'm going to come any second."

I chuckle against her. "Good. Then I can go for an encore." My mouth closes over her, suckling and flicking my tongue in a steady rhythm.

"That's the kind of work ethic I like." She clutches my shoulders, her short nails digging into my flesh.

I relish the taste of her and the way her hips rock with me. When she grows tense, I slip two fingers into her, and her moan of satisfaction is almost enough to send me over the edge. She's always been responsive, vocal, not afraid to tell me what she wants.

"Oh God," she pants.

Come on, Tay. I suck a little harder, and she rockets off the bed, her internal walls clenching around my pumping fingers.

"Holy shit," she mutters. "God, that was . . ."

I look up and smirk at her. "I'll take amazing. Sensational. Orgasmerific."

"Orgasmerific?" She stares at the ceiling, her expression pensive. "That's a word?"

"Definitely a feeling. You up for round two?"

She covers her face and lets out a husky laugh. "I'm dead. If you can get me to come again, you're a magician."

"Is that a yes then?" I reach into the nightstand drawer where the condoms used to be kept. She's staring at me but doesn't say a word. Blindly, I take one out and wag it at her.

"Yeah," she says, her hand stroking me. "Let's see if you've got any magic in you."

"I'd never claim it was magical, but I've got something in me dying to come out."

Her laugh is throaty. She takes the condom from me, ripping it out of the package and rolling it on. "No magic, huh? That's the only thing I'm interested in."

"Let's see what my wand can do. There may be some magic in it," I say, poised at her entrance. When I slide in, she arches her back to meet me, and our gazes connect. All teasing vanishes in a heartbeat, and we're united on a whole new level. I want to tell her I've missed her, missed this with her. The combination of sexual hunger and humor is rare. But I don't want to scare her off. We're not together, but that doesn't mean I can't make her wish for more.

With each stroke, I shift my position, drawing our bodies tight together, looking for the spark of lust I'll see when I get it right. Not all women can come this way, but with enough persistence on my part, she can. There's nothing magical about it—after six years, I still remember what gets her off as if we were together yesterday.

Another incremental movement, and she sighs. *Ah, there*

it is. She closes her eyes and moans. Bingo. Thinking about her has meant I'm not thinking about me, but as soon as I'm in the right position, I long to let go. Instead, I grit my teeth and concentrate on giving her the friction so crucial to her second trip around the stars.

"Look at me," I say. Tomorrow and the next day and the one after that I want her to remember I'm the guy who makes her feel this way. There's no one else. Fucking her is primitive and primal, competitive and possessive. I want her to remember forever what it's like to have me inside her, to be driven to the edge over and over by me.

Her gaze is dazed with desire. "You feel so good," she murmurs, her nails digging into my ass, keeping us tight.

All the things I want to say get caught in my throat. She's not ready to hear any of them. I kiss her roughly, and she meets the intensity without question, rocking in rhythm with me. "I don't know—" I break off because *fuck* she feels good. I bury my head in her neck and try to think of something else, but she's so wet and hot I can't hold on much longer.

"Keep going," she pants. "Please. I'm so close."

Even though it's killing me, I maintain the excruciating rhythm, and then she's crying out, clutching onto me and shaking with her orgasm. With a few more quick strokes, I kiss her deeply as my own surges through me.

We lie in silence for a moment, both of us breathing heavy.

"Apparently, it *is* a magic wand," she says with a sigh of contentment.

"Don't worry," I say, easing out of her. "I'll let you

borrow it whenever you need a little magic in your life." I head into the en suite to clean up.

"You're so generous," she calls after me.

"My kindness in this area knows no bounds." Already I'm wondering when we can do it again. When I come out of the bathroom, she's dressed.

I stand at the doorway, still naked, a frown on my face. "What'd you do, dress at the speed of light?"

"I'm hungry," she says, her voice defensive. "I'll heat up the food." Without another glance at me, she's out the bedroom door.

I rub my forehead, not so much confused by her attitude as annoyed by it. Would ten seconds of cuddling have killed her? I grab my clothes off the floor and get dressed. Already, a sense of impending doom is filling my chest. Either things will be awkward as hell or she's going to try to pretend I didn't just give her two orgasms with my magic dick.

When I come out of the bedroom, one plate is already on the coffee table.

"You can start eating," she calls to me from the kitchen.

Pretending it is. Great. "Thanks," I say, easing onto the sofa.

When she comes out carrying her meal, she sits at the far end of the couch, her plate cradled in her lap.

"Lots of room on the table," I offer, gesturing to the mountain of space beside me.

"I'm good here." She takes a bite of naan.

We eat in silence, and about ten different icebreakers rotate through my mind. None of them are what I actually want to say. Isn't Aaron always counseling me to be honest? "We're going to pretend like we didn't just have sex?"

"I'm not pretending," Tayla says, her tone indignant. "But I told you it didn't mean anything. Great sex is a dime a dozen."

Such fucking bullshit. I'd ask her the last time she had great sex, but I don't actually want to know. "Sure, yeah. I had great sex . . ." I pretend to think it over. "Just yesterday. Amazing. So common I bet everyone has great sex all the time, every day."

"Oh, good." She gives a dismissive wave of her fork. "Glad the man-whoring is going well."

"Don't sex-shame me. You're the one who just said it's as common as butter on bread." I scrape up the last bite of my food. My mouth is on fire. Did she put more hot sauce in this? I'm going to need to chug a gallon of milk.

"Look," she says, taking her half-finished plate and stomping to the kitchen. "We had sex. It's not that earth-shattering, and it doesn't mean we're getting back together. If I'd thought you were going to be up in your feelings about it, I wouldn't have initiated it."

Well, at least she's admitting it was her idea. Still, I'm not overly keen on being pinned as emotional. With a sigh, I follow her to the kitchen. So far, Aaron's honesty idea is overrated. I slide my plate into the sink. Tayla is at the fridge, the door open.

"I didn't think it would mean everything, but I thought it would mean *something*." That's the truth. How can she be so dismissive?

She glances at me over her shoulder, the tension easing

out of her. "It means we have good sexual chemistry. I thought we were in agreement about that."

"Then why devalue that admission by saying *you* have great sexual chemistry with *everyone*?"

"Maybe I do." She takes the milk out of the fridge and two cups from the cupboard. Tension coats her actions again.

I close my eyes and take a deep breath. "Name one other person."

"One other person what?"

"One other person you've had great sex with. Just one. Name them, right now without thinking about it, and I'll believe you."

"I don't kiss and tell," she says primly, pouring the milk.

"Bullshit. It's because you can't, Tay. Neither can I. Okay? Can you just admit it?"

She shoves the cup into my hand. "Why does it matter if I tell you that sex with you is better than sex with other people? It doesn't change anything between us."

"I want you to admit it." My jaw is set.

"So you can have your ego stroked?" Tayla gulps down her milk. "I already stroked something else tonight. I don't think I need to add your ego to it."

"You're being stubborn about this for no reason." I let out a frustrated noise.

"*I* am?" She slides her empty cup onto the counter. "Okay, Si." She sidles up to me, and her index finger trails down my chest. Under her eyelashes, she glances up. "You're the single greatest lover I've ever had." Her breathy voice causes my cock to spring to attention. "Did

I stroke the right thing this time?" Her fingertips graze the front of my jeans.

It annoys me that her clear attempt at mocking me still turns me on. "Your sarcasm and undermining my request should not be sexy."

"Can't account for what gets you going." She shrugs and heads out of the kitchen.

I follow her into the living room. "Tay."

She's at the front door with it open. "Your keys are there." She points to a side table. "We had dinner, and we both got off. Now I think it's time for you to go."

"You're kicking me out?" I snatch my keys off the table, and then I stop in front of her, searching her face. She's closed off again—almost as though the week of progress I've made is gone. Christ. If I knew having sex was going to set us this far back, I would have kept my dick in my pants.

"I'm asking you to leave. I'll see you Thursday as per our agreement. Don't send me any cutesy texts either. I'm not answering those anymore."

"Tayla," I plead. We've been exchanging texts for the last week without issue. Most of them are logistical, but many of them have been friendly, even flirtatious.

"We're not getting back together." She shoves my shoulder, and I stumble out the door. "Sometimes when something gets broken, you can't fix it. It stays broken."

Chapter Seventeen

TAYLA

The slab of flourless chocolate cake rests uneaten on the plate on my desk. Ruby gives me an expectant sigh from her chair. "I brought you cake. You're supposed to give me details. You're clearly not in a good place."

I wedge off a small piece of cake and chew slowly. "Things are going well with Pixie. That's a plus. Luis was over yesterday helping me train her."

"Luis is not the man you want to be helping you train that puppy. What's going on with you and Simon? You've been in a tailspin since Sunday."

With a deep breath, I dive into all the gory details, from Sunday's date and confession by Simon to my suspicions I pressured him into getting married, from us having sex to me kicking him out. "And he never answered me about the pressure to get married. Avoided it completely. Obviously, I'm right about that."

"You had sex with him and kicked him out? Seems like a reasonable response to his avoidance."

"I cannot help how my body responds to him. I can't, okay? It's like . . ." I falter. What is it like? A wildfire. A tornado. A collision course I can't avert. "He even made me say he's the best sex I've ever had."

Ruby's eyes widen. "Is he?"

"Hands down. But don't worry—I made it sound like I didn't mean it." I stab at my cake and shovel in a mouthful.

Ruby chuckles. She watches me eat for a minute. "I'm only gonna say this once. There's no shame in taking him back if that's what you want. You're both older, hopefully wiser. No one is going to think ill of you for following your heart."

"My heart doesn't get a say in this. My libido is raging out of control, but I'll pop a lid on that now too. Released the tension." *Twice.* "So cut it out. The only part of me that gets to weigh in on Simon is my brain."

"Why?"

"Because my heart got me into the last mess. My libido got me into the mess Tuesday night."

"Your brain took you to Soulmates Reunited."

"That's not a helpful comment." I point my fork at her.

"I'm just saying—isn't every part of this pointing to him? If you didn't care, you wouldn't be spinning out like this."

"How do I know this isn't all a game to him? How do

I know he didn't get the email and think, 'Oh right, yeah, that's the chick I used to have great sex with. Let's give that another go,' and that's why he came to my office?"

"Ask him."

"What?"

"Ask him. I know it might not seem fair, but maybe you need to put yourself out there a little bit."

"I have asked him why he came." My heart squeezes in my chest at the various answers he's given me. None of them have been remotely teasing. He was genuine and sincere when he said no one has ever matched him as well as me.

"What did he say?"

"Lots of things." I shift uncomfortably in my chair.

"Any of those things suggest he viewed coming after you as a game?"

"No," I answer grudgingly. "I just—I don't want him to be *the one*."

"Because he broke your heart."

"Yeah," I say, picking at the cake. I bite my lip. "It also feels like, as honest as he's being, he's still holding something back."

"Such as?"

"He freely admits he wanted to marry me. Planned a whole proposal, as far as I can tell. Then, at the last minute, he breaks up with me." I stare at her, tears welling in my eyes. "Do extreme cold feet account for that? Out of the blue? Something must have happened, and I don't know what it could have been. I always thought he was cheating on me with Jada. But he swears he wasn't, and he was surprised by the accusation."

"You haven't asked him what caused the sudden change?"

"Not really. He told me he wasn't ready to get married. I understand that. When I look back and try to be critical of where we were at, how I was feeling, how he seemed, I *can* see some distance between us leading up to the engagement."

"Really?" Ruby raises her eyebrows. "You've only just discovered this?"

"I think I knew it back then, but it was easier to be mad at Si than to admit I saw something changing in him and I didn't ask. I didn't want to rock the boat. I loved him so much. The idea of doing anything to cause that to change—I didn't want those discussions."

"I get that," Ruby admits, taking a bite of her own cake. "When you're not sure what sort of answer you're going to get, it's hard to take that first step in communication. I think that's why Dean and I have worked so well. We've both learned that lesson. Even when it's hard, you've got to try because if you're not trying, you aren't just rocking the boat, you're *sinking* it."

We eat in silence for a few moments while I consider her words. I don't know if I can trust Simon again, but if I never ask him the hard questions, if I never push him for the answers I need, we'll never figure out if we can get the good parts of our relationship back.

Well, the other good parts. The sex is still on point. I ripped off my sheets last night in a fit of rage because they still smelled faintly of him.

"You're having dinner with him tonight?"

"It *is* Thursday." I sweep the icing off with my fork.

"Put on your big-girl pants and ask him. You've got a week and a half until you get your money back. Wouldn't it be nice to know whether these three weeks were about the money or about the relationship?"

The thing is, I already know the answer to her question. I haven't thought about the money in days.

The Greek restaurant is an explosion of activity. There's no chance to talk about anything remotely serious over the hustle and bustle of live entertainment, dancing, and dinner. The white, blue, and gold decor suggests an atmosphere that should be more calming.

"I didn't realize we'd be going somewhere so loud," I call over the chaotic din.

Simon shrugs and sips his beer. "Change of pace." He searches my face and then looks away to watch the music. "The food is good."

After radio silence all day yesterday, and only a single text with the time he was picking me up today, my resolve over the whole "no cutesy texts" is fading fast. Cutting those out seems to have chopped off any sense of fun. We're surrounded by a bright atmosphere, and I'm anything but. "How was work?" He's been on day shifts this week, so his evenings have been free.

"Not too busy," he says, eyeing me. "You?"

"Good, yeah. Steady." I hold up my phone, which was resting on the table. "I'm the vet on call tonight, so I have to keep this close." When he doesn't say anything, I add, "Ruby came for lunch today."

"She bring you health food?" A ghost of a smile crosses his face.

"Chocolate cake," I admit. "This will be my first real meal today." We've already ordered, and I'm hoping they're prompt.

"Chocolate cake," he says, shifting in his chair to fully face me for the first time. His elbows hit the table, and he leans toward me as though he's about to say something secret. "That's crisis food. What's the crisis, Tay?"

"No crisis. I like cake." A flush heats my cheeks.

He chuckles and leans back, picking up his beer again, but the cake admission seems to have inflated him. Does he find it comforting that I might be struggling with what's happening between us?

"I tend to drink too much when I'm in crisis mode. Had a hell of a hangover today. Drunk-dialed Aaron last night." He shakes his head, lifting his beer. "Messy."

I must have upset him the other night. For a moment, I'm vaguely stunned. Tuesday night, I was too consumed with my own feelings to even consider what I was doing or saying from his point of view. He honored my request to leave me alone yesterday and today, but here we are now, and he seems torn between being his usual flirty self and keeping his distance. "Did I hurt your feelings on Tuesday?"

"Wasn't that the point?" He chuckles and sets down his beer.

"No. I wasn't really thinking about the things I was saying in relation to your feelings." I run a hand through my hair and flip it behind my shoulder.

"Not sure if that makes Tuesday better or worse." He grimaces.

"I didn't mean to hurt you, Si. Honestly." I fumble for the right words, but I don't get a chance to say anything more because our food is delivered.

We eat in silence for a while before he says, "So, what *did* you mean?"

I take a drink of my wine and then inhale deeply. "I really like being around you, and that scares me."

"I know what I want, and I'm not going to hurt you." His eyes soften as he gazes across the table.

"Did I put pressure on you to propose?" The thought has been nagging me since Sunday night.

He finishes chewing and rubs his cheek. "Not directly, no. Did you talk about other people getting married or engaged a lot? Did you compare the amount of time they'd been dating to how long we'd been dating? Yeah. But I'm not laying what I did at your feet, Tay. I made choices that hurt you. Whether or not I felt any kind of pressure in *any* direction says more about me than you."

We eat again in silence for a moment while I gather my courage. The opening is there. *Ask him, Tayla.* "What kind of pressure were you feeling?" His question from Sunday is starting to take a different shape in my head. "I—I did notice a change in you in the weeks leading up to our breakup."

"Did you?" He rears back as though I've said something shocking. "Really?"

"Looking back, yeah. Hindsight and all that. But you'd definitely pulled away, and I felt some anxiety about it, in retrospect."

"Why didn't you ask me then?"

"I think I was worried if I said anything we'd end up where we ended up."

"You thought saying you'd noticed a change would lead to us breaking up?"

"You were becoming distant. I mean, later, I thought you'd probably been sleeping with Jada behind my back. So I never thought about it much after that—the gut feeling I'd had. I thought I knew what it had been."

"You understand that's not what happened, right?"

"What did happen, then?"

He blows out a breath and runs a hand through his hair, his meal done. The waitress takes our plates and passes him the bill. He fingers the slip of paper, lost in thought.

"I feel like your ability to be honest with me is crucial to my ability to trust you." Ruby and I came to that conclusion earlier in the office.

"Let's get out of here," he says. "I'll pay, and we can talk in the car. It's too loud."

Secretly, I wonder whether the point of this venue was just that—no talking. I'm not going to argue with him about the change because the overly loud music is starting to give me a headache. He pays, and he takes my hand on the way out of the restaurant. He opens the car door, and I slide into the passenger seat.

Once he's settled, he doesn't start the car, instead turning to look at me. "I can explain the distance you felt. But if you don't mind, I'd rather leave what happened with Jada for another day. It's a complicated story."

"Does she have any bearing on why we split up?"

He runs his thumb and his fingers over his lips. "In a roundabout way. Not directly, no. I did not cheat on you. I would *never* do that."

I sigh. "We've got a week and a half left, Si. If you haven't told me everything by the last Sunday, you don't want us as bad as you say you do." My heart aches at the thought I might already want us to work out more than he does. Trust isn't built in a rush, though. It's built moment by moment—one action on top of another.

"You have my word, I will tell you everything before the last Sunday."

I hold his gaze for a beat. "I'm going to trust you mean that."

"Here goes." He takes a deep breath and runs his hands along the steering wheel. "I spent a lot of time working in the garage with my dad."

I nod. If Simon wasn't working and I was, he went to his parents' house with Rex to do some woodworking in the garage, or he went for a run. Those were his two go-to activities. Spending time with his dad or working out.

"My dad—in his defense, it turned out he was a very unhappy man—he spent weeks . . ." He seems to search for the right word. "Undermining my feelings for you." He rubs his face. "God, I feel like I'm throwing him under the bus. I take responsibility for letting it happen, and his comments were never so direct as to say he didn't think I should be with you at all. They were harder to pin down."

I swallow and stare ahead at the sign for the restaurant. "Can you give me an example?"

"I don't think I should. My dad and I are close again

after a long period of not getting along at all. He tore away at the fabric of my life, my mom's, and my sister's before he had the guts to be honest about his internal struggle. It was—it was when he took off to the monastery that I realized how deeply I'd fucked up my life on very poor, disillusioned advice."

"Did he give you this advice because he didn't like me?" My heart thunders in my chest.

"No," Simon says taking my hand in his. "It was because he didn't like himself, or maybe he was tired of pretending to be happy when he wasn't. Either way, his input had nothing to do with you."

"I know how much your dad's opinion mattered to you—"

"Too much." He shakes his head. "I let it matter too much."

His parents were so friendly, so kind. It's hard to imagine Simon's father the way he's painting him. But we spent less and less time with his parents in the weeks before we split up.

I try to slot this new information into the narrative I've held in place so long. In my head, Simon dumped me for another woman. The restaurant, the elaborate setup, and the champagne just to break up with me was baffling. "The night we broke up . . ."

His arms are draped over the steering wheel, and he rests his cheek against them, his gaze connecting with mine. "I planned to propose. Had the ring in my pocket. Went to the bathroom to collect myself." He sits back and flexes his hands on the steering wheel again. "And then my dad called. He was bawling. So upset. Begged me not to propose. I can't even—he was so upset."

I scan his face. My parents' opinions mean a great deal to me, so on one hand, I can see how his father's unraveling would have given him pause. On the other hand, he was sure enough about me to buy the ring, to arrange the night at the restaurant. I'm narrowing the decision to one phone call when he's already told me his father spent weeks drilling into the base of our relationship. Could I sustain my feelings for someone if one or both of my parents were like Simon's dad? "One phone call," I say. "When you were moments from proposing." My thoughts are scattered, and maybe I'm not being fair. "Was I really so easy to discard?"

Chapter Eighteen

SIMON

We're getting somewhere, and it guts me to let her believe for even a moment that letting her go was an easy decision. At the time, it felt necessary, but there was nothing easy about it. Maybe if I tell her how Soulmates Reunited pursued me relentlessly during the same time period my father was cutting into our relationship, my decision would make more sense.

Maybe.

Or maybe she'd ask me to drive her home, and she'd never talk to me again. At this point, either scenario feels equally likely. Without the ammunition to bring Soulmates Reunited to their knees and get her money, she's tied to me. Does that make me a terrible person? Even if I truly believe she's the right woman for me? Because if there's one thing I've figured out over the last weeks, whether or not Soulmates Reunited is a fraud, my feelings for Tayla are real. All-consuming, can't-stop-thinking-about-her, yesterday-not-talking-to-her-was-torture kind of real. I've wanted to prove the company wrong for years for thrusting Jada into my life, for causing me to doubt my connection to Tayla, but maybe there's something to their system. *This* match isn't wrong.

"To you it feels like one phone call; to me it was this man I'd hero-worshipped, this marriage I'd aspired to have, crumbling down around me. If he couldn't make a marriage work with my mom, what chance did I have? If he was this miserable, maybe I would be one day too. There was no guarantee I wouldn't become him, and I'd spent so much time wanting to be him."

"You thought I'd make you miserable?" The words seem to roll around in her mouth, her expression revealing their sour taste.

"That's not—" I let out a huff. "I don't know. I don't know what I thought. The point is that I wasn't sure. About anything. His crumbling dislodged my footing. I couldn't find that stability when I needed it."

Tayla stares at me in silence, and I have no idea if I've ruined everything. "I want you to take me home."

"Tay," I plead.

She shakes her head, and tears pool in her eyes. "Just take me home."

Rather than pushing her to talk to me, I start the car, and I guide us out of the parking lot and onto the deserted streets. We drive in silence for a few minutes, and I scramble to find something that might make her realize that I don't think what happened between us the first time had to do with *us* as a couple but rather *me* as a person. Except I feel like I've said that already, and she's not ready to hear it or accept it. I'll just have to hope she gets there within the next week and a half. Or else I'll be out of time and out of money, and I'm sure I'll never get another shot with her. If I blow this, I'm done.

I'm lost in thought as I drive along a section of road that is surrounded by forested areas with minimal streetlights. Up ahead, something dark is on the road. The shape draws me back to the present, and I slow the car, peering into the distance. "What is that?"

Tayla perks up in the seat beside me, leaning toward the windshield as we creep closer. "Oh Lord," she whispers. "It's someone's dog. Pull over. It must have been hit."

The dog is panting on its side in the middle of the road. Still alive. My heart constricts in my chest as we both climb out and rush to it. A black Labrador.

"Do you have a blanket?" Tayla asks, her hands skimming over the dog. "I won't know exactly what's wrong until we get him to the clinic."

I run back to my car, pop the trunk, and grab the blanket I keep with my first aid kit. "Do you want the first aid kit?" I call back.

"No," she says, her voice small. "There's blood, but no excessive bleeding. I'm worried about internal hemorrhaging."

After throwing open the car door and popping the

driver's seat forward, I go back to Tayla. "I can lift him into the back seat," I say. "You sit with him and do your thing to make him comfortable while I get us to your clinic." Carefully, I hoist him into my arms. He's a sturdy fella, well loved by someone. "Looks like he's got tags."

"I'll call from the car." Tayla slides into the back seat next to where I've placed the dog.

When we're all buckled in, I steer us to the clinic, careful not to jerk around corners but keeping a consistently high speed. In the back, the dog pants and whines. Tayla tries the number on the tag, but no one answers. She leaves a message, rattling off the information for her vet practice and where we found the dog.

As I wheel into the closest parking spot, Tayla hops out of the back and hurries toward the front door. "Can you bring him in? I'll get everything ready."

"On it." I wedge myself into the back of the car and lift the dog into my arms, cradling him gently. He's not light. I'm not sure what Tayla might have done had she come upon the dog by herself. She works out, but he's got to be eighty or ninety pounds.

She's propped the main door open, and I go through sideways, inching us past the narrowest part. Without waiting for direction, I head toward the back of the office where I know the surgery rooms are located. She directs me to lay him on an X-ray machine, and I grab a suit and gloves from the pile so we're both protected. We work in tandem as Tayla assesses his injuries and has me move the dog from place to place as carefully as possible.

When she's run all the tests she can, she yanks off

her gloves and tosses them in the garbage. The dog has a broken front leg. Probably a concussion, but Tayla isn't sure to what degree. There doesn't appear to be any internal bleeding, so surgery isn't necessary at this point. All in all, the dog is lucky. She fills a needle with pain meds to give him some peace.

Once he's secured in a kennel space, Tayla and I shed the protective clothing and wander to her office. There's a message on the answering machine from the dog's owners. She calls them back and gives them the rundown on his injuries. As I listen to her, I can't help but marvel at her calm, professional demeanor. I'd never undermine her choice to be a vet, but she would have been a hell of a people doctor too.

When she hangs up, I say, "They're on their way?"

"They are, yeah." She sighs and rubs her face. "Thank you for all your help."

"Of course." I shrug and shove my hands into the pockets of my jeans.

"I can walk home from here if you've got other places to be. The owners said they'd be here in about half an hour. Then, depending on what they want to do, I'll have to put him down or keep him comfortable so we can repair or amputate tomorrow."

I chuckle. "I'm not going to let you walk home alone in the dark." It takes a moment for the rest of her words to sink in. "They might put him down? Are his injuries that bad?"

"No," Tayla says with a shake of her head. "But if there's one thing I've learned over the years, it's that I can't talk people into something they don't want to do. Goes in both directions. He's their dog. I give advice, but I can't make decisions for them."

It's funny how our conversation mirrors, in a weird way, the one we had earlier about my dad. The hardest part of telling Tayla the truth is that we both know if I was one hundred percent committed to marrying her, nothing would have stopped me. Were there circumstances and conversations that undermined my certainty? Yeah. Too many, in the end. But I've learned to own my response. I wasn't ready for her then.

"I don't know if you want to hear this right now or not." I scan her face, trying to determine if I should plunge ahead or leave things, but when her gaze connects with mine, I decide to lay it all out. "I made a lot of mistakes in the weeks leading up to our breakup. A lot. I didn't communicate with you enough. I let my dad's unhappiness become mine. I listened to the wrong people about the wrong things. But I loved you, Tayla. I loved you so much it felt like you were lodged in the marrow of my bones." I take a deep breath. The streetlights outside the window cast a shadow across her face. It's hard to tell whether she's interested in what I have to say.

"Lodged in the marrow of your bones." She takes a deep breath and then rubs her face. "A pretty thing to say, but you only came to see me once after we broke up. Once. A year later. You refused to talk to me in the weeks after we split. I tried. I wanted to understand."

"I was screwed up. Talking felt like it would make things worse or more confusing because I didn't know what to say." I run a hand along the top of my head. "My dad had been spouting all this shit, and there was some other stuff." The other stuff being Soulmates Reunited springing Jada on me with all these love and soulmate guarantees. "Took me a year to sort through it all." I hesitate and grab the back of my neck, trying to figure out how to phrase the rest of it. "I came to see you. You didn't want to see me. I never wanted to be the guy who couldn't let go, who didn't know when to let go. My mom clung so hard to my dad when it was clear he didn't want her or their marriage anymore. I'd seen that desperation, and I didn't want it to be me, even though it felt a hell of a lot like me." I meet her gaze, trying to convey how mixed-up I was and how clear and focused I am now.

She stares out the window, her back turned. With her face hidden from me, her thoughts are invisible. She opens her mouth, half turning to speak, and the door flies open.

"Tayla Murphy?" A middle-aged woman and her husband burst the bubble between us. "Is Beau here?"

"He's in the back," Tayla says, slipping on her professional demeanor. "I gave him something for the pain. We can go into my office and have a chat about options after you've had a chance to see him."

She glances at me before leading them to her office, and I can't read her expression. I ease into one of the chairs in the waiting room and take out my phone, scrolling through the day's news. Not long after, the couple comes back, thanking Tayla profusely and indicating they'll be back tomorrow to pay. As soon as they're out the door, Tayla's shoulders drop.

"Oh, shit," I breathe out. "Are they putting him down?"

She shakes her head. "No, no. But they were worried about costs, so I dropped my fees down as low as I could go."

I rise to stand in front of her. She hesitates a moment before sliding her hands around my waist and pressing her cheek to my chest. Her hands inch up my back, and I wrap my arms around her shoulders, cradling her head. "You okay?" I murmur.

"I want to believe this is real. What we have is real. That Soulmates Reunited got us right. That maybe we're ready for each other in a way we weren't six years ago. But it's so hard, Si. So hard to forget how awful I felt the night you let me go."

I kiss the top of her head and squeeze her tight. How do I respond to that? "I can't change what I did in the past. I wish I could. But I promise, if you give me a chance, I'll never make you feel that way again."

She nods against my chest, and then she steps away, linking her hand with mine. "Do you think you can help me get him comfortable? If not, I can call someone to come in."

"Whatever you need," I say, following behind her to the back room. "I'm not going anywhere."

We work in tandem to get the dog settled, and when we're done arranging a space for him, I drive her home. At her front door, we stare at each other for a beat before I frame her face and kiss her tenderly. The sigh that escapes her before she deepens the kiss lessens the tightness in my chest. I'm torn between begging her to let me into her place, into her bed, and walking away. The other night didn't bring us closer, and I can't afford any more steps back.

"Will you call me tomorrow and let me know how Beau's doing?" I link our fingers, drawing our palms together. Goose bumps rise along her bare arms.

"Yeah," she whispers, her eyes darkening with desire. "Did you want to come in for a few minutes?"

"Yes, but no." Telling her I didn't enjoy being treated like a sex doll last time would be a lie. I *did* enjoy it. I just didn't like the way I felt afterward. "I've got Rex at home."

"Yeah," she says, staring at my lips. "I should get inside to Pixie too."

The temptation to scoop her up, sweep her into my arms, kick open the door, and find the nearest surface to set her on surges, and when she rises on her toes to kiss my cheek, I have to close my eyes and clench my jaw to keep from acting on it.

"I guess I'll see you Sunday," she whispers in my ear before opening her door and taking temptation with her.

Chapter Nineteen

TAYLA

I'm distracted. The kind of distracted that's borderline rude. Even though I know it, I can't seem to make myself focus on anything Luis says as we walk along the kennels at the SPCA. Thoughts of Simon are a disease, eating away at my brain cells.

"See any good ones?" Luis asks when we get to the end of the last aisle.

"Not today," I admit. Before we went through the kennel area, I asked one of the workers about well-liked dogs, and she mentioned one or two. We took a serious look at them, but after playing with them for a few minutes, I wasn't sure they'd work. Neither of us is opposed to slightly older dogs. The key is temperament.

Mine isn't in the right state today to be looking at dogs.

When we get outside, Luis nods at a pub across the street. "Did you want to get a drink? Maybe some dinner?"

The OPEN sign flashes, and I hesitate, a touch of guilt dogging me, before remembering Simon's evasions. We can't build real trust without complete honesty. Why close this door with Luis?

"Sure," I say, leading the way across the street.

Jada is still a mystery, and even if he didn't cheat on me, there's something weird about what went on there. If she wasn't somehow tied to our breakup, why would she have been at his house so much? Why would he be reluctant to tell me what happened?

Luis holds the door open, and his hand rests on the small of my back while we wait for a table. Normally, the contact wouldn't bother me. He's attractive. We have a good rapport. He's mentioned several times over the last couple weeks that he's single, and I cleared up the Simon mess, sort of, so he knows I'm single too. Like every other guy who came after Simon, he has the qualities that should make him a good fit for me, but I can't force the connection.

"You seem far away today," Luis says after the waitress seats us and gives us menus.

"Do I?" I avoid eye contact and search the food list. Since it's Friday evening, the place is bustling with life. The smell of spilled beer and fried food hangs in the air.

"Everything okay at work today?" He gives the menu a quick glance before closing it.

On my lunch break, I called Simon to give him an update on Beau's condition. Could I have texted him? Yeah. But I wanted to hear his voice. The admission, even if it's just to myself, has thrown me off. "Yeah. Fine."

If I told Luis about Beau, I'd have to admit I was on a date with Simon last night. In a week and a half, Simon will be out of my life. Luis and I will be working together on his project to turn shelter and rescue dogs into therapy dogs for months, maybe years. Especially if nothing comes of the exchange. No need to overcomplicate this relationship.

He gives me a long, appraising look when I close my menu, but he doesn't pry. Instead, he launches into a series of amusing stories about the puppy he's taken to train. I listen attentively, and we order our food. When it comes, we eat and chat, but the whole conversation on my end is distant, half my mind somewhere else.

When we get to our cars in the SPCA parking lot, Luis folds his arms over the top of his roof and meets my gaze. "You sure you're okay? You seem distracted. Not really yourself."

"No, it's—it's nothing." I shrug.

"You sure? I'm a good listener. I've got these broad shoulders that can take a little extra weight."

I offer him a small smile. He *does* have broad shoulders and a tapered waist. For so many reasons, I should be attracted to him. What if Simon had never walked into my office? Would I have reached out to Luis? Forged the connection eluding me now?

"That's a really sweet offer," I say.

His lips twitch, and he opens the driver's door. "Message received, Murphy. You don't wanna talk about it." He points at me. "Puppy training in the park Sunday at one p.m. You there?"

"I'm there." I open my car door and slide into the seat. Following him out of the parking lot, I point my car in the direction I want to go before I can second-guess myself.

♥

Ruby opens the door on the third ring of the doorbell. "Where's the fire?" she asks, peering around me.

"I need wine." I drop my purse near the entry closet.

"You're in luck," Ruby says. "I have a bottle on the go. I'll grab another glass."

I slouch into the couch and put my feet on the footstool. My stomach is tied in knots, and I can't decide if it's the meal that doesn't agree with me or the realization Simon has wormed his way into my head. I fear my heart is next.

"Find any more dogs?" Ruby pours me a glass of red from her bottle on the coffee table before taking a seat on the other end of the couch.

"No." I sigh. "I wasn't into it tonight."

"The dogs? Or Luis?"

"Can it be both? I think it might be both. God, I wish it wasn't both."

"How'd the date with Simon go last night?"

I chug the entire glass of wine and pour myself another.

"Are you sure you don't want beer instead?" Ruby laughs. "Yesterday's date went that well?"

"He finally told me why we broke up. Well, kind of." I sit back with my second glass. The first is already working its magic on my rising anxiety.

"Kind of?"

"He hasn't told me what happened with Jada."

"That's a red flag." Ruby purses her lips. "You realize that, right? If the guy can't tell you what happened with her, there were some dirty dealings. I know I told you to get back together with him if you wanted, but . . ." She wags her finger and flicks her long black braids over her shoulder. "Honesty is a cornerstone of a relationship."

She's not telling me anything I don't know. But the more time I spend with Simon, the less I care about getting the truth, and the more I care about getting in his pants. Put him within two feet of me and my libido goes into overdrive. Even when I don't like him, I still *want* him.

"Every time we drove past his house for months, she was there. On his front step drinking coffee, her car in his visitor's spot, talking to him at the doorway. So he says he didn't cheat on you. You believe him. That's fine. That's your choice. But if he's not telling you what happened, that's not okay. He's hiding something."

"It wasn't every time," I grumble. Maybe every other, and I only saw the two of them actually together once. She was just . . . there, sliding into my spot in his life the minute it was vacant. I close my eyes and sip my wine. "So, you think I'm being dumb to feel anything for him again?"

"I think you need to be cautious." Ruby sighs. "Granted, it *was* six years ago." Her index finger swirls around the rim of her cup.

When I glance down at my glass, it's empty, and I reach for the bottle to refill it. My mind won't stop orbiting

Simon. "What if he *is* my soulmate? What if Soulmates Reunited *is* right?"

She sets down her glass and draws her knees into her chest. "Do *you* think he is?"

"I know you think that after Simon, I've chosen all the wrong men on purpose or sabotaged relationships . . ." I search for the right way to tell her how I'm feeling. "There were a few men who, on paper, should have been a match for me. Right?"

Ruby looks at the ceiling. "Jake, maybe, or Victor."

"Exactly, see?" I point my glass. "Not all of them were duds."

"You *want* it to be Simon."

"That makes it sound as though I have a choice." I stare into my wine. From the minute he walked into my vet office, we've been on a downward slide, an avalanche. There's no steering. I'm just holding on for dear life, trying not to get buried. "We found a dog last night that had been hit by a car."

"Oh no!" Ruby sits forward. "Was the dog okay?"

"Considering it was hit by a car, relatively minor injuries." I meet her gaze. "But I can't imagine having spent last night with anyone else. He helped me so much by waiting with me for the owners to arrive, and he took such gentle care of the dog . . . and me. He was *exactly* the partner I needed."

Ruby examines me in silence, and I sip my wine, trying not to dwell on the emotions welling up—again.

"So, what was his reason?" Ruby's voice is gentle.

"I don't know if you remember his parents—"

"Great couple. Warm. Funny. The few times I went to one of their parties with you, they were great hosts. Simon was close to them, right? Which I remember you liked because you're close to your family."

"His dad advised Simon not to get married."

"Oh God." Ruby sucks in a deep breath. "Does that mean his dad didn't like you? How could he not like you?"

I take Ruby through everything Simon told me the night before, and when I'm finished, Ruby goes to the kitchen for another bottle of wine. When she comes out, she's got a cheese board. I smother a smile. In a crisis, I eat chocolate cake, but Ruby's go-to is cheese, a lot of cheese.

She gets comfortable on the couch, plucks a piece of cheese off the board, and takes a sip of her wine. "That's a tough one. My parents' opinion about anything wouldn't bother me. Neither of them are good decision makers. But you've always cared about your parents' opinions, and Simon was *really* close to his dad."

"Incredibly close," I agree. "So, part of me sort of understands why he didn't go through with the proposal. But to go from *almost* proposing to breaking up with me in the same night? I just—it still doesn't make sense to me."

"This is gonna hurt, Tay, but my instinct is to say he *was* cheating on you, and he's trying to find a way to dress it up as something else now."

"Trust me." I gulp my wine. "It's occurred to me. So many times." I run a hand down the side of my face and tuck my hair behind my ear. "He's sincere when he talks about her. I don't think he's lying, not really. Or, at least, not about cheating on me."

"He *must* have been dating her."

"Agreed." I nod. "Simon says they 'weren't really dating,' but guys can be so weird about labeling a relationship."

"Irrationally weird." She laughs a little. "Which is why I was glad to meet Dean through Soulmates Reunited. We both knew what we wanted."

"Where is he, anyway?"

"Speaking engagement." She swirls her wine. "What are you going to do about Simon? You've got, what? A week or so left?"

"Technically, next Friday is a month since Soulmates Reunited gave me Simon's name. I agreed to next Sunday as the last date." I refill my wineglass and cross my legs. "If he doesn't tell me the truth about Jada before next Sunday, we're done. No matter what. I need to know he's not going to blindside me again."

"You're going to let him go to the wire?" Ruby's eyebrows lift. "You've got it under control? No chance you'll slide back into something without all the details?"

"Not a chance," I say, the wine slurring my words. "All the details or we're done, forever."

"I'll drink to that." Ruby raises her glass, and then she takes another square of cheese and pops it into her mouth. "You staying here tonight?"

"Can't," I say. "I've got Pixie at home. My neighbor let her out earlier, but I can't leave her for too long."

"You can't drive."

"Uber, baby." I wink at her, the wine slipping down my throat. "I'll get my car in the morning before the clinic opens."

"Sounds like you've got it all planned out."

I do. And the more I drink, the better my plan sounds in my head.

Chapter Twenty

SIMON

"Si, can you be my Uber?" Tayla's voice is hushed.

I check the display on my phone. One in the morning. "Where are you?"

"Ruby's house. But I had too much to drink, and I can't drive. And I need to get home to Pixie. I can call a real Uber. Sorry. I shouldn't have called." She stifles a laugh. "I already told Ruby I ordered an Uber, and she's gone to bed. I'll just—I'll just order one."

"No, no." I sit on the side of my bed and rub my face. "I'm coming. I'll get you. Can you text me Ruby's address?"

"Bring Rex?" There's a hopeful slant to her voice.

A heavy silence rests between us on the phone line. She's asking me to stay at her place without saying the words. More time with her is a win, so I'm not saying no. But her speech suggests she might regret calling me in the morning.

"I really need a Rex fix," she says.

"Yeah," I say. "I'll bring him. I'll get there as quick as I can." Hanging up, I throw on some clothes and whistle for Rex. I'm out the door within five minutes and on my way to the address Tayla sent.

Middle-of-the-night booty calls have to be a good sign, right? Rex's head is on the console between the seats, and I scratch his ears while I turn down Ruby's street. Ahead, at the end of a spacious driveway, is Tayla, leaning against a post. She's going to regret however many bottles of wine she split with Ruby tomorrow.

I park in the driveway, and Rex perks up at the sight of her. He pants and whines, and when she climbs into the car, he frantically licks the side of her face. *Me too, buddy. Me too.*

"Rex." I give him a gentle shove off her, and Tayla giggles.

"Aww," she coos, scratching under his chin. "I've missed you too."

He licks her palm and stares at her adoringly.

"You okay?" I ask as she clicks her seat belt.

"Yeah, yeah." She waves me off. "Just, like, got a bit carried away talking to Ruby about stuff."

Stuff. Sounds loaded. Do I dare? She tends to be brutally honest when she's had a drink or ten. Might want to tiptoe. "You spent the night with Ruby? Was Dean there?"

"Conference or something." She stares out the window.

"I had dinner and drinks with Luis, actually."

My hands flex on the steering wheel, my knuckles whitening. "Find any more dogs?"

"Nope." She cocks her head in my direction. "The dinner and drinks were good, though."

Jealousy, hot and fierce, spikes in my gut. What is this? He got her warmed up on their date, and I'm her best follow-through? The thought is bitter on my tongue, and I press my lips together to keep it in. Even if it's true, she wouldn't like me saying it.

"Does it bother you I went out with him?"

My jaw is clenched, and I shift my focus from the road to look at her. "You're going to feel like shit tomorrow."

"Won't be the first time I've gone to work with a bit of a hangover." She shrugs.

When we get to her house, I pull into her driveway and unlock the door for her to get out. If she wants me to come in, she's going to have to say it. "Here you go."

She gazes at me for a beat. "You're not coming in?"

"Do you want me to come in?"

"Isn't that how a booty call works? I snap my fingers, and you drop your pants?"

A chuckle bursts out of me. She's never been shy or coy about sex. I open the door to follow her. Rex hesitates until I invite him along, and then he bounds to her front door, his tail wagging furiously.

Tayla fumbles with her keys. On her third attempt at getting the key into the lock, she lets out a frustrated huff. Gently, I take the key from her hand and slip it into the slot.

"Good thing one of us still has some coordination."

She leans against the doorframe, and our gazes connect. My pants tighten in response to the look in her eyes. The memory of Tuesday night ignites the air around us. "You're way better at finding the right hole."

I grin and shake my head. Booty call or not, I shouldn't sleep with her.

I open the door, and Rex bounds between us into the house. Pixie lets out a series of barks in response to the noise, but we're still standing on the threshold staring at each other. Her comments about Luis bang around my head.

"I wasn't sure you'd come," she whispers, her hand resting on my chest.

"Not sure I would have if I'd known I was the consolation prize for the night."

"What's that mean?" Tayla frowns.

"Never mind." I slip past her into the house. I'm horny and pissed off. Not a great combination.

"What's that mean? Consolation prize?" She grabs my arm, and I glance at her over my shoulder.

"You go on a date with another guy and then invite me into your bed. What would you call it?"

"It wasn't a date," she scoffs, heading to the kitchen.

"Why'd you make it sound like it was?" I shut the front door and follow her into the kitchen. She's chugging a glass of water and taking aspirin.

"I can't help how you interpreted dinner and drinks with Luis." She puts the empty glass in the sink.

"I interpreted it the way you meant me to interpret it. You wanted me to be jealous. Well, here it is. I'm jealous. Pissed off."

"I don't know why you would be. You get to have sex with me, not him."

For how much longer? Another week?

She doesn't wait for me to respond before heading for her room to greet Pixie. I'm starting to feel like a puppy trailing her around the house, begging for scraps. She scoops Pixie into her arms and takes her back to the front door, attaching a leash.

While she's gone, I stare at the bed and rub my face. Rex nudges my leg, and I gesture to the living room outside Tayla's bedroom door. "Couch for you, buddy." He tucks his tail and heads for the living room.

I shouldn't stay. My feet are rooted to the spot, unable to commit to staying, but not able to carry myself to the door. She's what I want, but I don't want her like this. I don't want to be an afterthought. The guy she turns to as a last resort. I rub my face with both hands and then leave her bedroom, snapping my fingers for Rex to get off the couch and follow me.

My keys are on the table near the door, and I scoop them up just as Tayla comes back into the house with Pixie. The two dogs circle each other excitedly. She unhooks the puppy, and then she meets my gaze.

"Are you leaving?"

"I think so, yeah."

"You think so."

"Yeah." We stare at each other. I jingle my keys and try to step around her. She steps with me. "Tay."

"Why are you leaving?" She looks up at me.

I keep my gaze averted, just over her head. A muscle

in my jaw twitches in frustration. "I don't want to be your booty call."

"I beg to differ." Her hand skims the front of my jeans.

"Are you gonna beg, Tay?" I brace my hands on either side of the door, boxing her in, and when I look down at her, she sucks in a breath.

She lets out a throaty chuckle and rises on her toes to kiss the side of my mouth. "You don't want this?" Her voice is breathy.

"No," I grit out. When she tries to slither her hand back down to my zipper, I pin her wrist against the hard wood.

"You're a liar."

"I'm not willing to be your second choice."

"What makes you think you're the runner-up?" Her lips skim against my chin.

I groan and bury my face in her neck, breathing her in. Her free hand strays to the button at the top of my jeans.

"I should want other men," she says, her breath hot against the skin on my neck. Her hand grips my length and moves in a leisurely up-and-down motion. "I *wish* I could choose another man."

"I don't want to be the one who gets your body while someone else is winning your heart," I rasp out.

"Oh, Si," she says, her lips closing over my earlobe. "No one's getting my heart. You might as well take my body."

"It's not enough." I lock my jaw and try to pull back. When I let go of her wrist, her arms snake around my shoulders, and she presses herself against me. Behind us, the dogs are playing in a rough silence. Right now, I'd take a Pixie intervention before I lose the last of my willpower.

"Are you gonna make me beg?"

She presses kisses along my jawline, and I grip her waist. My willpower is fraying, in danger of snapping. "Why'd you call me, Tay?"

"I was horny, and you're good in bed." She kisses me, and I return the caress of her lips, but I don't let her deepen it. She groans. "Si!"

"I'm *great* in bed," I amend. "Why'd you call me?" I rest my forehead against hers, willing her to give me more. Thoughts of her consume every waking hour of my day.

"I just told you." She huffs out a breath and tries to slip away from me.

"It's not enough."

"I've never had to work this hard to be fucked before." She glares at me.

"Am I your second choice? Did Luis turn you down?" I can't imagine anyone turning her down, but she's got me twisted in knots.

"You're killing my buzz." She slaps my chest. "I snap my fingers; you drop your pants. I didn't call you to talk about feelings."

"My pants *are* dropped." They're around my ankles. My boxer briefs are only half on. "But you've been drinking . . ."

"It's not like we've never fucked when we were drunk. What part of me doesn't seem willing?" She takes my hand and guides it between her legs, and there's no doubt she's as turned on as I am. "I know what I want."

"Take off your shirt."

She whips it off and tosses it toward the couch. Her hair

is a cascade of black around her shoulders and down her back. "Done."

I chuckle and trace the edge of her bra with my finger. "Impressive." My lips skim her shoulder, and I slide a fingertip under the strap, sliding it down her arm. She shakes and leans into my touch. "Tell me something real."

Her head rolls to the side, and she closes the distance between us, so our hitching breaths mingle in the space between us. "Just one thing?" she whispers.

"Just one."

"I can't stop thinking about you even when I wish I could think about anyone else but you."

It's enough, and I dip my head, capturing her lips. A sigh escapes her, and I swallow it, savoring her desire. She meets my kiss, digging her fingers into my scalp. I sweep her up into my arms, step out of my pants, and carry her to her bedroom.

Chapter Twenty-one

TAYLA

Being forced to confront the truth of how deeply Simon has wormed his way back under my skin should switch off my desire. I don't want to feel the things I'm feeling for him. I sure as hell don't want to be admitting them. All the alcohol in the world can't seem to drown out the truth. The connection we had six years ago hasn't been lessened by time and distance. I loved him then, and it would be so easy to love him now.

"If I can give you the triple crown of orgasms, will you let me sleep here?" He kisses along my stomach, his hand working magic on my core.

I let out a husky laugh. Why does he think I told him

to bring Rex? "A three-peat? You could probably ask for anything you want."

"I'm holding you to that," he murmurs before his tongue flicks along my center, and I moan, lifting my hips, begging for more. And boy, does he give me more.

After the second orgasm, he stares at me with a hint of a smirk. "Triple crown, coming up." Competitiveness comes naturally to him. In this case, who am I to complain?

"You think I'm that easy," I murmur while he sheaths himself.

"Not easy," he says, cradling my body as he slides into me. "Just always worth the effort."

Whether it's the endorphins or the alcohol, when he eases out and back in as our gazes connect, my stomach flutters. His green eyes are soft, the way he used to look just before he told me he loved me. The memory lodges in my throat. I run my hand along his cheek, searching his face. *Does he love me?* How can he? *Do I love him?* My stomach clenches at the thought. I can't. I won't.

His forehead touches mine, and then we're kissing and moving in sync. He draws me closer, tighter, and, unbelievably, my body begins to coil again, ready to spring free once more. Any thoughts other than how good he feels inside me fly out of my mind. I want this. I want him. Nothing else matters.

"You feel so amazing," he rasps.

"Don't stop," I murmur, digging my nails into his ass, keeping him pressed tightly against me. "Don't ever stop." I want this feeling to go on and on. Somehow, I want him to convince me we can have *this* again for more than these three weeks. I want to cling on, even as I'm free-falling over the edge, tumbling into another orgasm. When I cry out, Simon holds me closer, his breathing ragged in my ear, and races over the edge with me.

"If I get out of this bed," Simon says from beside me, "am I going to come back to find you fully dressed and watching TV in the living room?"

"I have to work in five hours." I throw my hand over my face, my body so spent, I'm not sure I'll be able to even move in five hours.

"I'll be right back," Simon says, throwing back the covers. He putters around the other room before coming back with Pixie cradled in his arms and putting her back in her crate.

I forgot about the puppy. What kind of vet am I? Totally forgot I have a dog, or at least, a dog for now.

"You're doing a great job with her," Simon says, sliding under the covers next to me and slipping his arm across my middle, tugging me against him.

"She comes to the clinic every day. Sandy does half the training, I swear." I turn my head to stare at him. "What happened with Jada?" The question comes out without being filtered through my brain first.

Thank you, two bottles of wine.

He tenses. "I told you—"

"I don't want to know in a week, or tomorrow, or any other time you decide. I deserve to know." I turn to face him, and the room spins for a second. "You can't tell me that you want more, that I'm worth the effort, and every other thing you've said over the last two weeks and keep the one thing I still need to decide whether *you're* worth the effort, whether *I* want more." Even as I say the words, I realize his answer might not matter. I'm in too deep.

While I scan his face, I'm memorizing the tiny lines in the corners of his eyes, the way the vivid green stands out against his impossibly long lashes. I used to look in those eyes and wonder what color our children's eyes would be. All the emotions I've been trying to keep in a neat little box are peeking out, daring to hope.

"Okay." He says the word slowly. "Okay." He turns onto his back and shoves one hand behind his head, focusing on the ceiling.

My heart plummets into my stomach. "Usually, when someone is going to tell the truth, they don't have to think about it so hard."

"After we split up," he says, taking a deep breath, "I went on a few dates with her."

"A few?"

"Three." He glances at me.

"That doesn't make any sense," I whisper, meeting his gaze. "She was at your apartment for months. I thought she'd moved in."

"You drove past my house?" He turns on his side to face me, his hands tucked between his head and the pillow.

"Ruby was my getaway driver." I mirror his pose.

A hint of a smile touches his lips. "I was a mess after we broke up, with my dad asking my mom for a divorce, the abrupt move to France. So I finally agreed to the dates, even though I didn't really want to go."

Agreed to the dates. Such a weird way to put it. "You make it sound like it was some kind of contract." I frown. "Unless she was, like, your house cleaner or something, three dates doesn't explain the number of times I saw her." Do I sound like a stalker? Likely. I'm too drunk to care. Her seamless integration into his life after we broke up ate at me. Still eats at me like battery acid.

"You probably saw her while I was at work." He purses his lips. "I didn't realize she was around so much. I knew she was . . ." He seems to search for the right word. ". . . obsessed with . . ." He winces. "I didn't know how bad it was until Aaron went over to let Rex out and found Jada sleeping in my bed."

My eyes bug out. "She had a key? You went on three dates, and she had a key?"

"Give me some credit." His lips quirk up, but the almost-smile isn't amused. "She broke in through a window I hadn't latched properly. Ground-floor apartments are great for pizza deliveries and break-ins."

"Aaron found her in your bedroom?" Is *this* the truth? Why would he hesitate to tell me about a woman who got too attached too quickly? My drunken brain gnaws on the details, slicing them up, rearranging them, trying to figure out what's true.

"Yep," he says. "A place, in case you're wondering, she'd never been during our three dates."

"What did Aaron do?"

"Called the police and reported the break-in." Simon

adjusts the pillow. "I shouldn't have let it get that far."

"Sounds like she was unstable." Did people think I was unstable when Simon broke up with me? I recognized the free fall, but I couldn't seem to stop myself. Driving past his house. Checking his social media. Hardly eating. Constant dreams about him. Love isn't always a blessing.

"Aaron took me to the police station the next day to file a for a personal protection order." Simon frowns and avoids eye contact.

"I guess after she broke in to your house—"

"There was a lot more than that. Looking back, it was . . . The break-in was just the point where Aaron thought I needed to snap out of it and put my foot down." He chuckles and runs his fingers along his forehead. "She didn't feel *dangerous* to me. Sad. Desperate. Obsessed with something that would never happen. He saw her behavior differently. I was burying myself in extra shifts. Who was I to argue?"

"Three dates and a protection order." I whisper the details, but they don't quite click into place. Is it because I'm drunk? Or maybe I just can't imagine doing the same thing myself, which makes it hard to believe? "This doesn't seem like your fault, Si. Why wouldn't you just tell me?"

"Other than you, the way I handled the situation with Jada is one of my biggest regrets." He loops his index finger around a stray strand of my hair and lets it slide through his fingers. "I made a lot of mistakes in a really short period of time."

I lace our fingers together and squeeze his hand. Tears pool in my eyes, and I sniff. For years, I thought he replaced me like I meant nothing. To realize the situation wasn't even close is both a balm to my soul and strangely compounds the lingering ache. Part of me wants to ask who disliked me enough to set him up with another woman right after we broke up, but I probably don't want to know. All those sleepless nights where I was so lost, wondering how I got our relationship so wrong. I *didn't* get us wrong, but we still went so wrong anyway.

"You had my heart, Tay. I could never give it to anyone else."

When I meet his gaze, the sincerity in his eyes erases the rough edges of the scar his abrupt departure left. Has he truly meant all the things he's said the last two weeks? "Do you really think we can get us back, Si?"

He traces the side of my face. "I wouldn't be here if I didn't." He shuffles closer and slides his arm around my middle, so we're mere inches apart. "I know you're not there yet, but I'm going to do everything I can to show you we're meant to be." His lips are soft and tender against mine, the kind of kiss that pulses with love and care, not desire or passion.

The gesture sets off the avalanche of feelings inside me again.

"I'm going to find a way to make you believe it, Tay."

The thing is, I think I'm already there.

Chapter Twenty-Two

SIMON

Sweat drips out of my hairline and runs in rivulets down the sides of my face. When a drop dares to take any other path, I brush it away impatiently. Rex keeps pace with me easily as we navigate the city streets. At seven, Rex won't be able to do these long-distance runs for too many more years. Music blares from my earbuds, and when my phone interrupts the stream, I tell it to connect without pulling it out of my running belt.

"Hey," Tayla says, after I say hello. "Where are you?"

I check the intersection as Rex and I cross the street. "Out for a run," I say. "What's up?"

"A run? Are you far away?"

I consider whether I should admit where I am or not. "I

didn't do this on purpose, but I'm about six blocks from your place." I put in my earbuds and went on Autopilot when I left my house. I wanted a long run to forget about Tayla training Pixie with Luis again tomorrow. He likes her. Who wouldn't? The uphill battle to win her over might be done, but I'm not sure we're on even ground yet. The light turns at the intersection up ahead, and I signal Rex to stop. Given that Tayla's been all I can think about, I guess my compass pointed to her without me realizing it.

"I just got home from work, and I was thinking about a late dinner. Did you eat yet?"

I scan the height of the sun and try to calculate what time it is without taking out my phone. "No, I haven't."

"Did you want to maybe have dinner with me?" Her voice goes up at the end as though she's not sure she should be asking.

I'm still at the light, even though it's changed once already. "By the time I run home, shower, and get back to your place, it'll be more like a midnight snack."

"You could just . . . you could come here."

I'm soaked through with sweat. "I smell—bad. You're not going to want to be around me."

"I have this new thing called running water. It's all the rage. Comes through pipes. Into your home." She gasps. "It's gonna change your life."

I chuckle. "Point taken. But I can't put these clothes back on."

"So don't." Her tone is a dare.

Christ, I'm standing in the middle of the suburbs sporting

a semi because just the sound of her voice is a total fucking turn-on. "I'm on my way."

Tayla greets me at the door, and while Rex and Pixie bound around the living room together, she leads me to her bedroom. In the bathroom, she starts the water, tugs off my shirt, and shucks my shorts and boxers.

"You're very dirty," she murmurs, running her hands along my torso. "Do you need any help getting clean?"

I grin down, and she glances up, batting her eyes in exaggerated flirtation. "Do you think you're up to the job?" I ask.

"You're not the only one who can rise to the occasion." A sly smile touches her lips as she checks the water temperature. Steam is already pouring over the top.

I wrap my hand in the hem of her shirt and tug her near. "Is this another booty call?"

"If you object, I can stop calling."

Securing her to me, I slide open the shower door and step into the streaming water with her still fully clothed. "I've got no objections," I say, as she laughs. I smother her laughter with my kiss as the hot water falls around us.

"Haven't seen it," I say as I grab another slice of pizza out of the box. Tayla flips through the Netflix options.

"Yeah, but it looks awful. An underfunded tiger zoo and an owner in a polygamous relationship." She shakes her head. "Nope, nope, nope. Those poor animals. The system is failing them."

"Not sure the men are any better off than the cats." I offer her some water from my glass.

We debate our options while eating through the whole pizza naked in bed. When nothing appeals to either of us, Tayla turns off the TV and sets the remote on the nightstand. She turns to face me, her head resting on her hand.

"Where do you see yourself in five years?" she asks, eyebrows raised.

"Five years?" I grab the empty pizza box and tuck it onto the nightstand on the other side of the king-size bed. "Ideally?"

"Well, yeah."

"With you. Maybe a kid . . . or two."

"Are you planning to give birth?" She arches her eyebrows.

I mirror her pose and trace a figure eight on the bed between us. "Maybe neither of us has to. All kinds of ways to build a family." I make eye contact. "All right then, where do you see yourself in five years?"

"In a stable, happy relationship. Still a vet. Maybe a kid . . . or two. Making a difference in my community somehow."

"Is that why you took this shelter dog to therapy dog gig with Luis?"

"I plead the Fifth." She bites her lip.

"What's that supposed to mean?" I brush her hair away from her face.

"I sort of contacted him out of spite, maybe?" Her dark eyes flash with mischief. "Luis is attractive, and we have a lot in common. He was a ridiculous flirt when he dropped off his business card. But I didn't call him until after you showed up at the office."

"Would you have called him?" The notion of her dating Luis, spending time with him, irks me. Whether it's because I've seen him in person or because I know they already have something in common that's important to Tayla, jealousy eats at me every time she says she's with him.

"Eventually, maybe. Not any time soon."

Am I supposed to read into that? If so, what am I supposed to get from that comment? Is he an option if we don't work out? Grilling her will probably lead to a fight, and since I showed up on her doorstep today, the atmosphere between us has been playful and relaxed. The cloud of indecision that seemed to hang over her whenever we were together before has vanished.

"Aaron has rented the rooftop patio of The Brew for Monday night. His car dealership had record sales, so he's celebrating with all of his employees. He asked me to stop by and said I could bring you, if you wanted to come."

"Monday night, huh? That's not one of our nights."

I'm not going to remind her that the last two nights haven't been scheduled date nights and yet we've ended up together. Any reminder on my part might lead to her kicking me out, and I can hear my clothes banging around in the dryer. Naked running is only fun when you're drunk and in college.

"The Brew is a great restaurant, and the view is incredible. You just gotta put up with the company." My lips quirk up into a slight smile.

"A great restaurant, an incredible view, and so-so company." She raises her hand. "I'm sold. Count me in."

I collapse onto my back and give a fist pump. "So-so company for the win."

She laughs and drapes herself across me. "I can think of worse ways to spend a Monday night."

On that we can agree because I can't imagine anything better than more time with her.

Chapter Twenty-three

TAYLA

Luis passes me Pixie's leash after we've finished our recall training in the local park and examines me. "You're in a much better mood today."

"Am I?" I smile and stare down at the pup, who is focused on me. We've been working on "eyes on me" with her too. She's a clever little girl.

"Yeah, but you're still doing the thing where you don't look at me. So it's gotta have something to do with another guy."

My gaze flies to his. "I—" I sigh. "You asked me a couple weeks ago what was going on with Simon, and I said nothing. At the time, that was true. But things have changed. We're . . ." What are we doing? Dating for money, initially, but I haven't thought about Soulmates Reunited in days. "I don't know. We're figuring things out."

Luis shoves his hands into his pockets. "You're still good to train Pixie with me? Help me find shelter dogs?"

"Yes! Yes. The two—in my mind—aren't related. It's just, I don't want to give you the wrong impression." It might have been the *right* impression a few weeks ago. But the romantic connection with Luis isn't there, at least not for me, and whether or not things go ahead with Simon, I shouldn't lead Luis on.

He squints into the sun. "Can't say I'm not disappointed." A hint of a smile touches his lips. "But I didn't come to your office looking for a date, I came looking for a partner for my pet project. So, from now on, I'll keep my comments strictly dog-based."

"My vet tech, Sandy, is really interested in the project too, if you wanted more help or were looking to expand."

Luis nods. "The doggy daycare I run along with my pet store has helped to get the word out about what we're trying to do. I'll stop by next week and chat with Sandy about what she might want to do."

"Perfect," I say with a smile. Sandy will be over the moon to talk to him again. While he isn't the right guy for me, he'll be a catch for someone else. I check my phone and see a message from Simon. He has something planned for us this afternoon. At this point, scheduled dates are probably silly. Simon's efforts are cute, though, and hard to stop. "I should get going."

"See you Wednesday for our shelter search."

"Wouldn't miss it!"

♥

Dusk is falling when we turn in to the gravel parking lot of the stadium on the edge of a town not far from Lake Michigan. Colored lights flash and twinkle on the other side of the gated entrance. We climb out of Simon's car, and the perfumes of cotton candy, popcorn, and fried pastries mingle in the air with so many memories. I take a deep breath, and my heart expands with it. Every summer as a kid, my parents took me to this county fair. Tears prick my eyes, and a pang of longing pierces my chest for my dad, who used to squeeze himself into the car of the "roller coaster" when I was too afraid to ride alone. I glance at Simon over the top of the car, floored he's brought me here.

"I did well?" he asks with a grin.

"I haven't been here in years." I take in the Ferris wheel, the games, and the dragon coaster. Off to the right of where we've parked, the stadium stands overlook a pit. "Oh my God. Is it demolition night?"

His expression makes my breath catch. He's staring at me with such a mixture of love and affection, the same emotions welling up in me. It's so easy to sink back into these feelings with him. Too easy. God, it's only been two weeks since we agreed to this insanity. How am I already in over my head?

"Did you remember?" I whisper.

"Of course I remembered." He shrugs and rotates to draw a line with his finger along the country road we traveled to get here. "We drove down here one time to get to Lake Michigan. My GPS wasn't working worth shit. Traffic jams were everywhere because of some big accident." He chuckles. "The windows were open, and your hair whipped around while you lit up telling me how great this fair was as a kid . . . I've never forgotten how joyous you were."

The memory comes back in an unexpected rush. "We didn't stop because we were meeting friends of yours for dinner at some restaurant by the lake, and we were already late." I meet his gaze. "And you said . . ." I hesitate, the words sticking in my throat. "'Don't worry. Someday I'll bring you back here.'" By the time "here" is out of my mouth, my voice is little more than a whisper. All the images from that day hit me in the chest. "God, I can't believe you remembered, and I can't believe I forgot. Your friend, what was his name again?"

"Drayton," he says with a grimace.

"Right." I tap the side of my head. "The longest, most awkward dinner. He and his wife . . . what was her name?"

"Sylvia."

"Yes! They were in some sort of weird standoff the whole meal. Barely spoke to each other. Shot barbs at one another and tried to pass them off as jokes."

"They'd been together since we were in high school," Simon says, not meeting my gaze.

"Are they still together? I don't know if it was a blip, but they seemed *really* unhappy." Simon and I left our dinner shell-shocked. To see a relationship fraying so badly and so publicly was disorienting.

"Divorced." He rubs the back of his head. "Married two years, and a really ugly, bitter divorce."

"Are you still friends with them?" I cock my head.

"Drayton, yeah. We meet up a few times a year. Text each other random, stupid shit." His smile is fleeting. "We've got about an hour before the derby starts. We can squeeze in some rides and games first." He holds out his hand.

I slide my fingers along his palm before locking our hands together. While we walk to the stadium, my chest floods with gratitude.

Two weeks ago, if someone from Soulmates Reunited told me I'd be grateful to be matched with Simon, I would have laughed in their face . . . and then maybe vomited.

But given how much he hurt me, I'm not sure I would have let him back into my life under any other circumstances. Soulmates Reunited, or maybe Simon himself, has forced me to see him in another light, through another lens. The hurt is still there, but it's been softened by the complicated circumstances surrounding our breakup and by his trying so hard to win me back. I don't doubt he wants a relationship with me, but I need to be sure I want one too.

Simon pays our entrance fee, and then we're scrutinizing the stretch of rides and games laid out in rows in front of us. "Where to first?" Simon asks.

"Gotta go with my favorite first in case we don't make it back to the rides after the derby."

"The Mega Drop," he says without hesitation, pointing to the tower in the middle of the fair.

I give him a quizzical look. "How'd you know that?"

"The first summer we dated, we went to an amusement park. You made a beeline for the Mega Drop when we arrived, then again after lunch, and one more time before we left."

"You have an incredible memory," I muse while we weave through the crowds toward the ride.

"Just where you're concerned." He kisses my temple as we get in line.

I stare up at him for a beat. "Thank you for bringing me here."

He frames my face before dropping a kiss on my forehead and then one on my lips. We move closer to the front of the line, and Simon tucks me into his side, dropping another kiss on my hair. I wrap my arms around his middle and close my eyes. The *bing-bing* of games, the screams of the people on the rides, and the announcer at the stadium calling for last bets on the derby are oddly soothing, and I give a satisfied sigh.

When we get to the front of the line, Simon and I select seats next to each other. I draw the U-shaped foam-padded bar over my head, securing it against my chest, and then I buckle the strap. Simon reaches over and pushes my bar a little tighter, and I chuckle.

"Are you going to be this nervous when you have kids?"

He meets my gaze, and there's a hint of a smile. "Probably. Safety first." He winks and settles into his seat.

The circular bank of seats rises into the air. At the top, we perch for a moment, and the whole fair is below us, noises muted. The nearest town twinkles in the distance. This is my favorite moment—the anticipation mixed with fear while I wait for the bottom to drop out.

"Happy?" Simon asks, his hand on my thigh.

"Yes!" Our gazes lock, both of us grinning, so immersed in the moment it's like magic has been sprinkled over us. Then the ride releases, and I let out a joyful scream while we soar toward the ground.

Chapter Twenty-four

SIMON

The rooftop bar here is one of my favorites in Grand Rapids. The view of the city stretches out before us as the sun sets. Denise, the pet shelter worker whom Aaron is now dating, says something, and Tayla throws her head back with a laugh. Warmth spreads across my body at the sound.

Aaron is talking to me, but I've only given him one of my ears. The other is tuned to Tayla's voice. Being with her again is like rediscovering an addictive substance. I recognize what this is, and yet it amazes me just the same.

"So, Soulmates Reunited brought you two together again, huh?" Denise says, her gaze traveling from me to Tayla and back again. "Funny how life works."

A frisson of unease races through me. Exactly how much has Aaron told Denise?

Tayla smiles, her eyes softening. "Trust me when I say no one was more disappointed than me when Simon's name popped up on that monitor."

My heart kicks, and a cold sweat breaks out across my lower back. Normally, I'd pretend to be hurt or fire a quick comeback, but words fail me. At any minute, Aaron could give me away. When he asked me if I'd told Tayla every-thing, I assured him I had. His gaze is trained on my face, and I'm sure he's putting together the pieces I didn't tell him the other day.

"What do you think now?" he asks, his tone mild.

"I don't know." She gives me a playful look. "He's all right, I guess."

"All right?" I pretend offense, recognizing I need to jump in before things get weird.

"Maybe they weren't so wrong after all."

Her admission causes another burst of warmth to flood my body. Christ, it's hardly a ringing endorsement, but given how resistant she's been, that small admission is a big win. "Soulmate Simon?" I suggest, raising my eyebrows.

"Still not sure about the alliteration." A hint of a smile threatens.

"It's easy to get thrown off."

Aaron's gaze travels between the two of us, and he shakes his head. "He was always crazy about you." He cocks an eyebrow at Tayla. "Hopefully he's making better choices this time around."

She glances at me and takes a deep breath before

focusing on Aaron. "Were you the one who set him up with Jada?"

Aaron chokes on a sip of his drink and waves his hands. "That was not me."

"Sorry—I just—I had to ask." Tayla flushes. "I didn't want it to be you."

"Anyone else?" Denise finishes her drink and waggles her martini glass.

"I'll come with you." Tayla slides off her barstool to follow Denise.

"For fuck's sake," Aaron growls. "You didn't tell her Soulmates Reunited is a fraud? That they drove all kinds of doubts into you? Compounded the bullshit your dad was talking? What the actual fuck?"

"I was worried she'd cut ties with me if I told her everything. She believes the soulmates shtick is real. And maybe—" I can't believe I'm going to say this. "Maybe I do too." I rub my face and sigh.

"She's gonna cut ties with you when she discovers you're not being open and honest—*again*. She thinks *someone* set you up with Jada?"

"That's not what I said." Up until now, I didn't realize she'd interpreted our conversation that way, but I can see how she would have made that leap. The more surprising part is that she hasn't asked me herself. "I'm going to tell her."

"When?" Aaron slides his pint glass onto the round table in front of us. "If you love her, you need to tell her tonight. Give her the whole picture. The whole thing. Don't wait until Sunday. Give her some fucking credit. She obviously still has feelings for you, and I've heard enough about how badly you fucked up with her to last five lifetimes. I don't need to hear it for another ten because you wasted *this* chance too."

"Tell me how you really feel," I mutter. "What if she hates me for not being honest from the start?"

"Look, man. You should have been straight with her from the get-go. But seeing the two of you tonight, what's between you is palpable. She's not going to ditch you unless you let her find out the truth from someone else."

Who else would tell her if Aaron isn't going to? "Does Denise know?"

"*Tell her*. The longer you leave it, the worse it gets. I thought you learned that lesson last time, but apparently, you're trying to see if the lesson has changed. It hasn't."

I sip my beer for a minute, staring at Tayla over at the bar, her long dark hair shimmering down her back while she talks to Denise, waiting for their drinks to be made. She'll be angry when I tell her I knew Soulmates Reunited was a fraud from the minute I received our match email. Will she forgive me for holding her money and her time hostage in a bid to make up for my past behavior? After two weeks together, I don't have a clue whether telling her will put the final nail in any chance we have or set us free to move forward. When she catches me watching her, her smile broadens. "I owe it to her, don't I?"

"You owe it to yourself too. Unburden yourself, so even if she walks away, you haven't held anything back to worry over for another however many years. You can't keep clinging on to any piece of the past. Build something new, but don't lay it down on top of shifting sands."

If I don't tell her, and somehow she finds out—a news story, a lawsuit, another unsatisfied customer, any of the people in my life who know—she'll never understand or forgive me for keeping the truth from her. Aaron's right—I have to build something that'll last. "When we get back to my place tonight, I'll tell her. I'll tell her everything."

"It's about fucking time." Aaron slaps me on the back.

Chapter Twenty-five

TAYLA

Simon has been weirdly quiet since we left the restaurant. I've tried to nudge him into conversation a few times, but unlike normal, none of my smart-ass comments are landing. He's distant and distracted.

He brings me a beer at his apartment and falls onto the couch beside me. "Denise seems nice."

"Nice and completely wrong for Aaron."

"Funny—Aaron said the same thing to me the other day when we went for coffee."

"So," I say, frowning, "why is he with her?"

"Best guess?" Simon's brows pull together, and he shifts in his seat. "The sex is good." He shrugs.

"God, men are shallow." I slouch deeper into the couch,

happy Simon is finally talking to me. I was starting to worry something was really wrong. He only gets quiet like this when something is weighing heavily on his mind. "Though I guess not all relationships are a love connection."

"Or even a good match." Simon stares at the bottle cap in his hand, pensive. "I need to talk to you about something, and I'm worried about how you're going to take it."

I frown and set my drink on the coffee table in front of us. Rex has curled around my feet, probably wondering why I didn't bring Pixie, but Sandy took her for the evening. "Okay." I swivel to face him. "Is it—is it about now or before?"

"Sort of both?" He winces and doesn't meet my gaze.

I stare up at the ceiling and try to slow my racing heart. As long as he doesn't confess to having cheated on me after all, I can probably take anything he throws at me in stride. The last three or four days have been so good, it's hard to believe anything he says can ruin how I'm starting to feel. "All right." I take a deep breath and search his face. "What is it?"

"It's about Soulmates Reunited." He flips a beer cap over his knuckles.

My phone buzzes in my pocket, and I press the Dismiss button without looking at it. "Is this about the money?"

"Sort of." He glances at me. "The email I got from them, the one with your name in it—"

My phone buzzes again, and I let out a frustrated sigh. "I just—I should check this in case it's a vet emergency. Sorry."

Simon gives a quick nod and takes a long drink of his

beer while I check my display. Luis has called twice now, back-to-back. "I'll call Luis back really quick in case it's important. I won't be long." When I stand up, Simon's shoulders slump, and I almost sit back down beside him, let him continue. But then my phone lights up with a text message from Luis asking me to call him.

I slip into Simon's bedroom, a mix of frustration and curiosity warring in me. I can't even guess at what Simon was going to say or why Luis would be calling me repeatedly on a Monday night.

"Hey, Luis," I say when he answers. "What's up?"

"Bruno is sick, and I'm trying to figure out whether I should be freaking out. Are you busy? I hope I'm not bothering you."

"No, no," I lie. "It's fine. Give me his symptoms, and I can let you know whether we should meet at the clinic." He's never abused having my number before, and since Bruno is one of the dogs we've pegged for the therapy dog program, we need to keep track of any issues he might have. Once we've gone through his behavior and I've given Luis a few options to try, I ask him to email me what Bruno has been eating. Sounds like a possible allergy.

I click into my email to make sure I have Luis's list, and another message loads. The sender isn't someone I know, but the subject catches my eye: *Veterinary Exchange.*

My breath releases in a whoosh. *Holy shit.*

I haven't thought about the program since I said I'd take anything on offer after one glass of wine too many. Before I can stop myself, I open the email and scan the proposed details. Scottish Highlands. A farm with a practice attached.

The man's planned exchange fell through, so he's looking for someone who can swap in the next month. I read the email a second time and sink onto the edge of Simon's bed. A farm would give me a chance to practice my large animal vet skills, something I've always hoped to do and have never been able to pursue in the city.

One month. That's fast. Faster than I expected. Can I get all my practice details sorted out in thirty days? Notify clients, talk to Mike, let Luis know about my new plan? As a single woman, there's no *personal* reason I can't pick up and go. Except . . . except . . . My thoughts drift to the past two weeks with Simon. Even when I knew he wasn't being completely honest, I couldn't control my lingering feelings. Our connection is a master class in chemistry. Almost like . . . almost like how I'd want a soulmate to be.

Oh God.

Someone who shattered my heart shouldn't get a second chance, should he? I sigh. But what have the last two weeks proven? We still fit together. We still have amazing sexual chemistry. When I'm in a bind, he's the guy I want standing next to me. What do I do?

I can go to Scotland.

I can stay here and see whether this thing with Simon sticks this time.

The email on my phone mocks me, and I almost wish it didn't exist. A week ago, I'd be replying right now, telling this man across the ocean to pack his bags because I'll make the timeline work.

Now the thought of leaving—of leaving Simon—causes a thin sheen of sweat to break out under my armpits. Simon or Scotland. Both options are risks. Which risk do I want more?

The doorbell rings, and I check the time. Who the hell is showing up at Simon's house at nine o'clock at night? Curious, I shove my anxiety down deep and head into the living room. Simon's broad back is shielding whoever is at the door, and his posture is tense.

Would someone be trying to sell something door-to-door this late? Do people still do that?

I start to pad toward the entrance, trying to peer around Simon to catch a glimpse of who's got him so on edge, but whoever it is, they're short. Then I catch a voice—female. My heart kicks.

Oh God. Is it an irate ex-girlfriend? I cringe. Did I ask Simon about any recent exes? Surely he wouldn't have been in a dating database if he was involved with someone, would he?

"Are you two back together?" The voice is accusing, angry. "You've been spending a lot of time with her."

Back together? How does this woman know we used to date? She knows who I am?

"That's not any of your business." His voice is tight. "You shouldn't be here."

"No, no. I should have come *sooner*, obviously. I thought—I thought once you got more women out of your system, you'd realize the truth. You'd know what I know."

"You shouldn't be here. Coming here again is a mistake. You need to leave."

I freeze in place, still not able to see who's at the door, but her words are clear from my spot on the other side of the couch. Listening to this is wrong, isn't it? Maybe I should go back into the bedroom. When she leaves, I'll ask Simon about her. I turn, ready to tiptoe out, when she speaks again.

"We're soulmates. We're supposed to be together. I've tried to be patient, but I don't understand why you'd give *her* a second chance when you never even gave me one in the first place." It sounds like she's crying. "You said you weren't ready for a relationship. I'm—I've tried to—I've given you space."

My heart roars so loud, Simon's reply is distorted. *Soulmates?* What the hell is going on? Who is this woman? Almost against my will, I creep closer to the door.

"You can't mean that," the woman says, her voice pitched too high.

"I do," Simon says, his voice gentle. "It's the truth."

I missed something. What did I miss? I peer around his side, and a cold sweat breaks out on my palms. Her blue eyes are focused on Simon. Her long brown hair is twisted into a knot on her head. She's older than I expected, but I guess we've all aged, haven't we?

"Jada?" I whisper. Why in the world is she at Simon's door now? Has he lied to me? Or is she breaking the protection order?

Simon turns to me, all the color draining from his face.

Chapter Twenty-six

SIMON

"Jada?" Tayla's voice is sharp with surprise.

I half turn to see Tayla's shocked expression. Not exactly how I was expecting the night to end, but the result might be the same. I don't know who I expected when I opened the door. Jada definitely wasn't it, and the sight of her sent a jolt of anxiety through me with Tayla in the next room.

"What are you doing here?" Tayla's glance bounces between me and Jada, whose tears have started to tumble down her cheeks. Finally, Tayla focuses on the woman on the other side of the threshold. We haven't seen each other since I filed the personal protection order almost six years ago. Stupid, maybe, but I assumed she gave up. Has she been here watching all along?

Jada slings an arm across her chest in a half hug while the other one swipes away her tears. "I—I wanted to see for myself if you two were back together." She lets out a shuddering breath. "He's supposed to be *my* soulmate."

Soulmates Reunited ruined her life . . . or maybe I did. Maybe I shouldn't have told her I wasn't ready. Maybe I should have told her she'd never be the one. I couldn't force what wasn't there—no matter what we appeared to be on a computer screen.

"Why would you think that?" Tayla's tone is measured and curious.

She's handling Jada's shocking return better than I am. I just want her gone, but Tayla, in typical fashion, is much more empathetic when faced with a situation she doesn't understand. I have a feeling that empathy isn't going to be extended to me once Jada leaves.

"Soulmates Reunited matched us," I say quietly before Jada can respond. "Six years ago, Soulmates Reunited said Jada and I were soulmates."

"What?" When her honey-brown eyes turn toward me, disbelief flashes before anguish settles in its place. "Are you serious?"

"Yes," Jada answers.

She's unable to read the change happening between me and Tayla. But I'm reading it far too well. She's going to leave me, and she'll never look back.

"We're soulmates, and he's never given me a real chance. I don't know if you know, but Soulmates Reunited is an incredibly expensive service, and they don't get these things wrong. He just needs to give me a chance." She must see something in Tayla's face, even though she hasn't taken her gaze off mine. "I'm sorry. I realize this is probably upsetting since you're sort of dating again."

"Oh," Tayla says, finally breaking eye contact with me. "That's not why it's upsetting. I'm going to let you two work this out. I'll grab my things."

"Tayla." I follow her into the apartment and try to grab her arm, but she evades me.

"It's a good thing I drove here, right? Otherwise, this would be superawkward right now. The last thing I want from you is a ride." Tayla scoops her purse off the couch and snatches her keys from the side table. "Looks like you've got lots of soulmate options." She glares in my direction and squeezes out the door past Jada. "Good luck," she calls.

"Tayla." I rush along the path behind her to the visitor parking spot.

"I cannot talk to you." She yanks on the driver's door and then whirls to face me. "I cannot look at you. I *never* want to speak to you again."

"I don't know what you're thinking, Tay, but I can explain. I was going to explain."

"When? Once you'd sucked me in so deep I didn't care anymore?" Her hand squeezes the doorframe. "So, you didn't cheat on me, but you signed up for a fucking dating service while we were still together?"

"That's not what happened."

She holds up a hand. "I. Don't. Care." Her jaw tightens. "I've been offered a veterinary exchange to Scotland. I leave in a month, so things were never going to work out between us anyway. It's just—we were never going to work."

I run my hands down my face while she drives out of the parking lot and speeds away. She's so fast, I'm surprised her tires don't squeal, that there isn't actual rubber left behind on the ground.

"She doesn't want you, Simon." Jada is still at my door, a smug look on her face. "You might as well give me a chance."

I shove my hands into the pockets of my jeans and gaze in the direction Tayla's car went. Aaron warned me this would blow up in my face, and I didn't fucking listen. Now I've got a woman I don't want on my doorstep and the woman I very much want no longer willing to talk to me. I sink into a crouch in the parking lot and rest my head in my hands. There has to be some way to make this right. How do I make this right?

A gentle hand touches my shoulder, and I flinch. I rise abruptly and step back from Jada, who must have left the front door without me noticing.

"Soulmates Reunited is a fraud, Jada." There's nothing gentle in my voice now. "Do you know how many women they've matched me to over the last six years? *Four*. Tayla's one of them. The most recent one. Besides you and her, there were two others. They aren't some elite, perfect soul-matching service. They're a fraud."

She scans my face, indecision and surprise written on hers. "But—but—" Jada rears back, stung. "My friend Stephanie was matched with them the year before me. They've been married for six years. It works. I—you're my person."

I shake my head and run a hand through my hair. "I'm

not. Maybe in another life I might have been. I don't know. But I met Tayla first, fell in love with her first, and I can't let her go. I won't." I cross my arms and peer into Jada's eyes. "I need you to hear me on this. Really hear me. I'm sorry you've spent the last six years hoping for something that'll never be. I—I thought you'd moved on after I got the protection order. I had no idea you were still . . ." I search for a word that doesn't make her sound unstable. ". . . monitoring my life. If I'd known, I would have told you about the others." Would I have? Maybe not. God, I've been such a dick. Not on purpose, but the result is the same.

"We're not soulmates?" Tears fill her eyes.

"Not any more than I was with two of the other women." I consider offering her a comforting arm rub, but distance is probably less confusing than consoling. Also, I don't want to touch her. It's not fair to blame her, but at this moment, she's ruining my life, had a hand in ruining it six years ago.

Soulmates Reunited's persistence wasn't her fault. The emails, text messages, their giving Jada my information in the first place—all of it muddled my mind in ways it shouldn't have. The phone calls were the worst, the same female voice in each one, calm and confident, more sure about their system than I was about anything. I can only imagine what that manipulation would have done to someone who already believed.

Should I blame Jada? She's the one standing in front of me right now. She can't help who they matched her with and how the company behaved to try to secure the match, wearing me down so far that I had nothing left to give.

I ease my fingers along my brow. Will Tayla ever forgive me? Listen to my explanation?

"Do you know what's it's like to be the one percent who has their match reject them?" Jada whispers. "All my friends knew I went to Soulmates Reunited. The money I'd saved for a down payment on a house . . ." She snaps her fingers. "Gone." She doesn't make eye contact. "My friend got married to the guy she met from the algorithm. Another friend who used them has been happy for years with the man they matched her to." She turns her big blue eyes up to me. "You gave me three dates . . ."

My heart softens a touch. Overall, this situation isn't her fault. There has to be some way I can make this right. Even if I was matched unwillingly, even if she's taken it way too far, they convinced her I was the one person in the whole world most suited to her. That had to be a serious mind-fuck when I rejected her so completely. I wasn't in a good enough place six years ago to take her feelings into account. I was too deep in my own. I can choose to be better this time. "I can't change the outcome for you, Jada. Your soulmate is never going to be me. I'm sorry." Then I dive into the same deal I made Tayla in a diner just over two weeks ago. "But I can help you get your money back. I can help make sure this never happens to another person who walks through Soulmates Reunited's door."

"How?" she says, her chin wobbling.

I take a deep breath and stare at the few stars visible. Am I going to do this? Am I going to take them on? How can I let this keep happening to unsuspecting women? To men like me who don't ask for this and quite genuinely don't want it? They're a scam. Even if the lawyer says I don't have a case, there must be something I can do.

"Give me a few days," I say, making eye contact again. "I need to get in touch with a couple people and make sure they're on board. Either way, I'll help you. We'll get your money back, and we'll expose them for the frauds they are."

"You'd do that for me?" Her eyes shine with a light I'm not so sure I want to inspire.

"For you and for anyone else they've ripped off in the name of love."

Chapter Twenty-seven

TAYLA

There have been a few days in my career where I've cursed how difficult it is to call in sick. If I didn't go to work today, a full day of clients would need to be contacted, appointments moved, and for what? Heartsick doesn't mean anything when so many people are counting on me.

At the end of one of the longest days I've worked, Ruby opens her door and slides a glass of wine into my hand. "Fucking Simon," she mutters.

"What a dick," I agree, dropping my purse on the floor by the door and following her into the living room. On the coffee table is a thick slice of chocolate cake, a bowl of raspberries, and a jar of caramel sauce. I groan and sink into the plush couch. "You, however, are not a dick."

"I made Dean stop at The Cake Shop on his way back from his lecture."

"I wish you hadn't married Dean. I'd marry Dean." I pour the raspberries and caramel sauce over the cake.

"So, the shoe dropped, huh?" One of Ruby's hands runs along the back of the couch, the other cradling her own glass of wine.

"Like a fucking bomb." I scoop a glob of cake into my mouth and moan. Nothing better than heaping calories for a broken heart.

"His Jada story never made sense to me. Why not tell you right away if he wasn't responsible somehow?"

"Signing up for a dating service while we were still together must have made him feel guilty." I spear another piece of cake and stop with it halfway to my mouth. "Fucking Simon."

"Is that what happened?" Ruby raises her eyebrows. "Dean went to some speed dating thing and was automatically signed up. Simon admitted to putting himself forward for Soulmates Reunited's algorithm?"

"How else would he be in there?" I set down my fork and take a big gulp of my wine. Pixie's at home, and I'm not calling an Uber tonight. So, as much as I'd like to drown my sorrows, I'm only letting myself drown in one glass.

"Strange that he'd be in there for Jada and again for you, though, right? Two matches is weird enough given what Soulmates Reunited claims, but six years apart?" Ruby purses her lips in thought. "You talked to him about it?"

"Uh, no." The next bite is halfway to my lips. "I drove out of the parking lot so fast I probably left half the tread from my tires behind. I just—I felt like a fool." He dangled everything I wanted in a partner in front of my face, and I fell for it again. There were gaps in his story, and I ignored them or filled them in. I wanted him to be someone he isn't.

"You left him alone with Protection Order Jada?"

I flush. Simon is well over six feet, and unless Jada had a gun, she wasn't going to be forcing him to do anything he didn't want to do. It didn't actually occur to me she might be dangerous. Delusional? Yes. Dangerous? Nope. But I didn't stay long enough to be sure. "I can check the news, but I think we'd have heard if there was a stabbing or shooting."

Ruby sips her wine without responding, and I eat my cake in silence for a few moments.

"I had to leave," I say, giving her the side-eye. "I couldn't stay once I knew he lied to me."

"You left because he lied to you?"

Did he even lie? He omitted details, but as far as I can tell, the information he gave me about Jada was honest. "She called him her *soulmate*."

Ruby plucks a berry off my plate. "If some other woman referred to Dean as their soulmate back when we were getting to know each other, it would have bothered me too."

"Simon and I aren't 'getting to know each other.'"

"Maybe not. Doesn't make it any less hurtful to hear." Her voice is gentle. "Especially if you were starting to genuinely think of him as that guy for you."

I hate it when she nails how I'm feeling before I realize it. Whether or not I want to admit it, I've spent the last few days thinking of Simon as *mine*. "Can I forgive him for signing up for a dating service at the same time he was considering proposing to me?"

"I mean, if that's what happened, he deserves to be hog-tied to the flagpole outside your clinic with the words *I'm a dirty dog* spray-painted on his body."

The imagery is enough to garner a laugh from me. "Where would I paint it? That's too many words for—"

"Seriously, if you bring up his dick again, I'm going to side with Simon about your penis fetish." Ruby holds up a hand.

"Wrong head, Ruby. I was going to say *fore*head." I throw a raspberry at her.

"Right. Sure you were." She grins. "You're distracting me with all this dick talk. The point I was getting to was that you don't know exactly what happened because you didn't stay to talk to him."

"You'd have stayed?"

"Aww, hell no." She waves a dismissive hand. "Doesn't mean I don't think you should talk to him now that cooler heads have prevailed."

"How do I know he'll tell me the truth?" I've had to drag every piece of information out of him, and at this point, I'm worried I still don't know everything. What if I go talk to him and it's even worse than I thought?

"You two broke up six years ago. He waltzed back into your vet clinic two weeks ago, and you're already head over heels for him again. Do you want to be wondering six years from now whether you made a mistake? Whether you should have gone to talk to him? Has he tried to call you?"

I blocked his number last night in a rage. I haven't

checked my voicemail for fear of hearing his voice and caving. "Um, I'm not sure," I admit and bite my lip.

"Life's hard enough without piling regret on top of it."

"Speaking of regret—remember that vet exchange?"

"I remember I suggested you wait until you knew what was happening with Simon before you went hog wild on a lack of restrictions. You also need money for that, which you don't currently have."

"Yeah, I didn't listen to you. Drunk decision-making seemed like more fun. I'm also counting on getting all my money back from Simon and Soulmates Reunited, so there's that."

Ruby drinks her wine and raises her eyebrows, waiting for my point.

"Well, last night, in another massive 'fuck you,' possibly to myself, I replied to a vet from Scotland with a 'hell yes.' So I guess I'm moving to Scotland in a month?"

"Scotland?" She chokes on her wine, and I pat her on the back.

"Yeah," I say. "In hindsight, I probably shouldn't have replied when I was feeling so emotional."

"Scotland," Ruby says again, shaking her head. "Have you told Mike or Sandy or Luis or your mother or your brother . . . or Simon?"

"I told Simon," I mumble, and then I pick up my wine-glass and take a sip.

"Ah," Ruby says. "Parting shot? Backed yourself into a corner?"

"I've wanted this exchange." Heat rises to my cheeks.

"I bet a day and a half ago, you wanted Simon more."

"You're not helping."

"I'm trying to make sure you don't leave the country on a whim with unanswered questions."

Last night, saying yes to the exchange seemed like the right thing to do. I'd applied for it. Scotland was an acceptable country. Once I expanded what I was willing to do, the farm was also acceptable. In fact, living on a farm would be fun and exciting, right? An incredible learning experience for me, about so many things.

Ruby is also correct, though. Had Jada not shown up at Simon's house last night, I wouldn't have emailed the vet exchange partner back in a flash of triumphant annoyance. I might not have said yes at all. "I don't want him to hurt me anymore."

"You've come this far. You're already hurt." Ruby squeezes my arm. "You owe it to yourself to be sure he's Fucking Simon and not Soulmate Simon."

Two days later, when I open the door to Aaron's car dealership, my heart pounds with nerves, and my palms are slick with uncertainty. Will Aaron talk to me? Should I be going to Simon instead? I've gone around in circles about the best way to tackle my Simon problem. When I replayed our conversation with Aaron at the party, some of his comments rang different bells. I'm sure he knew about Soulmates Reunited.

His office door is open, and I peer around the edge, my knuckles skimming the outside of the door. "Aaron?"

He glances up from whatever paperwork he's organizing.

The smile on his face slips a notch when he recognizes me. Not a good sign.

"Looking for a test drive?" Aaron asks.

"I already test-drove the Simon model. He seemed like a good fit, but I'm worried he's a lemon." I shrug and gesture to the seat across from his desk. "Are you busy?"

"Not too busy for you." He places the papers to one side and gives me his undivided attention. "So, Simon, huh?"

I take a deep, steadying breath and run my hands along the arms of the chair. "You've known him a long time."

"Since high school."

"So, you're aware of everything that happened when we broke up and what he's been doing this time as well, right?" I'm convinced he knows a lot, but I'm not sure he'll be honest. How deep does his loyalty to Simon run?

Aaron rocks back in his leather chair and observes me for a beat. "What do you want to know?"

Everything he's willing to tell me. Where do I start? "Did you know Simon had been contacted by Soulmates Reunited before?"

"Yes," Aaron says, his voice measured. "Si said you didn't give him much of a chance to explain—not that I blame you. He's an idiot."

I absorb Aaron's comment. "He was matched before? With Jada?"

"I get why you're asking me these questions." Aaron's eyes narrow, and he purses his lips in thought. "He wasn't completely honest with you about the circumstances around Soulmates Reunited, but I really feel you should be talking to him."

"I can't be sure he'll tell me the truth."

"If you can't trust him, Tayla, how can you build a relationship with him?" He rocks forward and puts his forearms on the smooth expanse of desk between us. "I can give you the straight-up facts that I know, but I can't give you the 'why' behind any of it."

"I'll take the facts." I swallow and cross my arms. "I'm trying to figure out if there's even anything to salvage between us. Maybe there's nothing to build."

"All right," Aaron says, locking his gaze with mine. "You're ready? I'm not going to sugarcoat what's happened. No sparing your feelings."

Sounds like these revelations will be unpleasant. Okay. I can handle whatever he throws at me. I already think Simon is a shit, so how much worse can he get? I clasp my hands in my lap. "Give it to me."

"Four women have been matched with Simon over the last six years. All of them through Soulmates Reunited. Of the four, the only one he met willingly and enthusiastically was you."

"Wait, wait, wait." I hold up my hand and peer at Aaron. "*Four* matches?" They've given him four *soulmates*? How is that possible? The foundation of their brand, their company, is their ability to find your one true partner. They match people in ways no other software can or does. Success is guaranteed. Ninety-nine percent of their matches are successes. All their ads boast their stats like a badge of honor. The six-episode series goes into great detail about their process and how accurate it is. Every podcast episode I listened to, the couple went on and on about how they couldn't imagine being matched with anyone else. How can they make those claims, allow other people to make those claims, and give Simon Buchannan *four* matches?

"Yep." Aaron's face remains stoic.

"Why did he keep signing up for Soulmates Reunited if he didn't want to meet anyone?" This doesn't make any sense. When I went, the whole purpose was to find "the one."

"That's a 'why' question, but I also happen to know the factual answer." Aaron holds up a finger. "He never signed up for *any* of Soulmates Reunited's bullshit. They data mine other dating sites for their unwitting prospects."

"So, Simon didn't sign up for Soulmates Reunited when we were dating, but he was on *another* dating site?" I slump into my chair. That's no better. One way or another, he was searching for an out from our relationship.

"All right, I know the answer to this one too." Aaron winces and sighs. "But any other questions, you've gotta go talk to him. Deal?"

"Deal." I give him a hard stare, prepared for the worst.

"Eight years ago, a few weeks before you and Simon bumped into each other at the bar, I convinced him to sign up for a dating website. It was free, and he was having terrible luck finding a woman who fit with him. Women who wanted him? No problem. Someone he had a genuine connection with? Awful. So, while we were predrinking before the bar one night, I got him to create an account."

The implication Simon was having lots of hot sex when we met stings a little. It shouldn't, probably, but it does. I search Aaron's face, but nothing in his tone or expression makes me think he's not being sincere. Was Simon actually the one who wanted a relationship? Or did he just let Aaron lead him into it?

"When Soulmates Reunited came at him with Jada and her 'perfect score' nonsense, they mentioned the free dating website as evidence Simon was on the hunt for a girlfriend. I'm pretty sure Simon never even logged into the website after he met you."

"Seems convenient," I say, scanning for any hint he might be covering for Simon.

"I forgot I made him sign up for the website until he told me Soulmates Reunited was hounding him with some chick they'd pulled out of thin air for him. His *perfect match*."

"Simon must have believed their sales pitch at least a little to break up with me. He must have bought into their soul-matching service or some part of it to go from proposing to breaking up with me."

"That's a 'why' question, and definitely not one I can answer." Aaron fiddles with a pen on his desk. "Are you going to talk to him about any of this?"

"When he got the email from Soulmates Reunited, why wouldn't he just tell me the truth?" I tuck one foot behind my knee and run a hand through my hair.

"You mean that he'd been contacted three times before you? Look, I suggested he should tell you." Aaron's mouth forms a tight line, and he eyes me for a beat. "If he'd told you, straight up, right from the moment he walked into your vet clinic, would you have given him even one more minute of your time?"

A huff of impatience leaves me, and I cross my arms

again. "He broke my heart, Aaron. What do you think?"

"I think a desperate man sometimes does desperate things." He taps his pen on the desk. "I also think it's about time someone took Soulmates Reunited down. As far as I can tell, they don't make matches, they ruin lives."

I ease my hands down my legs. Exposing Soulmates Reunited might not be a bad idea. "I need my money back," I say. "I just accepted a vet exchange to Scotland."

"Scotland," Aaron barks out, and his expression brims with amusement. "I suppose putting an ocean between you and Simon is one way to solve your problem."

Did my move solve my problems? Not really. Whether I'm in Scotland or here in Michigan, my feelings for Simon aren't likely to go away quickly. As much as I'd like to snap my fingers and have them disappear, prior experience with heartbreak tells me that's unlikely. Although I understand Aaron's point, I can't help wishing Simon had been honest from the start—or just earlier, or any time before Jada showed up on his doorstep.

Loving Simon is exhausting.

"I'll talk to Simon. I'll get my money back from Soulmates Reunited." I take a deep breath. "And then I'll put an ocean between us."

Chapter Twenty-eight

SIMON

Tayla walked out of my life four days ago, and I've thrown myself into working extra shifts. Right now, I regret accepting this one. The first patient I triaged had a beer can shoved up his ass. A drunken dare gone very wrong. Now I'm sitting on a stool picking maggots out of this elderly man's foot. Maggots. Out of a foot. One for the books.

While I remove the wiggly worms, I question my life choices. Turns out, Aaron might have been right—I should have told Tayla about Soulmates Reunited right from the start. She won't take my calls or even read my text messages. Maybe she blocked me.

Shit. What if she blocked me?

I deserve her anger, even if I was about to give her all the details. Too little too late.

With some sort of warped sense of making things right, I've reached out to the other two women who were matched with me to see if they want to help me go after the company. Neither of them has responded yet. Maybe it doesn't matter if they do. I've got the emails, so it's not as though the company can deny how many soulmates they've given me.

"Simon?" Another nurse, my shift supervisor, peeks around the curtain and scrunches up her face. "There's someone here to see you."

I frown and check the clock above my patient's bed. Another hour until my shift is done. "Who is it?"

"A woman. Dark hair. Slight build. Pretty. Ring any bells?"

Tayla.

Why would she come see me at work? "Is she injured or sick?" I drop my equipment onto the metal table beside me and tug off my gloves.

"Looks fine to me. You're due a break. You missed your last one with beer-can-up-the-butt guy." She grabs gloves out of the box by the curtain. "I can finish this up for you. She's at the front desk."

Tayla's here, and I don't have to keep maggot-picking? All my Christmases have come early. I slip out of the curtained area before my supervisor can change her mind.

I glance down at myself to make sure I don't have any maggots or blood or feces covering my scrubs. Nothing obvious. Not that I expect her to get that close.

When I get to the front desk, she's sitting in one of the

closest chairs. The sight of her causes a wave of remorse to crash through me. She rises, and my instinct is to slide my hands into my pockets to keep from reaching for her, but I don't have any. So, for a second, I fumble awkwardly until I end up crossing my arms. I scan her face, trying to decipher the reason she's come to my work.

"Is there somewhere we can go to talk?" She speaks as soon as I'm close enough but before I get a chance to say a word.

"Outside is probably best." I gesture to the sliding doors. She leads the way, and I follow, unsure whether I should drop to my knees and grovel for a chance to explain or brace myself for a diatribe. Tayla's never been the dramatic sort. I almost wish she'd rail at me, flush out some of her anger. When I open my mouth to speak, she holds up a hand.

"I'd really prefer it if you didn't talk right now. We're at your work, and I'm likely to blow up. I would have called or texted you, but I blocked your number, and I can't figure out how to unblock it. I have zero patience for figuring that shit out." She lets out an impatient noise and crosses her arms, so we're mirroring each other.

"Okay." Should I say more? Wait for her to continue? Have I ever seen her genuinely angry with me?

"I'm moving to Scotland in a month."

My stomach drops into my toes, and an ache spreads across my chest. Would she be leaving if I'd told her the truth earlier? If she hadn't found out on my doorstep from the worst possible person?

"But before I go, I need my money back from Soulmates

Reunited. All of it." Her jaw is tight. "Nothing romantic will ever happen between us again, but I need your help to bring Soulmates Reunited to justice."

I stare at her for a beat, and a deep sadness takes root at her words. I suspected she might dig me out, but I still had a seed of hope. "I can do that," I say. "I've already reached out to the other women who were matched with me. I was going to try to get everyone's money back."

She gives me a long stare. "How many other women?"

I grimace. Even though being matched wasn't my choice, admitting the number makes me feel like an asshole. "Including you, there have been four. Jada was the first."

Tayla releases a shaky breath. "I already called Soulmates Reunited, and they're refusing to give my money back. They said they have photographic proof you and I have been in contact."

I raise my eyebrows. "Photographic proof? That wasn't me. I didn't email them back, and I sure as hell didn't send them photos."

"I wasn't accusing you." She gives me a mild look that still seems to imply I'm an idiot. "My best guess is Jada. Maybe when she left your place she was so enraged she did it to prove a point. I don't know."

"She wasn't enraged when she left my house. I offered to help get her money back." I run a hand through my hair. "Maybe before she came to the door."

"She needs some sort of counseling, Si. Sure, I went to the company and paid a lot of money, but I didn't pin the rest of my life on the outcome. She's clinging too hard to something that's not real."

"I told her everything. I was completely honest with her after you left."

"That's nice, you know, that you were completely honest with someone."

That's a burn, and it stings. "I'll tell you whatever you want to know."

"Will you?" She gives a humorless laugh. "You've decided I deserve it now? Well, now I'm not ready to hear it. I don't *want* to hear whatever you *want* to tell me. I gave you two weeks—two weeks where I practically begged you to be honest—and you couldn't do it. Soulmates Reunited might be the assholes who matched us, but you're the one who weaponized that information." She takes a deep breath. "I will admit I didn't buck too hard against the manipulation because you're charming and attractive and make me feel all ooey-gooey inside." She avoids eye contact. "Doesn't everyone who's ever been dumped dream of the person coming back to them and saying they made the biggest mistake of their lives?" Her eyes brim with pain. "That would have been enough, Si. Telling me the whole truth and saying those words would have been enough." She stabs at her hair and flicks it over her shoulder.

"I made a mistake," I say, and she gives me a warning look. "I made *a lot* of mistakes. Last time. This time. I'll do whatever you want me to do to help get your money back."

"I need your help to build an indisputable case against them. We'll go after them in person first, but if they don't cave, we'll go to the media. Maybe your case is unusual, but maybe it's not. Maybe not enough people are speaking out about their negative experiences, too ashamed to admit they spent all that money on a gamble and lost."

"I have all the emails they sent me, and the emails I exchanged with the other women they tried to match me with. I'll send them to you."

"I don't just want your forwarded emails. I want you."

Her choice of phrasing slays me. She must read something on my face because her jaw locks again.

"Did you sign up for Soulmates Reunited or any other dating app knowing you'd be used for an exclusive and expensive soulmate matching service?"

"No," I say in a firm voice. "I signed up for a free dating profile a few weeks before you and I met. I never once looked at it after I met you. Forgot I even signed up for it until Jada came knocking and Soulmates Reunited pursued me so relentlessly."

A frown mars her forehead, but I'm not sure what I've said to put it there.

"What?" I ask.

"Nothing." She looks off into the distance over my shoulder. "When are you working tomorrow?"

"I'll be home by six."

"Come to my house at seven. Bring printouts of every communication you've had with Soulmates Reunited or with any of the women." She turns on her heel and walks away without a backward glance.

I head into the hospital to finish my shift, sorrow and hope mixing in me. Maybe I'm wrong to long for yet another chance, but I can't help wishing for one anyway.

Chapter Twenty-nine

TAYLA

Mike rubs his forehead and squints at me. "Scotland? And you've already said yes?"

At the doorway, Sandy crosses her arms over her ample bosom. We finished early, and all our clients are gone for the day. With the extra time, I finally sucked up the nerve to tell them I'm moving abroad for a year . . . maybe more. I'm short on cash, but I'm hoping that's temporary.

Angus, my Scottish exchange partner, is open to whatever arrangements we can make with visas and work permits. We've traded several tentative, searching emails, but we haven't spoken on the phone. Telling Mike and Sandy removes my last opt-out. If they're okay with the change, then I'll be going to Scotland in just over three weeks. Angus is waiting for my call after the conversation to confirm we're moving ahead. My stomach flutters, and I'm not sure if it's from excitement or anxiety. Any time I let myself question whether I'm making the right decision, I want to throw up.

"What about Pixie?" Sandy asks, the puppy sprawled in the hall outside Mike's office.

"I was hoping you might be open to taking over her training?" I purse my lips and glance in her direction. "She's with you most of the day when I'm working, and you've had her a couple nights when I've been away."

"Luis won't mind?" She bites her cheek.

"He'll be grateful for the help."

She searches my face for a beat. "Are you doing this because things haven't worked out with Fucking Simon?"

I should never have given him that nickname. While the guy is a dick, I'm not sure he deserves quite the invective the capital-F-word denotes. "You know I applied a while ago."

Is Simon the motivation now? Yes. How does that make me look? Like I'm running away. There is definitely some running, but it's *toward* a better future. I'm not running *from* Simon or his half-truths. This exchange is a positive out of a whole lot of negative. "I've always wanted to work and travel. Angus and his vet practice give me a great opportunity to do both."

"You'll be gone a year?" Mike chimes in, a frown still marring his forehead.

"That's the initial plan, yeah. Angus has said he's open to eighteen months or two years if we can make the legal aspects line up and we're both happy."

"Well, I'll miss you." Mike rubs his jaw. "As long as your half of the building's rent is being covered, it's really your practice that's at risk, your clients. Have you *spoken* to him? What's he like?"

"We've emailed back and forth the last few days. He's in the Scottish Highlands. Owns a farm. His vet clinic is attached. Getting close to retirement."

"So, you'd be running a farm too?" Mike's frown deepens. "Does he know you're in the middle of a city?"

"More like the outskirts of Grand Rapids. But yeah, he knows where I'm located, that my house is small and all that."

"If this is what you want and what you think is good for you, we'll welcome him with open arms." Mike rises from his desk chair and grabs his keys. "Three weeks, you said?"

"Yeah. I'll email all my clients tomorrow."

"I'll post a note on the front desk," Sandy offers.

"I hope your talk with him goes well." Mike ducks out of the office without another word, and Sandy follows me back to my half of the building.

"You're sure you're okay with taking Pixie?" I ask, though my options if she says no are extremely limited. My mom would probably take her, but my mother isn't much of a dog trainer. She wouldn't be the partner Luis was looking for when he approached me.

"Yeah. She's a great dog, and she'll be a wonderful pet for someone. I'm more worried about you. This all feels very sudden. I mean . . . a few days ago you had stars in your eyes over Simon."

"A lot can change when an offer like this comes along.

It's a great opportunity. I'd be a fool to turn it down." Or to take it. The jury is still out. Decisive action is needed. If I let myself sink into my feelings, I'll curl into Simon and pretend he didn't betray my trust, didn't try to manipulate me into a relationship under false pretenses. "I have to call Angus, actually, to give him the good news. So, as long as you're okay with taking Pixie, I should get on the phone and hammer out the details."

She gives me a pensive look.

"Change is good," I say with a smile.

"Change is good as long as it's for the right reasons. Change for the sake of change can be foolish." She shrugs and narrows her eyes. "You wanted this, a farm in the middle of nowhere, even *before* Simon?"

"Yes." The confirmation comes out with more conviction than I feel. Once I talk to Angus, my lingering anxiety will fade.

"All right," Sandy says, hanging on to the doorway for a beat.

"This is a good opportunity. I love traveling. I love my work. And I've always wanted a chance to work with large animals." Maybe not out in the middle of nowhere far from anyone else's help, but that's how this cookie is crumbling.

"I'm not denying the logic, just the motivation." Sandy holds up her hands.

"My motivation is fine," I snap and then let out an exasperated sigh. "I'm sorry." My hair falls around my face like a curtain, and I tuck it behind my ears. "I need to call Angus before I go home."

"I'll let you be," Sandy says, but I can tell from the way

MISS MATCHED

she leaves the doorway of my office that she's pissed at me. Rightfully, probably. I'll have to bring her some cookies tomorrow and apologize for my shitty attitude.

I shut my office door and sink into my desk chair, tapping a pen against the surface. *Make the call, Tayla.* On my phone, I locate the number and then use the office extension to dial Angus's number.

He answers with a thick Scottish brogue, and I question whether a phone chat is the best option. We go through the logistics of the exchange, details of our veterinary practices, cars, homes, and anything else we can remember to touch upon. I have to ask him to slow down and repeat himself a few times, and another zing of unease shoots through me. What if I can't understand anyone there?

"You're coming alone?" he asks, his tone tentative for the first time. "The farm's a lot of work for a young lass."

"I'm not afraid of hard work. You said your neighbors are helpful?"

"Yeah, but far." He takes a deep breath. "My wife always reckoned the isolation was the toughest bit."

"Is she coming with you here?" I wrack my brain to remember him mentioning a wife in any of his emails.

"She died almost a year ago. Reckon I need a change." His breath releases in a whoosh. "Too many days I wish I could rewind time and do it all over again, even the hard bits."

My mind strays to Simon, and I shake my head. I won't be doing any "bits" over again with him. We're done. "I'm sorry to hear about your wife."

"'Twas a privilege to love her. Not everyone gets a

partner they love even more at the end than they did at the beginning."

Again, my mind shifts to Simon, to how great the last few weeks were, to how it felt even better the second time around. Until it didn't.

God, why can't I stop thinking about him? The hurt look on his face when I went to see him yesterday surfaces. When he emerged from the ER to see me, my heart skipped a beat and my body lit with desire. It seems wrong to hate someone and want to rip their clothes off. I close my eyes and rub my forehead. In a couple hours, Simon will be sitting on my couch putting all my willpower to the test.

I really need to get out of this city. Start over. Bury him under an avalanche of new experiences.

"Are there any single men in the local village?"

"You in the market for a soulmate?" Angus chuckles. "That American company seems to have everyone in a tizzy to find the one."

My cheeks flash hot and cold. Apparently, the word *soulmate* has become a trigger, and not in a good way; I'm sure the company he's referencing is Soulmates Reunited. They really are taking over the world. "Oh." I give a nervous laugh. "Nope. Forget I said anything."

"I reckon you won't have any trouble gettin' some interest from the lads."

"So, does this situation work for you then?" I ask, eager to change the subject. Why did I ask him about other men? So ridiculous.

"Aye. And you? You'll be all right with the cattle, sheep, chickens, and dogs? I can send you more pictures."

"None of that puts me off." In fact, it's the part I'm excited about as long as I don't think about how isolated I'll be. Being part of a real, working farm will add another layer of adventure.

"You reckon you'd be happy here?" he prods.

"As happy as anywhere," I confirm. "Let's move ahead." Here's hoping some of those Scottish lads can banish any thoughts of a Michigan man who stole my heart and refuses to let me have it back.

Chapter Thirty

SIMON

Tayla's house isn't big, and although we've only been apart a few days, the distance feels enormous when I walk into her house and find her sorting through her personal things. Boxes are marked in bold letters with *storage* or *Mom's*, and they litter the small living room. Guess she's really moving to Scotland. I shove my hands deeper into the pockets of my jeans and try to ignore the crushing heaviness in my chest. Man, did I ever fuck up.

Tayla clears the couch of clothes and gestures for me to sit. Unlike before, she doesn't sit beside me. She takes the stiff-backed chair to the left of the couch. When I glance toward her bedroom, I can't decide what reaction she wants from me. The door is closed, and the Soulmate Simon plate hangs in the center. She might as well have a giant picture of me on a dartboard. Though I suppose the ugly, flaccid penis amuses her more than a photo of me. Either way, her *do not enter* is clear.

From my back pocket, I take out the printouts of the emails I exchanged with Soulmates Reunited and the women, and I pass her the sheaf of papers.

"This is all of it?" she asks, scanning each page before flipping to the next one. A crease forms between her brows.

"Yes," I say, my gaze straying to the plate again. Just weeks ago, that plate was funny. I was so sure I could win her back and the plate would become a joke between us, something we would both laugh at eventually. Instead, it's functioned as an omen, a reminder of what an ass I can be, a warning for her to keep me in check. I'm not the soulmate the top of the plate declares but the ugly dick depicted beneath it. I release an unsteady sigh.

When our gazes connect, her honey-brown eyes glint with steel, and then she follows where my focus has been. A hint of a smile tips up the edges of her lips. "Felt like a good place to hang it. I put a lot of work into that plate."

"All the others seem to serve their function in a dark cupboard." Why am I pushing the issue? It's not like I don't know why she put it there.

"Not true." She tries to lean back in her chair and is stopped short by the high, stiff back. "The Happy Birthday plate comes out every year. This one," she says, gesturing toward the dickhead on the door, "can serve a purpose every day."

Instead of continuing the conversation, which'll probably

go in circles and make me feel even worse, I opt for a subject change. "What's your plan with Soulmates Reunited? Did you book an appointment with them or something?"

"They won't see me," she says, her jaw tightening. "I've violated their contract by lying about whether or not you and I made contact."

"You've gotta be fucking kidding me." I run a hand through my hair. "Have you got the contract? Did Ruby or Dean look through it?"

"Neither of them is a lawyer," Tayla says, opening her phone and passing it to me.

"I, uh, I consulted a lawyer a few years ago about whether Soulmates Reunited's tactics could be considered harassment."

She stares at me, a question in her eyes, but she doesn't say anything, just waits for me to continue.

"No dice for me, but with the four of you, maybe there's some loophole we can find."

"With or without a loophole," Tayla says, "I want a meeting, and I want my money back." She picks up a high-lighter and opens my sheaf of papers. "They aren't who they say they are, and I'm going to prove it."

We read in silence for a few minutes. Words like *libel* and *slander* are mentioned several times throughout the contract. Have they sued people into silence before? Can we go after them through social media without incurring their litigation arm? Maybe I should get that lawyer to look through this before we do anything.

When I glance up, Tayla is holding a single piece of paper in her fingers with the others back on the coffee table.

"I can't believe they sent this to you." Her face is pale.

My gut clenches. "Which one is that?" I close her phone and lean forward, though by the expression on her face, I realize which email she's clutching. There's only one in the pile that could elicit that reaction. It's the message I received in the bathroom the night I didn't propose. When I printed the emails at Aaron's car dealership, a spike of anger shot through me at Soulmates Reunited's audacity. Of course, anger wasn't the most prominent emotion that night. It was resignation, a cloud of inevitability.

Her hand shakes, and she sets down the paper. The date is highlighted, and some of the words at the top are also highlighted. There's less color as the email progresses. "They didn't know me or our relationship. How can they possibly claim that you and I wouldn't be able to work? That a marriage between us would lead to misery and divorce?"

I slouch deeper into her couch. "They'd tried everything else at that point to get me to give Jada a shot. She was, I guess, hanging around my apartment. Tried to talk to me a few times. At every turn, I refused. For months after we broke up, I still refused her and the company because the thought of being with anyone other than you turned my stomach. Soulmate or scam, I just couldn't face what I'd done. Then Soulmates Reunited called me and said if I gave Jada at least three dates, they'd stop hassling me, and so would she." I pick a highlighter from the table and flip it around my fingers. "After the three dates they stopped, but she didn't."

"You got this the night you broke up with me."

"In the bathroom. Then my father called me, sobbing."

"Is *this* why you broke up with me?" There are tears in her eyes.

"What do you remember about that night?" I search her face and wish I still had the right to comfort her in some way.

She frowns, and a tear slips down her cheek. She scoops it away and shakes her head. "Private room, flowers, nice meal, the server brought champagne at exactly the wrong moment."

"Do you remember what I said when I came out of the bathroom?" My idiotic words are burned into my brain. The whole night has been buried so deep in my subconscious that no one has ever had every detail. I couldn't bear to take them out and examine them. Maybe if I'd gone to the server first and nixed the champagne we'd have talked, sorted out my confused feelings, but I came out of the bathroom shell-shocked by the email and my father's pleading voice. I didn't want to make a mistake.

"'I think we should break up.'" Her voice is firm.

I can't meet her gaze because reliving my biggest moment of stupidity makes my chest feel like it's being squeezed in a vise. "I said, 'I'm not sure I can do this right now,' and you said, 'You're breaking up with me?' And instead of denying it, I just sat there like a fucking moron."

"No," she says, her voice still firm. "I'd remember if you didn't say you wanted to break up with me." But her voice trails off at the end, as though pieces to a puzzle that never fit are slotting into place. She cocks her head and stares at me, a series of half-formed thoughts floating across her face.

There's no defense for how I behaved, and I'm not going to open my mouth and lay any blame on her. But the way she remembers that night isn't quite accurate. Was the result the same? Yeah. So I've never denied that I broke up with her. My vague language and then my silence got us here.

"So you didn't mean to break up with me?" Her voice is full of disbelief, hurt, a touch of anger. "Why didn't you take any of my calls the week after we broke up if you didn't *want* to break up?"

"I have no idea what I meant when I went out there, what I wanted. I had to throw on the brakes because I was so brutally mixed-up. My head was cotton balls and nonsense." I drag my hands along my cheeks, my fingertips scratching through the thin layer of stubble. I couldn't ask her to marry me with my mind so out of sorts, but then when she suggested we break up as though it was my idea, I couldn't respond. How does someone get to a proposal and not follow through without becoming a giant dick? I couldn't contradict her assumption because I didn't know what to say. *Uh, I think I want to marry you, but all these other people are telling me I don't.* Stupid. Unforgivable. I couldn't say that, so I said nothing.

"In one ear, Soulmates Reunited is telling me the love I feel for you can't be real, can't be something built to last, and we're destined for divorce. Marrying you would be sentencing you to a life of unhappiness. You read it." I toss my hand toward the paper. "In the other ear, I've got my father nattering on about how men aren't meant to marry. I might be happy now, but give the relationship another ten or twenty years and I'd be as miserable as him." I throw out my hands. "At twenty-six, I was no mental or emotional match for that tornado. I couldn't seem to find the right perspective. Who was right? Me, who loved you so fucking much? Or them, who told me that love would fade?"

I hesitate for a second, unsure how much I should reveal. But I've come this far; I might as well give her the whole avalanche. "Then my friend Drayton, who'd been with his wife since we were in high school, called to tell me he was having an affair and leaving Sylvia. He'd gotten this marriage and happily ever after thing all wrong, and he was asking for a divorce. That was like the day *after* I didn't propose."

"They were miserable, Simon. We saw how terrible they were together when we had dinner with them that night."

"Sure, yeah. But they weren't like that at all in high school or any of the times I hung out with them before the night we had our double date." I run a frustrated hand through my hair. "And my parents—who we both thought had a great relationship—were on the verge of divorce." I take a deep breath and release it. I fiddle with her phone before setting it on the coffee table. She's been stunned into silence, and I wonder what she's thinking. Probably calling me three million terrible names. "We couldn't even pick out a house together. Couldn't agree on a layout, and I think that freaked me out too. Stupid now. What the fuck do I care about a house? I don't. I don't care. I don't know why it was even a thing. But on top of everything else, it just felt like maybe we should be slowing down, except I let us go too far."

"You should have talked to me," Tayla whispers.

"I couldn't talk to you until I knew my head was in the

right place. Took a long time to get there. Then once I was there, standing in front of you asking for a second chance, my timing was awful."

"The worst," she agrees, the edge of the paper crumpling under her fingers. "Jesus, Simon."

The heat from embarrassment and shame starts in my neck and creeps up. "I am—" My voice cracks, and I clear my throat, shifting uncomfortably on the couch. "I've always been deeply ashamed of how I behaved that night. So when I—when I thought I could skirt around the whole truth . . ." I meet her gaze before glancing away. "I took the easy way out."

"*Again,*" Tayla says, and her voice is thick. "You took the easy way out *again*. You should have talked to me after that night, Simon. You should have come to me—even if you were a mess, you should have come. Because—" Tears overwhelm her voice, thickening it. "Because I loved you enough to help you, to forgive you. I could have forgiven you."

I meet her gaze, and my heart stutters at the tears in her eyes. Here I am, making her cry again. I'm the worst. "It sure as shit didn't feel like the easy way out back then, Tay. I get what you're saying. I get it. But I felt like I was walking through mud every day. Asking someone to wade through that shit with you when you're not sure how it's going to end? Didn't feel like the right thing at the time."

"That's what a relationship *is*, Simon. It's holding someone's hand while they walk through their darkest days, tackle their hardest things. Instead, you and I were wandering through these really hard years alone." She sniffs and stands up, running her hands down her shorts. "I need a drink. Do you want a drink? Or a piece of chocolate cake? I think I need cake."

Alcohol and cake. Our conversation must be stressing her out. "No, I'm—I'm good. Maybe I should go? I can contact the lawyer I've talked to before about this contract if you send me a copy."

She's already in the kitchen as I start to gather my things, but she ducks out to point a finger at me. "Don't you dare leave. We're not done sorting this out. Am I rattled? Yeah, but we've got work to do. Okay? Sit down."

I nod and sink into the couch. The pile of emails is on the coffee table in front of me, and Tayla is knocking around in the kitchen. Telling the whole truth, every last word, should be a weight off my shoulders. Instead, a bit of unease swirls in my stomach. Should I have been *that* honest?

She comes out of the kitchen with a coffee cup and a giant slab of cake.

"It's that bad?" Though she doesn't seem to have alcohol, so maybe not that bad.

"I'll let you know at the end of my sugar rush." She heads for the uncomfortable chair again rather than the more logical spot on the couch, where the coffee table is close.

It's silly for her to try to balance the cake on her lap. "Let's switch spots." I move toward her chair.

We shuffle around, our chests skimming each other; when I glance down, she catches my gaze, and the shuffling stops. Her hands are full of coffee and cake, and yet we can't tear our focus from each other.

"You must hate me," I mutter.

The tension in her face dissipates. "I hate what you did, Simon—both times—but that doesn't mean I hate you."

A piece of her hair falls forward, and my touch is tentative, light as a feather, when I smooth the strands behind her ear. *God, I love her.* She closes her eyes and sighs.

"I don't hate you, Simon. It would probably be easier if I did." Her voice is soft, and her gaze, when she opens her eyes, is softer, and all I want to do is sweep her into my arms and kiss her.

Chapter Thirty-one

TAYLA

He's staring at my lips like he wants to kiss me, and God help me, I want him to. Thankfully, my hands are full of cake and coffee, and I'm not so far gone that dropping this mess on the floor is appealing. Not gonna lie—the idea of tossing them toward the *table* and gluing my face to Simon's is still a fleeting thought. What are the chances the cake and coffee will land upright?

"We should come up with a game plan to go after Soulmates Reunited." My voice is breathy, and I hate how turned on I sound. We're not even touching. His hand is long gone from my hair, and our chests skim ever so lightly together each time we breathe, but otherwise, we have zero points of contact. The air around us crackles nonetheless.

He's catnip, and I'm the cat.

"Yeah," he agrees, his voice husky. "I—" He searches my face. "Do you think you can ever forgive me, Tay?"

Oh, jeez. That's a loaded question. In the kitchen, while I was getting my coffee and cake, I tried to process everything he'd told me, but I kept stalling on the email from Soulmates Reunited. It was awful and presumptive—as though they're the authority on love and matchmaking. Of course, they've since made a lot of money off their air of authority.

Despite my reservations, I watched my best friend meet and fall in love with the match they gave her. Then I fell for the marketing genius too. Who doesn't want to make this whole dating game easier? Your soulmate delivered on a platter? Literally, sign me up! So naive.

"I don't know how I feel. I can't answer that question right now. It's a lot to process, and I'm nowhere near doing that." I step past him and set my cake and coffee on the table, my fork rattling on the plate. "Taking down Soulmates Reunited is my number-one priority."

"And moving to Scotland." He eyes my boxes.

I flush. "Yeah, well, that might have been a hasty decision, but I'm doing it. I told him a definite yes. I dropped off all the legal and visa paperwork earlier today." Anxiety swirls in my stomach. The whole time I was filling in forms, paying money, and talking to people, I was cool, calm, collected, and one hundred percent sure of myself. Now, with Simon sitting in my house, the smell of his cologne wafting toward me, a different desire rises in me.

"One of the things I love about you," he murmurs. "Once a decision is made, you don't back down."

That's sort of what got me into this mess with Soulmates Reunited in the first place. One friend from college tried to talk me out of pouring my money into the algorithm. To her every concern, I held up Dean and Ruby as my stellar examples of how well the process could work. Until Simon's name appeared on the screen, I believed it would work for me too. Even now, gazing at him across the coffee table, pieces of me yearn to be next to him. To hear him use the word *love* in reference to me only strengthens my urge to abandon my cake and indulge in something infinitely sweeter.

I clear my throat and stab my slice with my fork. "You've spoken to Jada. What about the other women?"

"I tried to contact them, but I haven't heard back."

"Your rejection of them coupled with the substantial financial loss is a good reason to avoid you."

"Using the word *rejection* is a bit harsh."

"That's not what happened?" I take a bite of the cake and stare at him expectantly.

"I mean, okay, I didn't *want* to be with them. The real problem, as far as I can tell, is that I didn't agree to *any* of this. These soulmates kept being thrust at me, and I was expected to welcome them, be grateful for them."

"Why didn't you block them or send them to your junk mail or . . . anything?"

"Truthfully? I didn't realize how persistent they'd be. When I got the first email, I wrote back telling them there must have been some mistake. They had the wrong Simon Buchannan. But it didn't end there. Phone calls and emails. Chipping away at my already addled brain. They gave Jada my home address, which pissed me off. But I honestly didn't realize how often she was at my apartment until much later. I was working stupid hours." He sighs. "After Jada and the protection order, when I got my third match, I filtered my email to send anything from them to my junk mail." He rubs his forehead. "It's so weird because even back then, the company was building a good reputation. Everything I could find touted their uncanny ability to match people. Soulmates Reunited was selling something society was keen to buy."

I was keen, and maybe he was too if he thought our lives would be ruined by getting married because his dad, Soulmates Reunited, and his friend Drayton said so. It seems ridiculous to look at an algorithm for a seal of approval or a guarantee, but I did it, and I suspect part of him did it that night too. He wanted reassurance we'd work long-term, and instead he found naysayers.

"How'd you discover the email about me?"

"Junk mail when I was searching for a message about a bachelor party."

I ignore the flare of sadness that a soulmate was a burden, something someone junked. "We know they are or were buying information from other sources to use in their database."

"Yes. The other dating agencies and services sell their lists to Soulmates Reunited."

"Do you know that for sure?"

"No, I guess not. It's the only thing that makes sense, though. They told me to take down my free profile if I wasn't willing to be matched. I did. So I don't know how . . ." He glances at me and then looks away.

"You don't know how you got matched with me?"

"No," he admits. "They *said* they removed me. I don't sign up for online dating stuff. Not worth the hassle." A smile touches the edges of his lips. "Half the women in America become my match."

A soft laugh escapes me, and I give him a sideways glance. "A slight exaggeration." I sip my coffee. "If you'll give me the contact information for the women, I'll reach out to them to see whether they'll talk to me. Maybe they just don't want to talk to you."

"My information could be old," he says, passing me his phone. "It's been a few years since I had my last match."

"Can't win them all," I say, a hint of teasing in my voice.

"I'll try to set up a meeting with Soulmates Reunited." He rubs the back of his neck. "I'll get my sister to call. She owes me." He meets my gaze when he accepts his phone back. "Doesn't it seem a tad predatory that they only take women?"

"It does now, yeah," I admit.

The company's claim that women are better suited to their software is part of their marketing. With a more cynical lens, it seems like a way of establishing a hierarchy or sense of elitism. If only women can be matched, it puts men on the back foot, waiting. But they assured me the men in their database were there by choice. I didn't dig deeper, and maybe their claim isn't a complete lie. Simon *did* sign up for a dating website, but the way they mine content from other sources means their matches aren't up-to-date. Do they strong-arm and cajole other men into breaking up with girlfriends, abandoning wives, or otherwise choosing a different path once they're matched? Is Simon *really* an outlier?

"The company's questionnaire is detailed, and you have

to supply character references. They try to make it seem like you're getting your money's worth. Are you sure your sister is up to it?"

"Don't worry," he assures me. "She'll get the appointment. She's tenacious."

"I remember." My voice is soft. At one time, our families were on the cusp of joining together. He's gone quiet, and I wonder whether his mind has ventured to the same place as mine. All the family dinners, the special events, the opportunities to see if we fit together.

"She'll get the appointment," Simon reiterates, his voice hushed.

"I want to be there to confront them." The words leave my mouth before I can think them through. "As long as it's before I move to Scotland, of course."

He stares at me for a beat and then takes in the plate on the door again. "When do you leave?"

"Three weeks."

"Wow," he breathes out. "You're not messing around."

"Once a decision is made . . ."

"Yeah," he says. "I guess so."

"I'll get a stopover in New York on my way to Scotland if the appointment is cutting it close." Why am I saying this? The money is all I need; it doesn't matter if I'm there.

"Okay." His tone is sad, thoughtful. "Where are you going exactly?"

I take my phone out and open the map app. Before Simon got here, I was poring over photos of the village and surrounding area. "The closest place to the farm is called Kearvaig. I'm probably not pronouncing it right."

"A farm?" He peers at the map and then raises his eyebrows.

"A real farm with sheep, cattle, chickens, and herding dogs." A small laugh leaves me. "I think it'll be fun . . . or awful. It might be awful too." The farm is remote, which Angus warned me about, but checking the map today made me realize how isolated I'll be. No neighbor for miles.

"You'll learn a lot about the large animal arm of veterinary science."

"I know." I abandon my cake and coffee to head into my bedroom. "I've been brushing up on it from college." I grab a textbook off my shelf and turn to head back to the living room, but Simon is standing in my bedroom doorway, his hands shoved into the pockets of his jeans. The slouch of his shoulders indicates his uncertainty about following me.

When I get closer with the book, he holds out his hand. "You were always keen on exploring large animal services. Never expected you to be doing it on a remote farm in Scotland."

Me either, but I'm touched that he remembers how enthusiastic I used to be about it. Until I realized that large animals and city life don't exactly go together.

We're standing close, maybe too close, while he flips through the textbook. I drink him in and wish I didn't enjoy his company so much. He likes science and scientific things, and he loves animals like me. But there's no reason for him to be leafing through the textbook other than in a show of solidarity or interest in the things I love. My chest warms, and the feeling spreads throughout my body.

"So, you'd have a mixed practice? Wasn't that what you said you wanted your last year in vet school?"

I stare up at him, and my heart squeezes. He remembers. Our gazes meet, and I search his face, wondering how it's possible to feel so many conflicting emotions about one person. "Yeah," I whisper. "Except Mike wanted to focus on small animal, so I agreed to put our practice more in the city. He was probably right. We've got a good business going. I don't know if it would have been the same out in the country somewhere."

"Now you get to try it." His gaze moves from my lips to my eyes and back again. The textbook lies open in one of his big hands. "I'm happy for you."

But his tone isn't happy—it's sad, wistful. Does he wish we could rewind time? Fall back into each other's arms? Pretend like we never broke up, like he never broke my heart, deceived me? Staring into his deep green eyes, I almost forget why I'm supposed to be mad or disappointed or anything other than in love.

Love?

I step back and grab the book from his hand, slamming it shut and striding to the bookcase to pop it back into its place. Even if I do love him, love is nothing without trust. While he might have told me about all the moving pieces that contributed to our downfall six years ago, and while I might sort of understand why he was ashamed, I can't dismiss how he's handled our second chance. Manipulation isn't a good foundation for a relationship.

I stay across the room from him. Pixie, whom I put in her crate when Simon arrived, wiggles with eagerness.

"So." I don't trust myself to get close to him again. "I'll try to connect with those other women. You try to get us an appointment with Soulmates Reunited, and we can communicate via text. Okay? There's probably no reason for us to see each other again before New York."

Hurt flashes across his face before he can school his features. "Right. Yeah." He shoves his hands into the pockets of his jeans. "I'll get out of your hair." He turns in the doorway, and then he glances at me over his shoulder. "If you need that half of the money I owe you . . . or if there's anything I can do to help you get ready to go, just let me know. Move boxes or whatever . . . I can make myself useful."

The offer of money surprises me, though it probably shouldn't. We did have a deal, even if it feels like everything has fallen apart. And maybe I *should* take his cash. God knows I don't have much to get me to Scotland, but taking it feels wrong—a connection I want and don't want all at once.

It would be so easy to let myself fall into something with him again. I might not like it, might wish it wasn't true, but a part of me will always love Simon. He's in my bones. "Thanks," I say. "I plan to get all my money back from Soulmates Reunited, so I won't need yours, and a few other people have offered to help with moving, so I think I'm okay."

He catches his bottom lip with his teeth and nods. Then he's gone from the bedroom door, and I hear the click of my front door when he leaves.

Chapter Thirty-two

SIMON

Tayla's moving to Scotland, literally putting an ocean between us, and I've been having a shitty week at work too. Even things I'd normally find funny are depressing.

For instance, I'm up for experimenting in the bedroom, but I draw the line at sticking various foreign objects up my ass or the ass of my partner. You'd be surprised how many people don't share my philosophy. Last week it was that guy with the beer can. Tonight's patient has a rubber fist jammed so far up, I think he's tasting rubber.

"The doctor will be in soon." I draw the curtain around the guy, who's lying facedown on the table. He came in alone, and when I asked how the fist got so far up there, he was vague on the details. The plastic/shit taste in his mouth is probably throwing him off. A few weeks ago, a night like tonight would have amused me.

"You get all the best patients," my shift supervisor says when I wash my hands for an extralong time at the sink. "You're done in five, aren't you?"

"I'm going to miss out on watching the guy have a fist extracted from his ass. Shame, really." I smirk. Instead, I'm meeting Tayla and a gaggle of soulmates at a pub not far from here. She must have figured out how to unblock my number because she texted me to confirm the date and time for the stupidly awkward meeting.

"Before you're done, there's a woman in curtain two who asked for you to do her intake." She waggles her eyebrows. "You've seemed a little down lately, so I thought I'd let you cross paths with an attractive woman before the end of your shift. Makes up for all the ass work you've been doing lately."

"Dark hair? Slight build?" My heart kicks.

"You've got a type, do you?" She scans the chart in her hands. "This one is short, curvy, brown hair. Pretty."

I let my breath out in a large whoosh. Of course Tayla isn't here. If she were, she'd be hurt or sick. It's one thing to visit me in the waiting room, another to actually come to the ER. I take the blank chart and head to the second curtained area. There, on the bed, looking as well as can be, is Jada. I haven't seen her in the almost two weeks since she crashed my explanation date with Tayla.

I squeeze the clipboard and don't sit down in the seat next to the bed like I normally would. "Jada. Are you hurt or injured?"

She beams, and then she must read my unconcealed annoyance because her smile falters. "You haven't been answering my texts or phone calls."

That's because they've been nonstop since she saw me. I answered the first couple, but when it became apparent she would use my offer to recover her money as a way to weasel into my life, I stopped responding.

"This is my workplace. Are you injured or ill?"

"I just—I thought maybe we could talk." She squirms on the table.

"Yeah, no. Definitely not while I'm supposed to be working." I check my watch. "My shift finished two minutes ago. I'll get someone else to assist you, assuming you've got a legitimate problem."

"Oh, I can walk you out if your shift is done." She hops off the bed.

I pinch the bridge of my nose and try to suppress my frustrated sigh. In an hour, I'm supposed to be meeting Tayla at a pub, and I need to shower. "Jada, I'm meeting Tayla, and she wouldn't be comfortable with us having this conversation." I duck down to catch her gaze. "I think you should talk to someone about the mind-fuck Soulmates Reunited has played on you. You need to find a way to let this go."

"You love her? Really?" She stares up at me, pain and frustration mingling in her eyes.

"I do. Yeah. She's it for me."

"Then why did you break up with her six years ago? Why did it take you six years to get back together with her again?"

"I'm an idiot is the short answer." I huff out a breath of half amusement, half frustration. "Probably the more honest answer is that I wasn't ready for her or for how I felt about her six years ago. I don't know why, but I wasn't."

"And you are now?" Skepticism coats her voice. "All of a sudden?"

"Nothing sudden about six years, a monastery, and some therapy." A hint of a smile tugs at the edges of my lips. "There's no shame in talking to someone when you're struggling to cope."

"Like a shrink?" Her brows pinch together.

"Like a therapist or a counselor, yeah." I keep my voice soft and even. "For whatever reason, you're clinging on to an idea that isn't real. We're not real. We don't know each other. They lied to you. I'll do what I can to get them to return your money, but we won't ever be a couple." Under different circumstances, I'd invite her to meet with the rest of us at the pub. Help us figure out a plan. But she doesn't seem like she's in a frame of mind where she could handle that, and she's a sore subject for Tayla. The combination of the two would not be good.

She rubs her face with both hands and then drags them down, her shoulders slumping. "Do you . . ." Her voice shakes, and she stops to inhale a deep breath. "Do you know someone I could talk to?"

My hand hovers over her shoulder, but I withdraw it before I make contact. "I can get you some names. We keep them at the nurses' station."

She stares at me for a beat, and tears pool in her eyes. "I just wanted it to be you so badly."

I release my breath in a whoosh because I understand that sentiment. The boxes littering the floor of Tayla's house spring to mind. *Scotland.* My stomach churns at the thought. "The person for you is out there, Jada. You need to be ready when they come knocking."

"Like you were ready for Tayla this time?"

"I might have been ready, but I'm still not worthy." I let out a mirthless chuckle, and my lips twist. "Not sure I ever will be. But I've got to try." I rub my cheek, my palm grazing my stubble. "Listen, I'll grab that information for you, but I have to go or I'll be late."

Tears spring to her eyes again, and she nods. "Okay. Thanks. You're a decent guy, Simon. Tayla's lucky."

Not sure Tayla would call herself lucky at this point, but at least one person believes my heart is in the right place.

Three women with no physical similarities sit in a booth at the back of the pub. I weave my way toward them, but I've only got eyes for one of them. Thankfully, she saved me the spot beside her instead of forcing me to sit next to one of the other women. Tayla sees me coming, and for the briefest moment, her face lights up. Then, as though she's remembered she hates me, a mask falls over her expression. She gestures toward me, and the other two women turn, one pale, blond, and curvy, the other a dark-brown-skinned woman with hair the color of red wine. I've met them both before, but this gathering is a tableau of false starts.

"You've both met Simon?" Tayla asks when I arrive at

the table and slide into the booth beside her.

Our shoulders brush together lightly, and a bolt of aware-ness streaks through me. I wish I had the right to wrap my arm around her waist, draw her tight against me, and plant a kiss on her temple. I fucked that up, so instead of looking at Tayla, I focus on the two women in front of me.

"We've met," Sherri says and flips her wine-colored locks over her shoulder.

"Us too," Jennifer agrees, her full lips pursed. "So, what's this about getting our money back? That's really all I care about at this point."

"Don't need a man, just need my cash." Sherri flashes her diamond-adorned ring finger at me in triumph.

"As I explained on the phone," Tayla begins, and then she launches into my history with Soulmates Reunited.

While she talks, I go to the bar to get everyone a drink. It's the least I can do as their collective soulmate. When I come back, Sherri and Jennifer eye me with less hostility.

"How are you getting an appointment with Soulmates Reunited?" Sherri asks when I slide her gin and tonic across the wooden table.

"My sister is on a waiting list for an appointment. Their *elite* service only takes so many clients a week." I pass Tayla her wine and Jennifer her Diet Coke. Once I'm seated, I fiddle with my beer bottle. "We're not sure how long it'll take to get in."

"Took me months," Jennifer says.

She was woman number two, so that would have been four or five years ago.

"I got a cancellation." Sherri's tone is acidic. "So lucky."

"If it takes months, Simon will be going alone." Tayla sneaks a glance at me. "I'll be in Scotland."

I can't tell from her tone if she's glad she'll be far away while I have to deal with the Soulmates Reunited mess or if there's a tinge of regret in her voice.

"There's a fourth woman," I admit. "I've promised to try to get her money back too."

"Why isn't she here?" Sherri stirs her drink with her straw.

"We have a more complicated history." I'm not willing to paint Jada as unbalanced, although tonight's appearance at my work suggests she's not well. She took the names I gave her and promised she'd call one of them this week. Hopefully, she can talk through her issues, whatever they might be, with a professional. Lord knows I can't help her. Look at the mess I've made of my own life.

"Ah," Jennifer says. "You actually dated her?"

"Not really." I shake my head. "Soulmates Reunited convinced me to give her three dates. The ending was messy."

"So, you haven't dated any of your so-called soulmates? You've got no interest in finding love?" Sherri raises her eyebrows.

"We dated," Tayla says in a rush. "Didn't work out."

"Makes sense." Jennifer sips her Diet Coke. "There's an awkward vibe between the two of you, like you're hyper-aware of each other. Must have had *great* sex."

"What?" Tayla chokes on her wine. "Why would you say that?" She's flushed.

I'm sort of enjoying her discomfort and the use of the

word *great* as a reference point for our sex life. Not going to complain about that one.

"I'm an Instagram influencer. I read body language. People pay me to state the obvious." Jennifer winks at Tayla. "And your sexual chemistry is obvious. So the missed connection must be due to a personality clash."

"Something like that," Tayla mutters. "Probably better if we focus on taking down Soulmates Reunited."

"Ohhh, you struck a nerve." Sherri grins.

Tayla takes a long sip of her wine and doesn't meet my gaze. Jennifer's instincts are good, or her observation skills—maybe both. Tayla and I have been wordlessly coordinating our movements in the booth to ensure we don't touch. Whenever parts of our bodies graze, the vibe between us is stilted for a beat. Awareness pulses between us, and it's a type of foreplay I normally enjoy: ramp each other up and rip each other's clothes off the minute we're somewhere more private. I stare at my linked hands on the wooden table and try not to let my mind wander to my tightening pants. Great sex with Tayla is *not* where my mind should be right now.

"I need any communication you have with Soulmates Reunited so we can examine it. Simon has a lawyer who has agreed to look over the contracts and any correspondence." Tayla swirls her wine. "If we have to, we'll take this to the court of public opinion."

"I have two million followers," Jennifer says.

"Two million?" Disbelief coats my words, but her claim is a much-needed distraction.

"Love and interpersonal relationships are a big business,

hence the reason Soulmates Reunited is such a force. We're out here searching for a connection, hoping to meet people we can stand long enough to be with day in and day out. It's a tall order in love and business. People seek avenues that'll give them an advantage over others. I provide one." She shrugs and wags her finger between me and Tayla. "And I'm good at it."

"That many followers is incredible," Tayla says. "Leverage." She peeks at me and then seems to think better of it, her gaze sliding away.

"She broke up with you, huh?" Jennifer raises an eyebrow, addressing me. "Wouldn't have called that." She leans forward, elbows on the table. "I would have pegged you for a commitment-phobe."

Her observation cuts to the bone. "You're not far off," I admit. "I've had my issues. What happened or—" I steal a glance in Tayla's direction "—didn't happen between us is down to me. Even if I'm not the one who cut ties."

"Did you cheat on her?" Sherri sips her drink.

"God, no." I scowl, insulted she thinks I'm that kind of guy.

"If it's not that, seems forgivable to me." Jennifer waves a dismissive hand.

I'm not sure how we ended up in soulmate group therapy, but I'm not mad they're rooting for me. A tad shocking, but I won't turn down support. An ocean will be between us, and I'd swim across it if she asked.

"I've got nothing but time if you want to spill more tea. I don't mind hearing about other people's screwed-up romantic relationships. Makes me feel better about mine." Sherri smirks.

"Uh." Tayla shakes her head. "No. We're not doing that." She shoots me a warning look. "We'll get your money back, but you're not getting any gory details about what went wrong between me and Simon."

"Spoilsport." Sherri sighs. "All right." She tips up the last of her drink. "You'll let us know if we need to use our socials to demolish them? Until then, we need to forward emails and such to you, right?"

"Anything you have," Tayla agrees. "You've got my email address?"

Sherri scoots out of the booth, and Jennifer follows. They both flash Tayla's business card.

"I've got a good feeling." Jennifer taps her card on the table and meets my gaze. "Good luck to you two."

Both women leave the table, their heads bent together, talking and laughing as they saunter to the exit.

"Her good feeling seemed to be tied to ogling you," Tayla mutters before taking another sip of her wine.

"What?" I laugh.

"After the whole 'good sex' comment, she couldn't stop staring at you."

"She said *great* sex, actually." I twist in the booth to stare at Tayla.

"So, we're on a waiting list?" She makes eye contact before sliding her focus back to her glass.

Guess she's not keen to dissect the difference between good and great. "Yeah, according to my sister." I decide to let the topic of Jennifer and her horny gaze go. Sex with anyone other than Tayla doesn't interest me. The woman sitting next to me has consumed my thoughts—waking or sleeping. I've been dreaming about her, which has been fantastically awful. When I wake up and realize my sub-conscious tried to steal another slice of happiness, despair takes hold. Will I ever get another taste?

"You'll have to confront them alone."

"I should have pursued it a long time ago. Hard to say whether Ruby and Dean are the exception or the rule. I set up a Google alert for a while on the company, but whenever I checked, only positive posts showed. Saw some notices about content being removed, so I'd guess they are on top of squashing nonbelievers."

A comfortable silence falls between us, and I wonder if Tayla is thinking about how hard it might be to take on Soulmates Reunited like I am. She seems determined, but the lawyer I consulted a few years ago was clear on the mountain of evidence I'd need to take them to court. Maybe whatever my former soulmates have will be enough.

"The money is one thing, but for women like Jada who are so sucked into the process . . ." Tayla glances at me. "I think I feel worse for them."

"She came to the ER tonight."

"Oh no. She was hurt?"

"Nope." I take a gulp of my beer. "I gave her the contact details for a few therapists we refer people to."

"I can't imagine not being able to let go like that." She toys with her glass.

"Yeah," I agree, and when Tayla meets my gaze, I continue, "I understand how hard it can be to let go of something you really want."

She flushes and drinks the rest of her wine. "I should get home to Pixie."

Reluctantly, I scoot out of the booth, and Tayla follows. "What are you doing with her when you go to Scotland? I can take her if you need."

The tight expression on her face eases. "Sandy is going to work with Luis on finding and raising the puppies while I'm gone. We're easing into a transition for Pixie. I think I might miss her, though. It's been nice to have an animal in the house again."

"Going to have lots soon." I shove my hands into the pockets of my jeans. "You mentioned he has herding dogs?"

She swallows and stares up, searching my face. The space between us crackles. So many emotions war in her eyes, I'm not sure what will stick.

"Why did you have to be such a shit?" Her voice catches, and she grabs her purse from the seat of the booth and pushes past me out of the pub.

My gut clenches at the hurt expression that settled just before she spoke. I didn't expect those words, but I knew from her conflicted expression that whatever she wanted to say wasn't anything warm and fuzzy. I rub my face and grab my beer bottle off the table, chugging the last of it.

She's gone. But how can I ever let her go when she's entrenched so deeply in my heart? Jada's words from earlier reverberate around my head. *I just wanted it to be you so badly.* The ache across my chest pulses.

With a deep sigh of resignation, I drop a tip on the table and head for the exit.

Chapter Thirty-three

TAYLA

Ruby grabs a box and puts it in the pile to go to my mother's garage, and then she grabs another one and sets it in the pile for her basement.

"Are you sure you don't mind keeping my things for the year?" It'll save me an enormous amount on storage costs, money I can't afford to dish out until I get my refund from Soulmates Reunited. I tug on my ponytail and try to suppress the surge of panic. Am I really leaving everything behind and moving to Scotland?

"Yeah, it's fine." Ruby reads the next box and sorts it. "Did Angus ask you to get rid of so much personal stuff?"

"No, but I figured it was the right thing to do. This place is small, and I don't want him to feel like he's imposing.

He's going to live here." My voice trails off at the end. "God knows what I'm going to find in Scotland."

"A man in a kilt." Ruby smirks.

The last thing I need is a more complicated love life. Though I suppose I'm leaving my current complication behind. I meet her expression with a weak smile and a queasy stomach. *Simon*. He's been all I can think about the last few days as I've organized my life to leave. Why am I so impulsive? I press the heels of my hands into my forehead.

"You getting excited?" She eyes me before lifting and moving another box.

"Yeah, yeah, of course."

"You're a terrible liar. You're having massive regrets."

I stare at her, waiting for the *I told you so*, but I should know better. That's not Ruby's style.

"She told you not to apply for remote locations until you knew what was happening with Simon." Dean breezes in the front door to snatch another box to load into the moving van I rented.

Dean, on the other hand, has no problem calling anyone out on their foolishness. Probably one of the reasons he and Ruby work so well. At least one person needs to be capable of cutting through bullshit.

"There's nothing happening with Simon," I grumble and escape to my bedroom to lug more boxes into the front room. On the top of the stack in my room is a shoebox stuffed with souvenirs and trinkets from my relationship with Simon. Last night, I sat on my bed and eased off the lid for the first time in six years. Then I cried myself to sleep.

Stupid. So stupid. I should burn the box in a ceremonial fire the day I leave this house. A complete fresh start. No more reminders of Simon anywhere.

Except in your heart.

I curse my idiocy and stagger back into the front room with my arms full of stacked boxes. Thankfully, they're packed with light items, and although I can't see much, they aren't too heavy.

"Here, let me help with those."

My arms go weak at the familiar deep voice, as though thinking about him has conjured him into my tiny house.

"Simon?" I sputter as he takes the boxes.

He gives me a sheepish smile and sets the boxes on the floor, reading the tops and sorting them into their proper piles.

"Sorry to drop by like this, but my sister got a phone call from Soulmates Reunited this morning about a cancellation, and I thought you'd want to know."

"Oh," I breathe out. The sight of him after several days' absence kicks my heart into overdrive. I half convinced myself that this tingling across my skin whenever he's in a room isn't real. But here it is . . . the tingles, so strong I might as well be vibrating with need. "Is the appointment soon?"

"The twenty-fourth," he says, his hands deep in the pockets of his jeans.

"That's Friday." The day I fly to Scotland. I told Angus I'd be at his house and ready for my first day on the twenty-seventh. Can I get my flight changed? I bought a flexible ticket. I stare at Simon for a beat too long. *Should* I get my flight changed?

"I'll fly to New York on the twenty-third," he says. "Ruby said you leave on the twenty-fourth, so it looks like you'll just miss the meeting."

"I have a flexible fare." The words leave my mouth before I can activate my brain. Out of the corner of my eye, I swear I see Ruby's eyebrows hit the ceiling. "I can call to move my ticket so I can be there."

"We're going to take this load over to our basement," Dean says from the doorway. "We'll be back to get more in a bit."

"Oh," I say, going toward the door. "I should help."

"No need." Dean glances at Simon. "You've got things to sort here."

Ruby gives me a meaningful look on her way out the door that I can't interpret. Does she think I'm an idiot for offering to go to New York, or does she think I should try to work things out with Simon? What would I even say at this point? I'm moving to Scotland in less than a week.

Is the queasiness in my stomach because I'm leaving Simon or because I'm leaving everything? I don't know. I can't ask him to uproot his life if my anxiety is a regular case of nerves.

"Are you sure about changing your plans?" Simon's brow is furrowed.

No. "Yes, it'll be fine. It's not a big switch. Except for a few lingering appointments early this week, my schedule is clear. What time is the appointment on the twenty-fourth?"

"Nine in the morning."

"Ah, right." I twirl my ponytail around my finger. "I

should probably come to New York on the twenty-third too. Have you booked a hotel yet?"

"Nothing yet. I just heard from my sister an hour ago."

"Right, well, I liked the hotel I stayed at last time, and it was within walking distance of their office. I'll see if they have two rooms available, if that's okay with you?"

"Yeah. But do you want me to take care of that? I'm sure you've got a lot on your plate."

I wave him off and press my fingers into my temples. "I can handle it." This is good. Talking about logistics has calmed my racing heart, and that innate attraction running under the surface of every interaction with Simon is softened. Keep us away from anything remotely personal and I'm fine. Just fine.

"Are there more boxes in your bedroom? I can move them into the front room to make it easier for Ruby and Dean."

"Yeah," I reply absently, staring unseeing at what's left of the piles by the door. I've accumulated so much stuff. When I come back, I should purge anything I don't use.

"Hey, Tay?" he calls from my bedroom. "Is this box with my name on it for me?" His tone is both hesitant and hopeful.

Oh, shit.

"No!" There's an edge of panic in my voice, and my heart, which was calm, gallops again. "No, no." I stride into my room to find him cradling the box in both hands.

"It's not for me?" He cocks his head.

"Nope." I take the box from his hands. "It's—it's about another Simon I used to know. Popular name."

There's an awkward beat of silence.

"A Simon who was neither a *Fucking* nor a *Dickhead*, huh?" His gaze is tender when he catches mine.

"Something like that," I mutter and whirl around to leave, forgetting the rug I rolled up by the door. My foot catches on the edge, and I flail around, the box flying out of my hands while I try to keep myself from falling. An arm circles my waist, catching me just before I hit the ground. When I glance up at him, his green eyes are startled.

"Are you okay?" he asks.

I hold his gaze, and our lips are close enough for my libido to kick into overdrive. Whatever pheromone he possesses should be bottled.

"Thank you," I murmur. "This wood floor isn't very forgiving."

He eases me back onto my feet, far more gracefully than I would have had the situation been reversed. I'm not even sure how he got around the boxes to catch me. Nursing reflexes on speed.

When I gaze around, the contents of my Simon box are scattered across the floor. Concert tickets. Cheesy photo booth pictures. The coaster he doodled on the night we met. A bracelet. Holiday trinkets from trips we took. Cards from special occasions. Wordlessly, we crouch together, picking up pieces and putting them back into the cardboard holder. We both reach for the last one at the same time, and when our gazes connect, Simon's is full of questions.

"You kept all this?" His voice is hoarse.

I shrug and toss the last item into the box as though I couldn't care less. "Yeah. Don't ask me why." The reason causes tears to burn my eyes, and I shove the lid onto the top with force. Back when we were dating, I thought I was collecting tokens of our love affair, things to show our children someday. I'd been so *sure* of him. "Do you want the box?" The words tumble past my lips.

We rise to our feet, and Simon runs a hand along the top of his short strands. He winces and tries to catch my gaze, but I avoid eye contact. Already, I'm regretting offering him the box. Last night, I wrapped the Soulmate Simon plate in bubble wrap and stuck it into the middle of my suitcase. Why? A reminder that I don't need him for when I'm in Scotland and I get lonely. At least that's what I told myself when I shoved it between sweaters.

"If you're just going to throw it out . . ."

"I am." I meet his gaze, defiant. "There's no point in keeping it, right?"

"You kept it this long."

"Forgotten. Shoved in the back of the closet. I didn't even remember I had it." All lies. Why can't I stop trying to hurt him? I want a reaction, but I'm not sure what'll satisfy me. There's pain etched in his features, and it's not enough because it doesn't even come close to what's etched across my heart.

"I have a box too," he says and rubs his temple. "There's a box in my closet with your name on it too."

"Sure there is," I scoff, stepping past him to enter the

living room. His revelation makes me light-headed, and I sink into the couch just as there's a sharp knock on the front door.

Ruby pokes her head in. "We're back for round two," she says.

Simon covers his face and eases his hands down his cheeks. "Call or text me if your plans change, Tayla."

Then he slips out the door past Ruby.

"You okay?" she asks, and then she spots the box on my lap. "I thought you burned that?"

"I couldn't do it." Tears fill my eyes. "When it came down to it, I couldn't part with it." My voice catches on the last words, blurring them together.

She sinks into the couch beside me and drags me into her arms. "Oh, honey," she murmurs. "What are we gonna do?"

"I hate that I still love him," I whisper, saying the words aloud for the first time.

"Is it enough?" Ruby asks gently.

The box in my hands caves in a little at the pressure I'm putting on the cardboard, and my mind tries to answer Ruby's question. "I don't know," I admit. "That's the hard part. I just don't know."

"Are you really going to New York with him?"

"Yeah." I ease my grip on the box. "I need closure. One way or another."

"With Soulmates Reunited or him?"

"Both," I say. "I can't go to Scotland feeling like I'm being torn in half."

"More talking or more working?" Ruby gives me one more squeeze.

"Working." I survey the boxes littering my front entranceway. "I need a distraction, and I only have the van rented for today."

"The right path will show itself." Ruby hoists a box into her arms.

I hope the fog in my head and heart clears in time to find that path and take it.

Chapter Thirty-four

SIMON

I've traveled through New York City a few times on my way to somewhere else, but I've only been here to sightsee once, and that was with Tayla seven years ago. Our first trip together. Does she remember? That time we sat next to each other on the plane, giddy with impending discoveries. This time, we were on opposite ends.

The hotel lobby buzzes around us while we wait in line to be served. In sync, we take a step forward.

In the box of mementos she dropped, there was a New York City shot glass. I don't remember when or where we bought it, but she must. All the things she valued about our relationship were scattered across her floor. The pressure in my chest when I realized we both kept things, held on to the past so tightly, was crushing.

Does she realize this is our last trip together? The book-ends of our relationship. Once we're done with Soulmates Reunited, I doubt I'll hear from her ever again. She offered to *give me* that box as though she couldn't care less. Her indifference is stinging. We'll never recover.

This last week, the only communication we exchanged was about hotel reservations, flights, and sharing taxis. She's nothing if not practical. Can't stand to be around me, but why pay full fare?

We're the last people in line, and it's our turn at the reception desk. When we're waved up, I follow Tayla.

"Reservation for Tayla Murphy," she says, hoisting her bag higher onto her shoulder.

She put her other two suitcases in a temporary holding spot via the concierge when we entered the hotel. Her life jammed into two suitcases and a carry-on. She's got guts, I'll give her that.

"One room with a king-size bed?" The receptionist clicks through various screens.

"No," Tayla says sharply. "Two rooms. I definitely booked two rooms." She roots around in her purse for her phone.

She forwarded me the reservation, so I pass my phone with the email open to the receptionist. He frowns and scrolls through it, and then he double-checks the information on his screen.

"Just wait here a minute." The receptionist hands back my phone and goes down the bank of check-in slots to someone who must be a manager. They have a brief conversation, and then the manager comes over with the receptionist.

They both click through various computer screens, and the manager sighs.

"Sorry about this, folks. We're booked solid because of a conference down the road, and it looks as though this booking and another came in at exactly the same time. Shouldn't happen, but sometimes there's a glitch."

A fucking *glitch*. Under different circumstances, I'd laugh. Soulmates, hotel rooms . . . The honorable solution stares me in the face, even if it means I'm unlikely to see Tayla until our appointment in the morning, and then probably never again. At least if we were in the same hotel I might have caught a glimpse of her at breakfast, passed her in a hallway, shared an elevator.

"It's fine," I say. "I'll go to another hotel as long as we're refunded."

"We've processed the refund. That's not a problem. But another hotel might be an issue," the manager says. "I'm happy to call around for you since this is our mistake, but the media arts conference this weekend is huge. I've heard everything within ten blocks is booked solid."

Of course it is. Fate is determined to drive me as far from Tayla as possible. *I get it, okay? I don't deserve her.*

She glances at me and bites her lip before turning back to the receptionist. "Do you have any rollaway beds or anything? We can share a room if we have to."

Even with reluctance wafting off her like a bad perfume, hope rises in me. Two nights of close proximity. That's a chance, isn't it? One last opportunity to show her I might be Fucking Simon and Dickhead Simon, but I'm also Soulmate Simon. Maybe that won't be enough, but I have to try.

The manager nods. "I'll have one waiting in your room when you get up there."

"Great, thanks." Tayla doesn't meet my gaze while the receptionist makes our keys and passes us the cards along with a guide to NYC.

We walk to the elevators, and I flip through the guide, remembering all the things Tayla and I did the last time we were here and recalling the things we didn't have time for. "Your flight is Saturday morning?"

"Bright and early." Tayla punches the Up button and crosses her arms. Her bag slips off her shoulder, and she tries to heft it up again.

"May I?" I slip my fingers under the strap and lift it. "Let me take it."

She passes the bag over, and I'm surprised at its weight. I helped her with the suitcases, but she clung to this bag as though it possessed her life force.

"I'm tired," she admits. "It's been a long week."

"Was it hard to say goodbye to Pixie?"

"It's been hard to say goodbye to everything." Her voice is thick.

We wait for the elevator, and I wonder if I should tell her not to go or that she doesn't need to move to Scotland to get away from me. I probably should have said that earlier. Has she sounded excited about the move at all? Determined, yes. Defiant. But genuinely excited?

The elevator opens, and we step inside followed by three other couples. I select the button for our floor, and we ascend in silence. Everyone else gets off before we reach our destination. She exits first, and I follow her down the hall, carrying both of our bags.

She opens the door and stops so suddenly I almost run into her.

"What's wrong?" I peer around her.

The room is tiny. The bulk of the space is taken up by the king-size bed, which leaves the tiniest space for the cot to be wedged in.

"We might have to rearrange some furniture." Tayla scoots around the cot and dumps her purse onto the bed. "I forgot these rooms were *this* small."

I squeeze around the open door and the cot, navigating the bags. With the placement of the beds, it's impossible to get to the bathroom without going over one of them. "This is . . . cozy."

"I should have made a bigger fuss at the check-in counter. Refund or not, it's unacceptable they overbooked."

"At least we both have a place to sleep." I set Tayla's bag on the bed and my backpack on the cot. The springs squeak with the weight. Not a good sign.

"I'm getting ready for bed." Tayla crawls across the bed to get to the bathroom.

I can't say I'm upset about her technique. A solid score of ten. What I wouldn't give to have her crawling across that bed to me.

I try to figure out whether there's a better place for the cot. But this is really the one spot it'll even fit. I take out my toiletries, and when the bathroom door creeps open, I glance in Tayla's direction and do a double take. She's in a lacy negligee that leaves very little to the imagination. I swallow.

Wow.

She shields her gaze from mine and stands at the edge of the bed. "This is all I packed to sleep in. Sorry. I—I wasn't expecting to share with anyone. Obviously. And I don't have enough clothes in my carry-on to just wear something else."

"No." My voice is gruff. "It's fine." Her barely-there negligee is *more* than fine. I wait for her to crawl across the bed back to her purse, but it becomes clear she's waiting for me to go to the bathroom before she makes another move. Then I remember she's probably not wearing any underwear, and I'm not sure I can get myself into the bathroom fast enough.

I clamber across the cot, the springs groaning and screeching in protest. After I shut the door, I rub my hands along my face and stare into the mirror.

Get it together, Si.

Fate is having a laugh. An actual laugh at my expense.

Once I've brushed my teeth, I realize I also didn't bring anything to sleep in. I press my palms into the counter and contemplate sleeping fully clothed. Knowing that she's a few feet from me, I've got two nights left in her life, and she's wearing *that* might cause me to spontaneously combust.

Well, I can't stay in here forever, staring at my reflection. She's probably already wondering if I'm in here rubbing one out at the sight of her. Maybe if we had those separate rooms . . .

When I come out of the bathroom, the only light is a bedside one. She has her back to me. I shed my clothes, and then I slip under the covers.

"You good?" she asks.

"Yeah, thanks." Good? Not sure there's a word for how I'm feeling right now. Intensely grateful to be here and equally frustrated to not be over there.

I shift around in the bed, trying to get comfortable. Each time I move, the springs are a chorus of squeaks and squeals. This cot has seen better days. The tension and awareness in the room tells me Tayla is still awake. Is she wishing things were different between us, like I am?

She lets out a deep sigh, and her sheets rustle.

I bounce around on the rollaway. Two nights on this is better than being ten blocks away. But it sure as shit isn't comfortable.

"I can't sleep with you making so much noise," Tayla says.

There are only two other options in this room. Her bed is off-limits. "I'll sleep on the floor." I sit up to strip the blankets off the cot.

"No." Resignation colors her voice. "You can sleep here. It's a big bed."

A better man would probably protest or at least question whether this is a good idea. Given the choice of this shitty cot, the hard floor, or half of a king-size bed that has Tayla on the other side, it's a no-brainer. I toss my pillow to the head of the bed and scramble over the covers to my half.

Tayla takes the extra pillows and lines them up in the bed between us, a wall. "Your side," she says, pointing to where I've slipped under the sheet. "My side."

"You built that wall for me? We both know who the cuddler is."

"Good night, Simon." She flops back into bed and hauls the duvet up to her chin.

"Night, Tay." I shove my pillow under my head, and when her breathing evens out, I listen to her for a few minutes, relishing her closeness, until sleep pulls me under too.

Chapter Thirty-five

TAYLA

When awareness seeps in, I realize I'm warm. That in itself isn't a problem, except the source of my delicious warmth is the wall of solid flesh under my cheek, hand, and leg.

Abs. So many abs under my fingertips. Each one a ridge of deliciousness.

I've breached the pillow barrier I set up between us. I might not mind if my unconscious self cuddled like a normal person. But no, that would be asking for too much. Both my cheek and my hand rest on his abs, and my leg is thrown over his, effectively immobilizing him. My elbow is dangerously close to brushing against something else that's likely hard and rigid.

How long have I been like this?

I stifle a groan. He's probably wishing he slept on the floor. With slow, careful movements, I try to extract myself from him. If luck is on my side, he won't even realize what's happened.

"You must have been an octopus in another life," Simon mumbles from the head of the bed.

"Sorry," I mutter, and I scoot away from him to my side. Pillows litter the bed as though I didn't just breach the wall but blew it up for good measure. I yank the duvet over my half naked body. Of all the sleeping attire I could have packed, I had to pick this flimsy piece of fabric. At the time, I was aiming for cool and light. With Simon in the room, it quickly fell into the *barely clothed* category.

"I'm not complaining." Simon shifts on his side to face me.

He's all sexy and rumpled. Heat pools in my belly while an ache spreads across my chest. How is it possible to miss someone when they're right beside you? My raging hormones are playing havoc with my mind.

"You sleep okay?" he asks.

"Like an octopus."

"Funny, you didn't change colors during your REM sleep."

"How do *you* know about that?" I frown.

"Decided to do a search on my phone while you were wrapped around me last night. Didn't allow for much movement." A sly grin floats across his face.

He's enjoying my discomfort. Asshole. "You could have woken me up."

"What fun would that have been? You'd have moved."

He stretches, his lean muscles flexing. "You were softer and warmer than that wall of pillows." He rotates onto his stomach and shoves his pillow under his head. "I'll let you do it again tonight, if you want. Don't worry. I don't feel used."

I shove his shoulder and can't help laughing. On the nightstand, the alarm on my phone rings, signaling it's time to get ready to face off with Soulmates Reunited.

"Did you want to shower first?" He trails my figure with his hot gaze.

My body ignites. "You calling me dirty?" The flirty tone is automatic, and I squeeze my lips together, annoyed with myself. We've slipped into our usual easy rapport. "Forget I said that." I lean forward, ready to crawl across the bed to the bathroom, but if I do that, he'll get a hell of a show. I sit back and bite my lip. There's no dignified way to do this. No matter what, I'm scrambling over or across a bed.

"Want me to close my eyes?" He smirks.

"Would you keep them closed?" I give him a wry smile.

"I don't need to look. My imagination is excellent."

"Probably better than reality." I gather my things from the bedside table.

"I said I didn't *need* to look, not that I didn't *want* to." He tugs at a corner of the pillow. "You're my dream woman, Tay. I'm not giving up any opportunities with you."

I purse my lips and hold the edges of my temper together. "But you did. You gave up all the opportunities with me."

He bunches the pillow more, the muscles in his back flexing. "When I went to the monastery to stay with my dad, they had a counselor there. You know what he told me? That it is possible to love someone and not be ready for them. The two don't always go hand in hand. Sometimes you can be ready for an experience and not be able to find it, and the opposite is also true. You can have something and not be in the right frame of mind to embrace it. I wasn't ready for you six years ago. I am now."

"But that makes me feel like I wasn't enough." My heart squeezes in my chest.

"That's not it at all." He runs a hand along my arm and laces our fingers loosely. "Watching relationships fall apart, having Soulmates Reunited whispering in my ear . . . I wanted a *guarantee* we'd work. I didn't want to just feel sure in my gut, I wanted to somehow be able to predict the future. That probably makes no sense to you, but that's how I felt. Does anyone enter into a marriage thinking they'll get divorced? But relationships fall apart. All the time."

"All the time," I agree, thinking of some of my friends whose marriages didn't make it past a few years. "There's still no guarantee, Si. If Soulmates Reunited is a fraud, we're not soulmates. We're just Tayla and Simon. The same people who couldn't make it work six years ago."

"I'm not the same guy."

I raise my eyebrows and draw my fingers away from his. "Color me unconvinced."

He turns on his side and rests his head in his hand. "I trust myself and my feelings a lot more than I used to. I don't *need* any external validation that we'll work, that we're capable of succeeding." He searches my face. "I've always loved you. When I came back from the monastery, I thought I'd blown all my chances with you or I would have come knocking again. I've never stopped loving you."

"Then you blew the next chance you got too." The words are out of my mouth before I can catch them. The dam I've built around my heart the last few weeks is leaking, and I'll plug the cracks any way I can. He can't love me. I can't love him. I'm moving to Scotland. We aren't right for each other. I can't do this. Why would he tell me this now?

He runs a hand down his face. "If I could rewind time, I'd go back to your vet clinic. I'd tell you everything—the whole truth. Then I'd woo you hard. So fucking hard. 'Cause what's between us is lightning in a bottle. We caught it, and I don't want to let it go, even if I should. Even if it's not fair to cling this hard. Even if I might get burned."

He's stunned me into silence. My heart pounds in my ears, and I scramble off the bed, not caring about the view he'll get anymore. I slam the bathroom door and press my back against it. There's a chance I might be hyperventilating. I can't catch my breath. Why is he always fucking up my life?

A soft knock sounds on the door. "Tay? Look, if I went too far, I'm sorry. But I didn't want you to leave without—"

"I need a minute." *Or a year*. Tomorrow I leave for a *year*. I rub my face in a furious, frustrated motion, trying to get my mind to focus. His words replay over and over. I turn on the water for a shower.

Then I'd woo you hard. So fucking hard.

If only that was what he did.

Is it okay that he wasn't ready before? That he kept things from me this time? While I shower, I let myself linger over what's happened between us the last few weeks. Even if everything he's said is true, I don't know if I'm capable of risking my heart again. Do I love him? Yes. But if I bow out now, I'll recover in Scotland. I'm not in so deep I can't recover. So, for the next twenty-four hours, I need to keep my distance.

With a renewed sense of purpose, I sweep my negligee off the floor, tighten my towel, and throw open the door. Except I've forgotten how tiny the room is, and I run smack into Simon's chest in my attempt to appear confident and in control.

"Oof," I say, bracing my hands on his chest to steady myself.

He chuckles, and a touch of amusement lights his gaze for the briefest moment before he takes in my annoyance.

"Where are you going in such a hurry?"

"We've got an appointment. The sooner we can get this mess sorted out the better." I tug away from him and step to the side to stand next to the nightstand. "Your turn to shower." There's no way I'm going back across the bed with him standing here. I might not have cared about giving him a show earlier, but I'm not keen to give him another one.

"So, that's it then? Back to business as usual?"

"You expected something else?" I tip my chin up.

"Not expected. Never expected. Hoped." He takes a step toward me, and I step back, my ass hitting the nightstand.

"I'm moving to Scotland for at least a year. Maybe more. Angus said he's open to more than a year if I want."

"Message received." He runs his hand along the top of his head and meets my gaze. "You don't want this. I won't—" He swallows. "I won't say another word about any of it." He steps into the bathroom and shuts the door.

The tightness in my chest makes it hard to breathe. I close the distance to the bathroom door and raise my hand to knock. Then I freeze. What will I say? I *don't* want this. I press my palm against the wood and shake my head.

He let me down. I can't give him a chance to do it again. I'd never survive a third heartbreak. What's that old adage? Fool me once, shame on you. Fool me twice, shame on me. Three times would make me a freaking idiot.

With that thought in my head, I grab my clothes out of my bag and prepare myself for battle.

Chapter Thirty-six

SIMON

When we're outside the multistory Soulmates Reunited building, I take a deep breath. Today is the reckoning for years of deception, and I want to feel triumphant, but I can't quite get there. Not that I believe in the soulmate thing. Or at least I didn't. I might not have given any of my other matches much of a chance, but I know what I had with Tayla. She was my once in a lifetime, and it makes me vaguely ill to realize how badly I've fucked everything up.

"You ready?" I ask.

"I've got all the emails, the list of things to hammer that the attorney gave us, a highlighted contract, and their Super Soulmate Simon. 'Battle ready' is an understatement."

"I have a feeling they're not going to roll over easily." At this point, I'm not convinced they'll roll over at all. Once Tayla decided to go in this direction, there was no talking her down, even when the lawyer I consulted said this was a long shot.

"I'm fighting for what's right. They're pedaling a lie. Screwing with people's lives and taking their money. It's not right." She glances at me before grabbing the handle to enter. "Game face on."

My insides are rioting. I've been trying to pretend Tayla didn't crush my last shred of hope in the hotel room earlier. A year in Scotland is a long time, but having her tell me the timeline is flexible by *years* was a knife to my heart. Maybe she'll find someone else there and never leave. My stomach lurches.

We wait for the elevator in silence until Tayla turns to me. "I'll do most of the talking, but if I forget something, jump in."

"Sure, yeah." I nod and shove my hands into my pockets. Will they even honor the appointment when they realize Tayla and I have shown up unexpectedly? There's a chance we won't get to talk to anyone. Though if that happens, the lawyer gave us a nice official-sounding letter about legal action for false advertising and a bunch of other mumbo jumbo. Sounds good on paper. Don't have a clue what any of it means.

Tayla presses the button for Soulmates Reunited's floor, and the elevator rises. My palms begin to sweat, and I slide them along the sides of my jeans. Why am I nervous about confronting them for being the shittiest company in the world?

"Nervous?" Tayla glances at my hands and then meets my gaze for a beat.

"Is that weird?" Shouldn't I be energized to finally confront them? To tell them to go fuck themselves?

"They've popped into your life at random points for six years. I think I'd feel weird if I were you."

Except, now that she's said that, I'm wondering whether what I'm really nervous about is saying goodbye to *her* tomorrow morning. If the queasiness in my stomach is related to this being our last joint venture. Once we've confronted them, what tie do we have? One more night in a shared hotel room. After that, an ocean between us.

The elevator chimes. We stand for an extra beat staring at each other while the doors slide open. My heart is in my throat, aching to be released one more time. *Stay, Tay. Don't go.*

"You can't look at me like that," she whispers. "You shouldn't look at me like that." She bites her lip and leaves me to exit the elevator behind her.

She's already at the reception desk when I make it through the main set of doors. Left me in the dust of my own longing. I probably deserve it. I stop for a moment and take in the large reception area. Hearts hang from the ceiling like some high school dance gone wrong. All the photos littering the walls are happy couples, each with some sort of plaque below them. The urge to read through them seizes me, but I quash it.

When I wander up behind Tayla, who is already talking, the receptionist raises his eyebrows in question.

"Can I help you, sir?"

"We're here together." I gesture toward Tayla.

"You're not here to be matched?" He gives me a baffled look and then transfers it to Tayla.

"Oh." Tayla laughs lightly. "I've already been matched. But . . . so has he. Four times, in fact. Can you imagine that?" She leans her elbows on the high counter and bats her eyes at him. "Why would a company that guarantees a ninety-nine percent accuracy rate match anyone *four* times?"

"Right." He takes a deep breath. "So, that's above my pay grade. I'll see who I can get to assist you."

"To be clear," I say from behind Tayla, "we're not leaving until *someone* assists us."

"Have a seat." He motions to the oversize white chairs behind us.

I sink into one, and Tayla leaves a seat between us.

"Looks like Cupid threw up in here," I observe, taking in the abundance of hearts and red, white, and pink floral arrangements. Does the floor have actual rose petals? Nope. Just a petal pattern.

"The decor did give me a moment of hesitation when I arrived." Tayla laughs.

"Only a moment?"

"Every story I heard everywhere kept pointing in this direction. *They* were the solution. Desperate times and all that." Her purse is on her lap, and she drags it closer to her chest.

"I never asked you why," I say, staring at my feet instead of looking at her.

"Why what?"

"Why you felt desperate enough to chuck all your money away."

She tucks her dark hair behind her ears and doesn't answer right away. "Dean and Ruby are happy. They met through Soulmates Reunited. I'd tried other methods. Dated other people. No one seemed to fit with me, or I didn't fit with them." With a sigh, she makes eye contact. "I'm not saying this to be an asshole, but no one was you, Si. What we had . . . I couldn't seem to find it again."

Earlier I said I wouldn't push her if she truly didn't want anything to do with me, but dropping a comment like that in my lap is practically begging me to persuade her we *can* work. She thought my one attempt at reconciliation was weak last time. Maybe it was. I was afraid of being a Jada—or truthfully, my mother—someone who didn't know when to let go. What's the right thing to do? Forge ahead or bow out?

"Excuse me." The receptionist has returned. "Michael and Jessica will see you in the conference room. Before we go there, you'll need to be searched by security and go through our metal detectors."

Metal detectors and security? I have a feeling we aren't the first unsatisfied customers they've encountered.

Tayla and I exchange a glance before rising to our feet and following him. Instead of taking the opaque glass double doors in front of us, the receptionist holds open a heavy metal door to the right. We climb a steep set of stairs to another floor, and he uses his key to unlock the entrance. At the top of the stairs, we pass our things through a metal detector and a scanner. On the other side, two guards pat us down before a waiting woman indicates for us to follow her.

We wind our way through hallways of closed offices. Unlike downstairs, everything up here is sleek, modern, impersonal, the opposite of the warm vibe they are clearly trying to create in the matching area. Who works here?

At the end of the hallway, a large glass-walled conference room sits with the city on display through the floor-to-ceiling windows. Even from a distance, the view is stunning, and I wonder whether they picked this place to meet with the hope that the landscape would be distracting and impressive. A company in New York couldn't get this kind of Central Park view without paying some hefty money to either purchase or rent part of this building.

The people I'm assuming are Jessica and Michael are standing on the other side of the conference table, manila folders open in front of them. She's dressed in a figure-hugging red dress, and the suit he's wearing oozes money.

The woman guiding us opens the conference room door, and we're ushered in.

"Tayla," the woman behind the table says, a smile slicing across her face. "I'm Jessica, and this is Michael." She gestures to the man beside her. "We're the owners and developers of Soulmates Reunited. We understand you've been unhappy with your service."

Jessica's voice is like being transported back in time. I rock back on my heels and cock my head. Is it possible?

"You," I say, a frown marring my forehead. "You're the one who called me so many times when I was matched with Jada."

"I'm sorry. Do we know each other?" Her frown matches mine.

"Simon Buchannan." I wait to see whether my name will ring any bells, but she continues to look at me as though I'm the one being an idiot. "I've been matched four times by Soulmates Reunited."

"We are aware of a few anomalies in the system." Michael glances quickly at Jessica. "You're one of them."

"That might explain the first three." I forge on. "But I should have been out of your system before the fourth."

"Why do you think that?" Jessica asks, her frown still creasing her forehead.

I wish she'd stop speaking. Hearing her voice grates on my nerves. Whether she'll admit it or not, I'm positive she's the person who called me several times both in the run-up to my breakup with Tayla and afterward to get me to at least give Jada a chance. If I could shake or slap my past self, we might not be in this position right now.

"After my third match, I called and asked to be removed from your database."

"And you were told . . ." She stares at me.

"That I'd be removed."

"Ah," she says. "We have our customer service repre-sentatives better trained now. Did you read the terms and conditions when you signed up for your online dating site?"

My stomach drops. Does anyone read all the terms and conditions? Those things are usually pages of legal jargon. When was the last time I read every line of the terms and conditions before I signed on the dotted line? Plus, Aaron and I were drinking the night I filled out my profile. "No."

"Well, if you had," she says, opening a folder to her right and removing a highlighted page, "you'd have seen this clause in section four, subsection thirty-four, paragraph ii." She slides the page across the table to me.

"The terms and conditions on a free dating website are that expansive?" Tayla's tone echoes all my disbelief.

"Of course." Jessica's answering tone borders on scathing. "Nothing is *free*. Seems a bit naive for a veterinarian and a nurse to believe otherwise."

"So, you lure men into a dating database you created to prop up a pool for an exclusive service directed at women?" Tayla draws her purse closer to her body as though they might try to snatch more money out of it.

Michael tilts his head back and forth in a gentle motion. "More or less. I'm sure you didn't come here to talk about how our service works. You're unhappy with the outcome, correct? But we have photographic proof of you meeting your match." He nods at me. "Several times in the last few weeks."

They already told Tayla about the photos, probably trying to prevent her complaints from going any further. Clearly, they don't know Tayla, despite their extensive questionnaires. Once she's made a decision, it takes a mountain to move her.

"Doesn't matter," Tayla says, reaching into her purse. "You breached your contract."

"How?" Michael slides photos of us across the table. "The only breach appears to be yours from our side of the table. We agreed to return fifty percent of our matching fee if your match made no contact."

"You matched me with an ex-boyfriend."

"Whom you appear to have a very strong connection with. You're trying to pretend, for some reason I can't understand, and every time he looks at you, he's got his heart in his eyes." Jessica sweeps her hand back and forth between us. "Coming here to tell us we got it wrong, when we *clearly* got it right, is foolish."

"You've matched him *four* times," Tayla counters. "It's not possible to have four soulmates."

"It's possible to have multiple matches, sure." Michael purses his lips. "We don't offer that service, but yes, you can be matched with multiple people."

"Your slogan—" Tayla begins.

"Is branding. Effective marketing, and actually true. Ninety-nine percent of our matches are successful. We don't claim they all end in marriage. More and more people are opting for alternative relationships that don't require cohabitation or an arbitrary piece of paper to legalize their commitment to one another," Michael explains.

"Sounds like spin," I say. "I went on three dates with Jada. What column did that get slotted into for your company statistics?"

"We have to have benchmarks and criteria in order to create statistics. There's nothing wrong with that." Jessica shrugs. "We don't hide those results from people. They're included on page one hundred and forty of our company story."

"Oh my God," Tayla says. "You counted those dates in the 'win' column."

"What is it you were hoping to get out of coming here today?" Jessica asks.

"The truth," Tayla says. "You're scamming people."

Jessica cocks an eyebrow. "What if I told you most people come here looking for a guarantee, and we provide as close to a guarantee as you can get? Our complex algorithms match people successfully every day."

"But if you're counting success as three dates, it's a faulty measure," I say even as I internally cringe at her use of *guarantee*. There are no guarantees. Life is what you make of it. It took me a while, but I get that now. I glance at Tayla. She can leave America hating me, but I won't have her leave thinking I didn't try hard enough again. My resolve solidifies.

"What's your real issue, Miss Murphy? Is it that you were matched with an old flame or that it didn't work out this time?" Michael asks.

"Both," Tayla says, straightening.

"We can offer you a second match as compensation. We've done that for . . ." He flips through the pages in front of him. "Here it is. We did that for Sherri Smith and Jennifer Espinoza when their matches with Mr. Buchannan weren't successful."

"What?" Tayla and I exchange a look of confusion. They sat across the table from us and acted as though Soulmates Reunited had done them equally wrong. Sure, they didn't get a refund, but it wasn't quite the one-and-done situation they allowed us to believe either. Our whole argument is built on Soulmates Reunited being deceptive liars who don't give people a second chance. That this whole program is an elaborate scam, at least for some people.

"Sherri Smith was matched a second time. Also unsuccessful, but she rejected him. We have her listed as married now, so she must have found someone on her own. Jennifer Espinoza was also offered a second match, but she opted not to meet him."

"Did they tell you that?" I mutter to Tayla almost under my breath.

"No," she whispers back.

"What about Jada?" I counter.

"She's refused all interventions on our part." Michael lifts a thick file from beside him on the right and slides it across to me. "I think you'll find a rather colorful documentation of your dating history for the last six years, including a copy of the personal protective order you issued."

"You knew she was still keeping track of me and didn't tell me? I got a fucking restraining order." I'm not opening that file. Nothing good will come of seeing it laid out across this table. My relationships have been short but plentiful. To think she's been spying on me, albeit from a distance, causes my stomach to roll.

"Company emails are filtered and sorted based on subject line. We didn't realize the file your initial match had compiled was that large until Miss Murphy was paired with you. At that point, we offered Miss Murphy the fifty percent reduction if you made no contact."

In other words, they created a folder for all Jada's craziness and filtered it there to avoid dealing with her anymore. They didn't have a problem digging into it when Tayla asked for her money back, though.

My head hurts from all this new information coming at me all at once, and I rub my temples.

"I want my refund," Tayla says.

Have we abandoned the others? I think we have.

"Or?" Jessica asks, eyebrows raised. "You must have come here thinking you had something on us. We've explained Mr. Buchannan's involvement, the history with his other matches, and our position on branding and statistics. Nothing is hidden."

"But you make the information hard to access."

"The book outlining our company policy, statistics, and branding is a free e-book. Anyone can read it." Michael takes back Jada's file when it's clear I'm not touching it. "We have a podcast and a six-episode season on a streaming service. Season two comes out soon. There's a wealth of information available to the public."

"But does *anyone* read that e-book? You're cherry-picking what to tell your clients, what the public sees or hears," I say. They're probably suppressing anything that isn't flattering for the podcast or TV show. I'm convinced they've done that with blogs and chat room posts.

"Of course we are," Jessica says, exasperated. "What company doesn't select their most flattering statistics for advertising and promotion purposes? The fact is: our system works." She gestures between the two of us. "Tell me you two aren't the least bit compatible. Mr. Buchannan, if you'd given any of those other women even a little bit of a chance, they'd have been compatible too."

I turn and stare at Tayla because I've made myself clear. For me, she's it. There is no one else in the world I'd rather spend the rest of my life with. But if she'd rather have her money back than admit we're compatible, I'm not going to hold her back.

Tayla takes a deep, shuddering breath, and I hold mine while I wait to see what she'll say.

Chapter Thirty-seven

TAYLA

As much as I want my money back, I can't crush Simon when he's standing right next to me, and when he's as aware of the truth as everyone else in the room seems to be. Are Simon and I compatible? Yes. Does that mean Soulmates Reunited isn't a fraud? I don't know.

"We are compatible," I say carefully. "But when I expressed dissatisfaction at the match, I think your company should have immediately offered me another one."

Beside me, Simon shoves his hands into the pockets of his pants, his shoulders slumping.

That is how I felt the day we were matched. Now? I'm in a tailspin on a ride I didn't sign up for, or rather signed up for in a drunken fit, and I'm not sure how to get off. Tomorrow I'm moving to fucking Scotland.

All morning, my mind's been on a Tilt-a-Whirl circling everything Simon said in bed. My brain is mush, and I really need to be at the top of my game during this conversation. I want my money back, but given those women weren't exactly straight with me, I'm less concerned about getting their costs returned. No one told me Soulmates Reunited would offer other options; instead, I've believed I was riding to the rescue.

"What you were told or not told is a training issue, and we will address that for future clients," Michael concedes. "To the best of our knowledge, your experience of being matched with an ex has never happened before. We don't have any documentation of it happening. Your concern should have been escalated, and for that, we apologize."

Jessica takes a slip of paper out of the folder in front of her. "At this point, though," Jessica says, "according to subsection twenty-six of the contract, we've fulfilled our legal and moral obligations to you. You were matched. You met your match. You *dated* your match, and it hasn't worked out."

"If I can't get my money back, I'll tell everyone that I think you're a fraudulent company," I say.

"I wouldn't suggest that route." Michael gestures to the glass door behind us, and another man in a suit steps in. "Our team of lawyers is well practiced at winning libel cases behind closed doors. That would be an expensive mistake."

My mind is already ticking through how I can turn this around. If my money is gone, I'm screwed financially until I can start getting payments from the veterinary practice in Scotland. Surviving isn't impossible—Angus offered to cover some things if my refund didn't come through (though I never told him what I was being refunded for)—but finances will be incredibly tight. Not at all the experience I hoped to have.

"I shouldn't have contacted her," Simon says. "At least give her the original half you offered."

"Did you go on dates?" the lawyer asks, circling the table to stand beside Michael.

"You know we did," I say.

"Then, as I'm sure Jessica said, Soulmates Reunited fulfilled their part of the contract. As terrible as it might seem to you, the company met its legal contractual obligations." The lawyer flips open one of the slim folders that have been resting in front of Jessica and Michael. "I can take you through the contract in depth if that'll help you reconcile how you've ended up here."

"No," I whisper. "That won't be necessary."

"I want out of the database. I never want to be matched again." Simon runs a hand through his hair before shoving it back into his front pocket. "Can you guarantee this won't happen again?"

"Absolutely. We can ban your email address; if you do sign up for *any* online dating again, we won't collect your account a second time." Michael takes out papers from a folder and passes them across the table to Simon.

The thought of Simon dating someone else, being with someone else, is a vise around my chest. Tears prick at my eyes. Why hasn't this reality crossed my mind before now?

Think of something else. You can't cry in here. Focus on this moment.

They didn't know we were coming, but they've managed to get the relevant paperwork together with so little notice. It makes me wonder how many times they've done this, and it makes me realize how unprepared we were in coming here. The lawyer said this was a long shot, but I didn't want to hear it.

Even now, it occurs to me that I should do more digging, but the truth is, given that I'm leaving the country tomorrow, I have bigger things to worry about than whether Soulmates Reunited is deceiving other people. In less than twenty-four hours, I'll be living on another continent. No matter how many times the thought pops up, it doesn't get less weird. With Simon so solid and present beside me, the reality that we'll never be like this again is sinking in, and my insides are threatening to revolt.

I am a liar. I've been lying to myself, to him. I lied to them. I'm not sorry they matched me with Simon. Maybe I should be, but every time I look at him, all I can think about is how much I don't want to leave.

Whatever pulses between us can't be denied, shoved down, or rejected. Comfort. Connection. Desire. Simon was right earlier. What we've found in each other is lightning in a bottle.

Why did I agree to move to Scotland?

Jessica clears her throat. "Was there anything else we could help you with today?"

The tone of her voice grates on me, but the truth is, they've won. I can't afford a libel suit, and like Simon's lawyer predicted, getting blood from a stone turned out to be impossible. We didn't have enough. Simon's case, especially when they accommodated his other matches, is only a disaster for us.

Jessica picks up the phone beside her and turns away from us to speak to someone. When she faces us again, there's a tight smile on her face.

The same woman who showed us to the conference room opens the door behind us. "I'll show you back to reception," she says.

While we wend our way to the reception desk, we're both quiet. I'm not sure how Simon is feeling, but I'm in shock about how differently that went than I expected.

We exit the stairwell, and in the front room, the receptionist is greeting another woman and showing her through the double doors. Was that really me a few short weeks ago?

Simon stops a few paces in front of me and looks back. "You okay?"

Funny how some stretches of life can alter a person so completely.

Coming here didn't work out how I expected it to, but I'm not sorry I came. I might not have gotten what I wanted out of the experience, but I think I've gotten what I needed in the end.

Simon holds the door open, and I follow him through to the bank of elevators. We ride to the main floor in silence, and I don't have the guts to ask him what he's thinking. Is he as twisted up as I am?

Outside the building, we watch traffic go past—on foot, in vehicles—and we still don't speak.

"Guess that lawyer was right after all," I say. "We were never going to be the ones to prove them liars."

"No regrets," Simon says. "They wronged you. They even admitted that much. We had to shoot our shot." He takes a deep breath. "Listen, Tay, I can give you at least half the money. More, if you want. Like we originally agreed."

"I don't want your money, Simon." When I glance up at him, our gazes lock. I'm not sure any of this has ever been about the money, even if I could use it now.

"Less than twenty-four hours until you'll be on a plane," Simon says, his voice husky. "Spend the day with me. I know you're leaving, and you're not going to change your mind. But the thought of ending things like this—of never seeing you again—"

His voice cracks, and my heart cracks with it. I've been so focused on getting my money, moving to Scotland, and getting away from Simon that I haven't fully processed what *getting away from Simon* actually means. Spending the day with him might make leaving tomorrow one hundred times worse, but the idea of not spending today with him makes me want to curl into the fetal position on the dirty New York sidewalk. My heart, which I've tried so hard to suppress the last couple of weeks, is waging war on my head. *This is it* is on repeat, and the realization we might never see each other again causes a heaviness to settle inside me. I just want to ignore what's gone wrong and bask in what's good between us one more time before I let it—and him—go.

"Let's give ourselves one last good memory." Simon cups my face, and I fall into his green gaze. I don't ever want to crawl back out.

"Yes," I whisper. "Yes."

Chapter Thirty-eight

SIMON

I'm trying not to read too much into her breathy "Yes" in the middle of a New York City sidewalk, but there's a massive amount of hope stirring in my chest.

I take out the NYC guide from my back pocket and unfold it. "We're close to Central Park," I say. "And if I remember correctly, you've always wanted to do the rowboat thing."

"Yeah." She glances up at me, and her eyes are soft with something I don't dare name. "Is that okay with you?"

"I could row us around a piddly lake." I flex my bicep for her. I'm defaulting to humor, desperate to unsettle the weight of her leaving.

"You're right." She squeezes my bicep, but her tone

isn't as carefree as I'd expect. "These muscles could do it." She falls into step beside me, and after a few minutes, she says, "Did you know they have egrets and herons and loons on the lake?"

"Trust you to know the local wildlife." On instinct, I kiss her temple and draw her into my side. We lost our battle with Soulmates Reunited, but I don't want to miss one second of whatever time I've got with Tayla today. This long goodbye will have to tide me over for the rest of my life.

We wander toward the nearest entrance to Central Park, and Tayla's hand slides down my arm until our fingers are linked. Holding hands? My heart kicks. *Don't question it. Don't read into it. You asked for one last good day, and you're getting it.* The reminder she's leaving makes my gut clench. Whatever she wants, I'm going to give and give and give until I've wrung myself dry. There will be lots of time for regrets, but I'm not going to let today, any part of today, be one of them.

When we get to the lake, I pay for the rowboat, and we climb aboard. Once we're settled, I follow Tayla's directions, and we row out into the lake, careful to carve our own space.

"So, why Scotland?" There's no point in pretending it's not happening. Tomorrow she'll be gone.

"Angus was the first one to email me?" She bites her lip and doesn't meet my gaze.

That sounds desperate more than determined, and my inkling about her reasoning for going to Scotland grows. "You only get limited options for the exchange?"

"No." She sighs and leans back on her elbows, staring

out over the water. "You can set as many limits as you want. I changed mine when I'd had a bit too much wine, and I agreed to this exchange in a burst of pettiness."

"Well, that's . . ." I struggle with how to respond. "Honest."

"Now I'm—now I'm having emailer's remorse." Her voice grows thick.

"Tay, if you don't want to go—"

"I can't back out now. I leave tomorrow. Angus is arriving at my house sometime today. It's too late for backing out. Maybe once I get there, it'll be great. Maybe I'll love it."

Except she's already clearly miserable, and in my experience, going into anything new with so much reluctance doesn't tend to turn out well. "Okay," I say carefully. "Tell me one thing you're excited about."

"Easy. The farm." She takes a deep breath. "Only I'm a bit worried about figuring out how to balance the work."

"Angus must have help?" The rowing rhythm is soothing and makes it a little less stressful to discuss her walking out of my life.

"He's been doing it alone, but he's left me contact info for some people I can hire if it's too much for me."

"I wish I had some good advice for you, but I've lived in the same apartment in the same part of the city since I left college. I didn't even go to college out of state." Up until now, how stationary I've always been hasn't occurred to me. Could I do what Tayla's doing? Would I even want to?

"But you like to travel." She meets my gaze. "You've always liked to travel."

"It's one thing to vacation. A whole other thing to transplant your life someplace else." For the most part, I've been content with my life in Grand Rapids. Not sure I could label my days and nights as happy anymore, but I'm not unhappy either.

"You don't think you could do it?"

"Move to another country like you're doing?"

"Yeah."

Is this a test? If she asked me, I'd go. "For the right reason—for the right person—I'd move in a heartbeat."

"You don't think you'd feel like you were giving up too much? Your apartment, your job, visits with your sister's kids . . ."

There's a chance I'm reading her line of questioning wrong. Is she considering asking me? Would she do that? "Do you feel like you're giving up too much?"

"I don't know yet." Her expression is thoughtful as she searches my face.

Well, all right then. Throw down the gauntlet and I'll wade through the blows. If she hasn't made up her mind, I'll give her something else to think about. "I don't think I'd feel like I was giving up too much in a situation like yours, since it's only a year."

"A lot can happen in a year," she says, her voice quiet. "People move on, go in different directions."

"Depends on if there's something worth waiting for, I guess." If she's not going to ask me to come, if she's trying to suggest I wait for her, I can cover that answer too. Any sliver of hope, I'll grasp. I've already waited six years. What's one more?

"I guess, yeah." Her voice is wistful, and she stays focused on the view. "I think maybe I'm just nervous because it's such a big change. Once I get there, I'll be fine."

All the hope blooming inside me withers and dies. She'll be fine without me. Will I ever be fine without her?

It's a gorgeous summer day, so we spend the rest of our daylight hours wandering Central Park and occasionally dipping out to sample other highlights of New York City. After our conversation in the rowboat, Tayla steers clear of her impending trip, laughing or chatting about whatever comes to mind while clinging to my hand or my bicep or slinging her arms around my waist. Apparently, she's not just an octopus in her sleep. The connection should buoy me up. It almost feels like she's not leaving at all, like maybe we're a couple on a long weekend away.

But in the back of my mind, there's a constant niggling thought—*This is the last*—and while I try not to let it taint our interactions, it's not easy to pretend to be carefree when my heart is so fucking heavy.

"Dinner?" I suggest when she mentions her feet are aching from all our walking.

She bites her lip and checks the time on her phone. "An early one? At the hotel? My flight is so early. They have some sort of rooftop bar and restaurant. That'd be nice, wouldn't it?"

"It's your last night in America. Whatever you want, I'll deliver." My smile is fleeting.

Our hands reconnect, and then she lets go to wrap her arms around me as we walk the few blocks back to our hotel. I'm not sure how to take this clinginess, but I'm worried if I point it out, she'll go back to building a wall of pillows between us.

She's nervous about leaving. I'm the only familiar person in NYC, so I'm probably reading more into her behavior than I should. If she wanted me to come with her, or if she wanted me to wait a year, she'd ask, wouldn't she? Is it fair for me to suggest either one? The whole reason, as far as I can tell, that she took the exchange was to get away from me. Inserting myself isn't exactly giving her the space she was so keen to achieve.

We shift around each other in the tiny hotel room, bodies grazing, gazes connecting, and the atmosphere is charged with sexual tension, once muted, now cranked to full blast. The ruse is wearing thin, and I'm not sure how much longer I can pretend we're solid and happy and in love before my heart cracks open at her feet.

"It's been a good day, hasn't it?" she whispers, her honey-brown eyes on mine when I come out of the bathroom, showered and dressed for dinner.

"The best." My voice is gruff because I've just spent the last fifteen minutes steeling myself to let her go tomorrow. *Twelve hours*. Her reminder of how good we can be together slices through me.

Across from each other at the table on the rooftop terrace, I search her face, and it's the first time I've sensed sadness clinging to her the same way it's been clinging to me.

"Thank you," I say after the waiter has taken our order and we're alone with our drinks.

"For what?" A hint of a smile.

"For giving us today. I'm gonna—" I clear my throat. "I'm gonna cherish the memories from today."

Tears fill her eyes, and she breaks eye contact. "I don't want to be sad, okay? Tomorrow is going to be hard no matter what, but I don't want it to bleed into today."

I take a deep, shuddering breath. *Pretend. Pretend. Pretend.* Then fall apart. Seems easy enough, right? "Yeah. Okay." I rub my face and stare out at the view across the city. "Is your brother going to come visit you?"

She perks up at the shift in topic, and she's off on a ramble about her brother. While she talks, I sip my beer and drink her in, savor how surreal it is having her across a table from me, giving me pieces of herself.

"Do you ever think there're people we're meant to meet?" I ask when she peters out.

"Like a soulmate?" She gives me a wry smile.

"Despite the fuckery of Soulmates Reunited, I actually do believe there are some connections that are once in a lifetime." An answering smile tips the edges of my mouth.

"So, what's the point when it doesn't work out?"

I suck in a sharp breath. "I'd like to think we learn something from all those people in one way or another." Sadness isn't allowed, but apparently bluntness is fair game.

"What'd you learn from me?" She takes a gulp of her wine.

"How important it is to be honest." There's no hesitation. Had I been honest with her six years ago, six weeks ago, our lives would be completely different. Today wouldn't have been a bittersweet dream—it would be my reality. She would have clung to me because she loves me, not because she's afraid to leave everything she's ever known.

"Tell me your truth right now. Tell me something you don't think I want to hear."

The challenge is clear. She wants ugly, but there's no ugliness left. There's just my heart in tatters, but I'm fairly sure she doesn't want it. Whatever hope rose between us earlier, her comment about relationships not working out is a clear retreat.

I take a deep breath and maintain eye contact because I want her to know I mean this, mean it with everything in me. "I'd toss out my whole life and follow you to Scotland if you asked. I'd do long distance like a champ for a year if you wanted me to wait. Hell, I'd just wait, even if we weren't together, even if you wanted the year to be sure I was worth it. I'd wait as long as you wanted."

Her eyes have grown very wide and glassy. "I don't—I don't know what to say."

"It's okay." I drop my gaze from hers as the waiter approaches with our food. "You don't have to say anything, but that's my truth." My heart beats a heavy staccato rhythm in my ears, and the food, which looks delicious, could be rocks for all the taste I'm absorbing while I chew.

A long silence settles between us, and I wonder if I went too far, revealed more than she wanted to hear. But I held my truth too tight last time, and it crippled us. At least now she knows, without a doubt, where I stand.

"One of the things I loved about you from the minute

I met you was that you never discouraged me from going after what I wanted, even when my dreams might not have aligned exactly with yours. The big dreams were the best ones with you," she whispers.

Our gazes connect over the expanse of table. There's so much warmth spreading across my chest that I think I might be able to heat the entire surface of the patio. Her words don't stanch the bleeding in my heart at the notion that our dreams aren't aligning, but the sentiment makes me feel like maybe she won't hate me when she leaves the country. That it's possible I didn't completely ruin everything twice.

"My dream is you, Tay. It's just you. Everything else can be replaced." It's my last-ditch attempt to get her to ask me to come. I won't insert myself into the life she's seeking if she doesn't want that, but I can't have her leave wondering if I truly would do anything to be with her.

"I'm not sure I'm in the right frame of mind to be making any sort of big, life-changing decisions tonight. This move is a bit terrifying, and whatever I'd say to you, I don't know if I'd mean it. I think I should mean it."

"There's no pressure. I get how badly I fucked up. But I—if the choice is mine, I choose you. Any road that leads me to you, I choose that one." I cannot possibly be any more blunt, but I don't want to leave New York with the sense that if I'd said one more thing or put myself out there a bit more she might have let me stay in her life, might have welcomed me back into it fully. She's not saying yes, but it's not a no either. Right or wrong, I'm clinging to that.

Until she slams the door in my face again, there's still hope.

Chapter Thirty-nine

TAYLA

We're at the door to our hotel room, and I press my back against it, not getting out the key to let us in. Simon braces his hands on either side of the frame and stares down at me. Green eyes so vibrant they almost don't seem real. A maze I could get lost in.

Fear shouldn't drive a decision like this, should it? His words from dinner keep circling, refusing to lie still. I can't ask him to uproot his life because I'm afraid to go alone. Is that what I'm feeling? Afraid to go alone or afraid to lose him? If I ask him, it should be because having him anywhere but there just doesn't make sense.

A wave of sadness crashes into me at the thought of never seeing him again. If I don't ask him to come or to wait or something, if we leave things as they are now, tonight will be the end of us. I've been afraid to stay, and now I'm afraid to go, but more than anything, I've been afraid he'll hurt me again. Instead, I wonder whether I'm just hurting myself.

When our gazes meet, I frame his face, and then I kiss him like I'm leaving tomorrow, like we'll never get another night like tonight. Because no matter what, tomorrow afternoon I'll be alone in Scotland. We'll never be in New York City staring down this abyss of uncertainty again. If we ever come back, we'll be different people in a different place. Somehow, through fate or chance or circumstance, we found our way back to each other, and I don't want to waste this time being angry or wishing we came together another way. Whatever path we took to get here, this is where we are.

His arms circle me, one hand between my shoulder blades and the other gripping my ass, drawing me close enough to feel how much he wants me.

"Are you sure about this?" Simon asks between kisses.

"I'm sure." Being with him like this might be the only thing I *am* sure of right now. The feel of his body against mine is all I want—no thinking required.

I fish the keycard out of my purse, slipping it into the lock and opening the door while drawing him into another kiss. He walks me backward, and I bang into the rollaway bed.

"Ow," I cry when my calf hits the sharp metal corner.

Simon swings me into his arms and walks over the beds until we're just below the headboard. He lays me down, takes off my shoes, and examines my calf where I clipped the bed.

"I think you'll survive," he says, gazing up at me under his lashes, my foot still in his hand.

"Not if you don't get up here. No one wants to spend time with my feet right now."

"Believe me when I say I've spent time with much worse." He chuckles.

"Oddly," I say, tugging his shirt over his head, "I don't need any of those stories right now."

We shed our clothes in a flurry of rushed movements, but once we're skin to skin, Simon traces his index finger along my body, and the air in the room shifts from frantic to something bordering on melancholy.

"I don't want to be sad tonight," I murmur. Tears are likely to be constant companions tomorrow. They don't need to ruin these last moments together like this.

"You think this is sadness?" Simon asks, his gaze following his finger. "This is reverence."

"You revere me?" A smile blooms. Simon has a romantic soul.

"Oh no." He chuckles. "Just your body."

I punch his shoulder, and he laughs more before cupping my cheek and kissing me deeply.

When he breaks the kiss, he plants another on the crown of my head and then dots kisses down my body. "I revere you from the top of your head," he says, "all the way down to the soles of your feet. Forgive me for doing a little memorization work tonight." His voice catches on the last sentence.

A burst of sadness, the thing I've been fleeing all night, seizes me, and I thread my hands through his short strands. "Come with me to the airport tomorrow?"

He slides back up my body, braces a hand on either side of my head, and stares down at me. "You want me to ride with you in the cab?"

"Yes. Please." Tears fill my eyes. "Maybe come into the airport to see me off?"

"Aww, Tay. Of course I'll come."

I wrap my arms around his neck and drag him down into a kiss. My heart feels like it's breaking even as he drives my body to the brink.

I love you. I love you. I love you.

But the words never leave my lips.

When the alarm goes off in the morning, I cuddle closer to Simon and keep my eyes closed. He reaches over me and bangs the snooze button.

I take a deep, shuddering breath, bolstering myself for probably the longest morning of my life. Thoughts of leaving, ones I was able to keep mostly at bay yesterday, are seeping in, threatening to drown me in sorrow. I shouldn't be sad to go to Scotland. I should be excited, but there are tears pricking at the backs of my eyes.

He kisses the top of my head and envelops me in a hug. "I'm a phone call, a text, an email away. You're never alone if you don't want to be, okay?"

"When did you learn all the right things to say?" My voice is husky with the tears I'm trying to ward off.

"Maybe after saying all the wrong things first? I'm a trial and error kinda guy."

I've been holding back my feelings for him as a last bastion against potential hurt. The words are there, begging to be spoken. Maybe if we'd had more time together in Michigan, things would be different. I'd be able to get past what's happened between us this time, trust him again, say those words with all the feeling and none of the uncertainty. The hurt and the love are so hard to separate.

He kisses me on the forehead and then stares down at me for a beat. "I brought you something, and I wasn't sure if I should give it to you. But I think I should. You can open it when you get to Scotland." He climbs off the bed and pads to his backpack. From inside, he draws out a box wrapped in paper, slightly smaller than a shoebox, and brings it to the bed. "My heart, wrapped in a box." There's false brightness in his tone, as though he's trying not to bring me down.

"I can't open it now?" I wipe away the stray tears sliding down my cheeks.

"You might miss your flight if we hang around here." He glances at the bedside clock.

I have room in my carry-on, and I wedge the box inside. My heart hammers at the thought of opening it alone in Scotland, but at least it gives me something to look forward to once I'm unpacked. One last parting gift—a thought that doesn't help my melancholy mood.

We get dressed and double-check the room for any stray items, and then we're in the cab headed to the airport. While we were still organizing ourselves in the hotel, I could almost pretend this was the end of any vacation. Now that we're in the cab headed to the airport, with only hours before Simon flies back to Grand Rapids, all I can think about is how much I don't want to leave.

A couple of times I ready myself to speak—a quip, a quick remark about something—but the words die on my tongue because putting voice to meaningless words makes me want to burst into tears.

He squeezes my hand in the back seat as though he can read my mind. Maybe his thoughts are the same as mine.

At the airport, we cling to each other for as long as we can before I have to exit the main terminal to get to my gate.

When I can't avoid leaving any longer, we stand at the entrance to security. He frames my face in his hands and kisses me deeply.

"I love you," he rasps.

A sob gets stuck in my chest, and I can't breathe. *Oh God.* I'm going to be that asshole at the airport who can't get herself under control. When the sob rises, Simon holds me against his chest and lets me cry.

"Just tell me what you need, Tay. Tell me what you need, and I'll do it." His voice is thick with tears. "You're breaking my heart." He rubs my back in soothing motions.

But I can't get the words out. I'm not even sure what they'd be. All I know is that I don't want to leave, that the thought of leaving is ripping me in half. The urge to cancel everything is surging through me—to toss aside the exchange and stay here, even though I know I can't.

The responsible side of me can't leave Angus's neighbors caring for the animals when it's supposed to be me. I agreed to this. Foolishly or recklessly, I said yes to living in the middle of nowhere in Scotland for a year. Really, I was saying yes to being away from Simon, and now that's the last place I truly want to be.

"Call me when you get there. Whatever time. Doesn't matter. I just want to know you got there and you're safe." He squeezes me tight. "I love you. Go be amazing."

I close my eyes and breathe him in one last time before I drag myself away. The weight of all the hasty decisions I've made over the last few weeks lies heavy on my back. I weave my way through the rows of partitions until I've joined the line to show my passport. *Don't look back.* If I see him again before I'm through security, I might become a puddle on the floor.

The security person gestures for me to join a line to send my things through the X-ray machine and metal detector. Just before I disappear inside the closed area, I glance back, and Simon is still at the back of the rows, one hand in his pocket, his other wiping his cheek, a lost expression on his face.

My heart. My fucking heart.

The urge to drop everything and run to him storms through me, and I step in the wrong direction. The person behind me makes an annoyed noise.

Simon glances up, and we make eye contact. His stooped shoulders straighten, a hint of a grin tugs at the edges of his lips, and he blows me a kiss.

Instead of crying, an answering smile breaks out across my face. The unexpectedness of the gesture is strangely soothing, as though he knows I need that boost of reassurance more than our shared grief. I blow one back, and the person behind me grumbles about "holding up the line." With an almost unbearable tightness in my chest, I slip inside the enclosed area, and Simon is gone from my sight.

Chapter Forty

TAYLA

Angus's house is a flat-fronted two-story made of some sort of stone. A large expanse of grass stretches out in front, and behind is a series of barns in various states of repair. Sheep and Highland cattle graze in the fields. The dogs wander over to me, tails wagging, and I crouch to give them a reassuring scratch.

"We're going to be roommates," I whisper, and I try to keep the anguish out of my voice. Every minute since I left Simon has felt like torture. The box he gave me sits heavy in my carry-on, but I'm afraid if I open it, I'll fall apart, and I need to get settled.

Angus said these were indoor and outdoor dogs, and he lets them decide where to spend their time with a rear entrance at the back of the house that has a doggy door and their crates for sleeping. Not quite what I'd call indoor, but letting them sleep in my bed would really confuse them when Angus returns. Could they adapt? Rex only sometimes sleeps with Simon.

Simon.

I close my eyes and take a deep, steadying breath. Every time he crosses my mind, the wound of leaving is reopened.

Instead of going into the house, which feels a bit like invading Angus's life, I leave my bags outside the front door and start with the clinic. Although the outside resembles a low barn, the inside is filled with clean spaces and rooms, state-of-the-art equipment, and a fully functioning computer system. Angus sent me photos, but it's hard to get a sense of a place from a snapshot.

Back at the front door, I gather my courage and use the heavy metal key his neighbor hid under the mat earlier today. Angus assured me there wasn't another soul for miles, so leaving the key under the rug wasn't an issue. I suppose by that rationale, they could have left the door unlocked or even wide open. Though both those options would have freaked me out. Wouldn't have been a great start to being out in the middle of nowhere by myself.

On the way here, I hardly understood my cab driver. While he rattled off all sorts of helpful local tips, I wondered how many times I could ask him to repeat himself before I seemed completely inept.

I haul my suitcases into the front hall, which has white walls and black accents. To the right is a narrow set of stairs and what looks to be a sitting room of some sort.

With a deep breath, I peruse the house, taking in the modern kitchen, the older but still comfortable furniture, and the various photos on the walls of Angus and his wife through the years. They never had any children. The thought brings Simon to my mind again, though he hasn't been far from my thoughts since I left New York.

Children with Simon.

I'm in the main bedroom when there's a knock downstairs on the front door.

"Hello?" a male voice calls out.

At least I can recognize that word.

I hustle down the stairs, and an older gentleman stands in the entryway. He lights up when I appear, a grin stretching across his weathered face.

"Aye, you're just a wee lass. Angus asked me to pop in. Said you'd need help gettin' a few things."

"You must be John." I offer my hand in greeting, and his rough, callused one encompasses mine. I hadn't expected him until tomorrow, but the sooner I can get groceries and a phone, the better. I badly, badly need a local cell phone. "Do you mind showing me around?"

"Nae a'tall. Shops close in an hour. We best be gettin' on."

I grab my purse off the top of the pile and follow John out of the house.

After my shower, I come into the bedroom and spot Simon's unopened package on the dresser. Once I returned from shopping with John and texted Simon that I'd arrived safely, I dug out the box and set it here. Part of me wanted to tear it open, have that sense of closeness with him again. Is what's inside funny or sweet?

Since the moment I left him at the security checkpoint, I've teetered on the edge of regret. Should I have asked him to come? What would it be like to be here with him? Better, I think. For so many reasons.

I finger the edge of the wrapping. Cross-legged, I sit on the bed, the package in my hands.

What does Simon Buchannan's heart in a box look like? Isn't that what he called it?

The tenor of his voice, the pitch of his laugh, the exact shade of green in his eyes, and the way his gaze softens when he tells me he loves me are all deeply lodged in my heart. Whatever is in the box might tip the scales in some direction. Convince me I made the right choice or mock me for being an idiot. Maybe whatever is in here will ease the constant sense of loss that's dogging me.

Carefully, I remove the paper and stare at the beat-up box. It looks well used, as though it's been opened and closed a thousand times. My breath catches. Didn't he tell me he had a box in his closet, the same way I had one in mine, now locked in Ruby's basement? *My love* is scrawled across the top in black Sharpie along with a start and end date. I recognize those dates all too well. A memorial of sorts.

My heart pounds, and I lift the lid. Tears spring to my eyes at the trinkets and mementos littering the inside of the cardboard box. Ticket stubs, souvenirs from trips we took, notes I slipped into lunch bags, cards from birthdays and anniversaries, photos of us he had framed in his apartment. Each piece draws out an answering memory in me. My chest swells with love, and tears slip down my cheeks. He kept all of it. I had no idea he clung to us the same way I did. We might have sealed up the memories, but our feelings were merely hibernating, waiting for the thaw.

Goose bumps rise on my arms. Six years. We spent six years apart. Asking him to move here isn't selfish—it can be freeing, healing. A fresh start. A new life together. He'll come if I ask, and for so long after we broke up, I wished I could call him and ask him to come back, that it was possible to rewind time. While I can't rewind what's passed, I can make sure the path ahead is one I want to walk.

As much as I've wanted to deny it, wished at times it weren't true, the person I want beside me through anything is Simon.

Beside me on the bed, my phone vibrates, and Simon's name pops up on the screen with an answering text message.

Glad you made it okay.

The three dots appear and disappear as though he's writing a long message. More likely, he's writing and deleting things. Tears prick at the backs of my eyes for the hundredth time since I said goodbye to him at the airport.

His heart is scattered around me, and any hint of uncertainty vanishes. I love him, and he loves me. The distance I've put between us doesn't need to be there. We can walk this path together.

I slide my finger across the phone and hit Call. Before he can get out any words after a surprised hello, I say, "Move to Scotland. Come live with me. I opened the box. I don't want to be away from you anymore."

"What?" He lets out a startled laugh. "Move to Scotland?" There's a beat, and then he says, "Yes. I'll move. If you're serious, I'll move."

"I love you. I want you here, but I've—God, Simon, I've been so afraid to believe we could have this again. Neither of us can go back. We can't change any of the decisions or choices we've made. I don't want to lose you this time because I'm too afraid to voice my fears and feelings."

"Christ, Tayla. I love you too. Never loved anyone the way I love you. If you want me there, I'm there."

"I do. I do want you here." I choke on a sob. I take in all the mementos spread out across the bed, and another wave of certainty sweeps over me. "I want to make more memories with you. Come make memories with me, Si. I think—I *know*—we can make it work."

"I know we can too," Simon says, his voice warm and gentle across the distance. "Not a doubt in my mind."

We fall into an easy banter as we work out the details of his move. Underneath our conversation, a new calmness sweeps over me. Soon we'll be standing shoulder to shoulder tackling this new experience together.

"You sound happy," Simon says.

"I am," I admit. For the first time in weeks, a decision I've made is inspiring a rush of certainty instead of confusion. "I can't wait for you to get here."

♥

A month later, I lead Simon out of the barn at the end of his tour, Rex at his heels. I can't remember the last time I felt this buoyant. Light. As though I could float off into the sunset, perfectly content.

After I picked him up at the airport, we spent most of the day mapping each other's bodies and celebrating his arrival. To see him again in person has been exhilarating. Whoever said absence makes the heart grow fonder must have done some serious long distance because when I caught sight of him at the airport, it felt like my heart was going to fly out of my chest.

When he enveloped me in a crushing hug, I couldn't get close enough. So we spent the rest of the day being as close as possible.

The farm introduction has waited until now, and Simon has shown his usual enthusiasm for the animals and routines in place. Just before we get back to the house, his steps stall in the gravel behind me.

"Wait," he says.

I turn to face him, and the fields are bathed in the fading light of the sunset. Pink and orange dust the sky, mixing with the pale blue. He draws me against him to gaze out over the property.

"Pretty, isn't it?" I say.

We stare out in silence, the sound of the farm animals breaking the stillness once in a while. The decision to ask him to come here feels right, even better than I expected. This is where I'm meant to be, and Simon is who I'm meant to be with.

"Thank you," Simon says, his voice thick with emotion.

I glance at him over my shoulder, and I link my fingers with his at my waist. "For what?"

"For giving me another chance, for letting me back in, for showing me that fear of the unknown can be beautiful instead of scary. What an adventure we're going to have." His voice is husky.

I turn in his arms and frame his face. "I'm going to love you forever, Simon Buchannan."

He kisses me, and I pour my heart into the embrace, give him every ounce of love I've been storing up for weeks, months, years. Then he sweeps me into his arms and carries me toward the house, and there's no doubt in my mind that, if soulmates do exist, he's mine.

Epilogue
TAYLA

Simon and I have four weeks left in Scotland. Our adventure has almost come to an end. Although we've adjusted well to this new life, Angus hasn't enjoyed living in a city as much as he thought he would. Too busy. Too noisy. Too much. At one point, we feared he might cut the exchange short. He's toughed it out, but he's not keen to go even one day more than necessary.

I wave to my vet tech, Eleanor, as she climbs into her tiny car and starts her journey home. With the door to the vet practice locked, I take in the surrounding hills and green pastures. There's been something soul cleansing about living out here, completely removed from almost all the noise of my old life. We've found our rhythm, and we're even talking about investing in our own version of Angus's life in the Michigan countryside, assuming we can find the right location.

Simon emerges from the barn, wiping his hands on a cloth, Rex trailing behind him. "All done?"

"Until the next emergency strikes." That's only partially a joke. Being a large animal vet in the middle of nowhere has led to some harrowing experiences.

"Shower?" he suggests, and he glances up at the cloudless sky. "Looks like a nice night. Pasture picnic?"

"You are a man after my own heart. You're going to smell good and take me on a picnic?" I tease while he loops an arm over my shoulders, drawing me into an embrace. "Animals are all fed and watered?"

"Yes, ma'am. Wouldn't want to disappoint the boss lady."

"I hear she's a real terror."

"Only on the second Tuesday of the week."

"Those damn second Tuesdays," I agree.

He chuckles and kisses the top of my head. "Okay if I shower first, and then I can get everything ready for the picnic?"

"Or," I say, "we could shower together, and then I can answer a few emails while you pack the basket?"

He backs me up against the front door and stares down at me. "You drive a hard bargain, but I can agree to those terms."

"Maybe we can negotiate a few more things in the shower?" I murmur against his lips.

"Probably shouldn't be striking any deals while I'm

immersed in something warm and wet." He kisses a line up my neck.

"I guess we'll find out," I say, tugging him into the house and up the stairs.

I peer out the window after answering my last email. "Do you think it'll be too dark?"

"We've still got at least an hour of light," Simon says, circling my waist with his arms. "Unless you don't want to go anymore?"

I glance at him over my shoulder. "I love our pasture picnics. Only four more weeks, so I'm not going to say no."

He laces his hand with mine and picks up the picnic basket. I grab the blankets we use to keep warm, and Rex and the other dogs trail behind us out into the fields. There's a small stream at the far edge of the property, and we often walk out there to eat meals and daydream about what life will be like once we leave here.

With little else to do besides work on the farm or solve a veterinary crisis, we've had a lot of time to talk. No subject has been off-limits, and I feel like I know Simon, understand him in a way I'm not sure I would have if we hadn't experienced this exchange together.

While he gets the food arranged on plates, I lay out the blankets. When he passes me my share, I can't hold back my smile.

"Where'd you find these plates?" I ask, taking in the hearts around the edges. Whatever is in the center is covered by my food.

"Back of the cupboard." Simon leans back on an elbow and stares into the distance, his plate on the blanket between us.

"I'm going to miss this place." I mirror his pose.

"Me too. But even though everyone has come to visit, it'll be nice to see our friends and family whenever we want."

His father's visit was particularly awkward, but one morning when we were both up earlier than Simon, he actually apologized to me for the part his fears had played in Simon's state of mind almost seven years ago. It was so much easier to be gracious when Simon and I have come so far from the people we were then. We trust each other with the hard questions and answers in a way we didn't before.

While we chat about our days, I pick away at the food on my plate. There's definitely something written underneath. I cock my head, trying to make out the words without moving the rest of the food.

Simon whistles for Rex, who has been trailing the working dogs, getting into mischief. He comes over and sits in front of me.

"What's going on?" I ask. There's something attached to Rex's collar.

"The plate you're eating from—I made it," Simon says, making eye contact. "I made it for you."

I brush aside the last of the bread and grapes on the plate and gasp. There, in Simon's neat handwriting, are the words *Will You Marry Me?*

"Are you serious?" I trace the letters on the plate before meeting his gaze again.

He scoops the tiny bag from Rex's collar and opens the drawstring. On one knee, he presents it to me. "Tayla Murphy, there is no one in the world I love more than you, no other person I can imagine spending the rest of my life with. You are my other half, my soulmate, my perfect match. Will you marry me?"

With a trembling hand and tears in my eyes, I hold out my fingers for him to slip the ring on. Once it's settled, I launch myself at him, knocking him onto the blanket with an oomph.

"That's a yes?" He chuckles. "This feels like a yes."

"Yes! Yes! A hundred, million, trillion times yes." I shower him with kisses, and then he cups my face, drawing me into a deeper kiss.

"Thank God. I was so fucking nervous," Simon says when we draw apart.

"About proposing?"

"Mostly about Rex losing the ring." He grins. "I was trying to act all nonchalant because I didn't want you to know what I had planned until you were done eating, but when he went into the stream for a drink, I almost dove in after him."

I laugh and roll off him, so my head is cradled on his arm. I turn my hand from left to right, letting the ring catch the fading light. "I'm going to be your wife."

He kisses the top of my head.

"You made me a plate," I whisper, remembering the red hearts, the careful, neat letters.

"All your best moments are celebrated with a plate. How could I not?"

"I knew we'd get married at some point because we talked about it, but this was perfect." Out here in our favorite picnic spot, on a plate Simon made me, delivered by the dog we picked out together so long ago. I can't imagine a better moment. "I love you, Simon."

"I love you too, Tay. The future might not always be easy, but it'll be better for having you at my side."

I squeeze him tight and sigh into his chest. Wherever life takes us, we'll navigate it together.

Acknowledgments

I am incredibly blessed to have an understanding spouse and two kids who can cope with me being glued to my laptop from time to time. Thank you to Jay, Hannah, and Autumn for being so supportive as I pursue this writing dream.

Without my dad, who loves spending time with his grandkids and loaning me a desk in his basement, I wouldn't be able to focus when edits roll in.

My Wattpad and marketing family have been extremely helpful in getting this book to where it is today. Deanna saw a spark in the story, Margot helped me brighten that up, Andrea polished my timeline, and Lee gave it one last pass to really make it shine.

Lesley Worrell's cover design is such a fun, bright interpretation of Tayla and Simon's romance, and I'm grateful for her time and expertise. I fell in love with the yellow-and-red design the minute it landed in my inbox (much like Tayla did with Simon ;)).

Thanks to Monica, Rachel, Anna, and Literally Yours PR who've helped to put this book in the hands of readers.

Writing can sometimes feel pretty isolating, and I feel blessed to have the support of Avery, Cole, the Nottpad community, the Wattpad Creators community, and all my readers on Wattpad who cheer me on from the comment section.

I can't wait to see what comes next.

About the Author

Wendy Million is a high school teacher and Watty Award winner whose contemporary romances about strong women and troubled men have captivated her loyal Wattpad readers. She is the author of the romantic suspense series The Donaghey Brothers, the contemporary second chance romance *When Stars Fall*, and the sports romance *Saving Us*, which all began on Wattpad. When not writing, Wendy enjoys spending time in or around the water. She lives in Ontario, Canada, with two beautiful daughters, two cute pooches, and one handsome husband (who is grateful she doesn't need two of those).

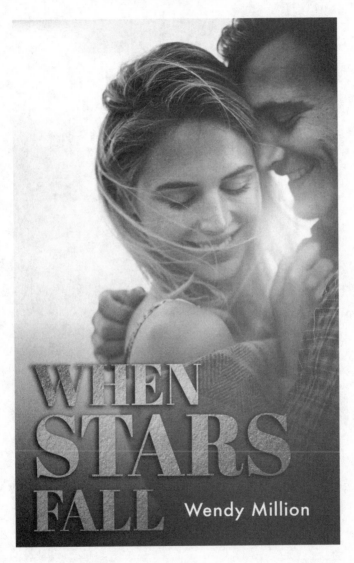

ONE

Wyatt

Ten Years Ago

As soon as the Rolls-Royce pulls into the driveway, I'm out the door of the rambling brick bungalow we share in Bel Air. I haven't seen her in weeks—since I was on location in Shanghai, and she flew home to visit her family.

Before Kyle can get to her door, I take Ellie's hand to draw her out of the back seat. "How'd your visit go?" I cradle her cheeks in my hands, scanning every peak and valley of her face. Something is off. She's hollowed out.

"Fine. Just tired." A weak smile rises, and she closes her eyes briefly.

"Grab her bags, will you, Kyle?" I sweep her up in my arms and carry her through the foyer into the huge open-concept living space. She could walk inside herself, but after so long without her, I'll seize any excuse to hold her close.

"Sure thing, sir," Kyle says.

"Have you eaten? I can make you something." She's lost weight, and she doesn't have a pound to spare. "Did some tabloid say something shitty about you again?"

"No, nothing like that."

When we get to the couch, I set her down. "Talk to me." I sit beside her and then shift to get a better vantage point. "Do you want a Perc to take the edge off?"

"I don't want anything." She twists her hands in her lap, a sure sign she's nervous. If she starts playing with her hair, there's definitely something wrong.

"What's going on?" I ask.

She doesn't say anything for a beat. "I've been thinking a lot lately. About us. Our relationship. About where we're headed."

There's a ring sitting in my underwear drawer. I dragged Isaac with me to choose one a week before he died. I haven't been able to face the diamond since, but I understand what I want.

She leaves the couch and goes over to where Kyle dropped her bags. From a side pocket, she takes out some pamphlets.

Maybe she discovered the ring and spent the week looking at wedding venues in Bermuda. She wouldn't want the chaos an LA wedding would bring. Wherever she wants to get married is fine by me. There's no need for her to be nervous. Not like I'll be mad about any of it.

"What's this?" I try to stifle my amusement.

She tries to pass me the pamphlets and flyers. My brain stalls, and it takes a moment for me to process the bold headlines claiming effective treatment for addictions. A chill streaks across my body. This has nothing to do with weddings and nothing to do with our future. I remove the bottle from my pocket and shake out a Vicodin, then throw it back. I'm not addressing what's written in these things. She's going to have to say it. I set the bottle on the coffee table between us.

After a deep breath, she says, "I think—I think if we want to have a future together, we should be doing that clean and sober."

"This is bullshit." I grab the pamphlets and toss them onto the table and they scatter everywhere. Some of them fall to the floor at her feet. My chest is tight with disbelief. She knows better than anyone what she's asking.

She tucks her hair behind her ears. *Shit, her hair.* She doesn't say anything.

An uncontrollable rage rises in me. "What the hell happened to you on that damned island? We've been together for three, almost four years and you've never asked me to quit. You've *never* said my using was a problem. In fact, Ellie, you do it with me."

"I haven't touched anything since Isaac died."

"You're a liar. We've gone out lots of times." Even as I say those words, I can't remember the last time she accepted a pill or took a drink or did a line of coke. My younger sister, Anna, started calling Ellie a No-Fun Nellie. "Nah, I don't believe you. I would've noticed." She must be lying, otherwise my intake has been much higher than I realized.

She points at a pamphlet on the table. "My mother says this one is very good. The best."

"You think I don't know about rehab programs?" I scoff. "You think I don't have friends who've tried it? Rehab doesn't work. It won't work. I'm not going."

"We're getting older. Maybe we should be considering a family." She rubs her face. "Kids, possibly, someday . . . maybe."

She can't even make eye contact when she says that. She's not serious. Wherever these notions are coming from, she needs to send them packing back to Bermuda. A week ago, she and I were just fine, and now she's returned with a truckload of bullshit ideas.

"No, Ellie. No. You're twenty-four, not forty-four. Don't play the kids card. What the fuck do kids have to do with anything?"

She stares at me, indecision on her face, and then her expression cements into a stubborn mask. "You're out of control."

I take the pills off the table and shove an oxy in my mouth, this time to dull the memory of this conversation, which will hang over us like a cloud. Tomorrow, I won't want to remember she even suggested this. "The only person who gets to decide that is me."

"I want you to quit." She crosses her arms. "Deal with Isaac's death, deal with your parents being terrible. Whatever underlying issues make you want to do this, be like this."

"You knew who I was when you went home with me that first night. I've never lied to you," I say with a harsh half laugh.

"You haven't, but I'm asking you to be better. To want more for yourself—for us."

"Now that you've fucked your way into better jobs and higher paychecks, you think you can dictate some terms?" I shove the coffee table out of the way, and the metal legs shriek against the stone floor. "Come on, Ellie. Where would you be without me? Still pretty far down the call list." The second pill was a mistake. Words are tumbling out of my mouth and I can't stop them. Her tears fall faster than she can brush them away. "Sure, Ellie. Sure. Bust out the tears. They won't work. I'm not going to rehab; I'm not quitting any of it. We were fine until you went home to Bermuda. Who's been pumping you full of this shit? Your mom?

Your sister, Nikki? One of your old high school buddies who saw something on TMZ?"

"*I* want you to go to rehab." Her voice is thick, garbled.

"You're the only one." I throw out my arms. It's incomprehensible that she'd ask this of me.

"I'm not." She shakes her head. "I'm not the only one."

"Your family doesn't count." Her mother has never liked me. Maybe her sister doesn't like me now either. Someone has been feeding her these lines. My Ellie is full of softness and understanding. She doesn't give ultimatums.

"Producers, directors, people who know you have been asking me to do something. To intervene. You're not coping."

A surge of anger courses through me, but not at her—at the people who put her in this position. "They have no idea what they're talking about."

"You'll lose jobs. People won't want to work with you anymore."

"Bullshit. I make people money. I've made you a lot of money over the last four years. Being tied to me is the best thing that ever happened to you."

"It could be," she says. "If you'll get help. You could be the best thing to ever happen to me."

"I don't need help, Ellie. I'm fine. *We're* fine. Screw the rest of them who don't understand."

"*I'm* one of those people. Me. I don't understand anymore either. You need help. I can't—I'm not capable of giving you the help you need."

My mind is muddled. She doesn't ask me to do impossible things. She'd never ask me to choose. We had a pact. "Who put you up to this?"

She takes a deep, shuddering breath. "No one. It's coming from my concern for you. I love you."

"I was clear from the start. If there's a choice, the choice is easy." If she loved me, she wouldn't be asking me to do this.

"Still? After we've been together almost four years?" Her voice catches on a sob.

My resolve wavers. I always let her win. She's not winning this one. Once she cools down, she'll realize I'm right. There's nothing wrong with us. "I told you never to ask."

She snatches a pamphlet off the floor, thrusting it at me again. "Try one of them. Any of them. Just go. Even for a little while. Doesn't matter which one. If you won't get help, I can't stay. I won't watch you spiral." Her rambling pleas are almost incoherent through her tears.

"There are plenty of others who will." I grab the pill bottle off the coffee table. "I'm going out. You have two choices. You can stay and accept that this is who I am, or be moved out by the morning. I'm not going to rehab, and we're *never* having this conversation again."

"Wyatt!" My name is a frantic call as she chases after me to the front entrance. "Wyatt. Stay. Please. We need to talk about this."

"We're done talking. If my not being clean and sober is suddenly a deal breaker for you, then we're broken. I'm serious. Forget about rehab or move out."

"You don't mean that." Her face is already puffy from crying. She's crying so hard I barely understand her words.

"I do. I really do." Before I can reconsider, I slam the door behind me.

She won't leave. Even if she wanted to, packing up and being gone in the next twenty-four hours is impossible. Our lives are too intertwined. Tomorrow, when I come back, we'll pretend like this conversation never happened. Maybe we'll even laugh about it. Ellie loves me. I know she does.

When I climb into the back of the car, my pills press against my leg through my pocket. I take out the bottle, pop off the lid, and stare into the container. Shaking out an Adderall, I throw it into my mouth. A little something to take the edge off, make me completely forget this conversation so I'm not so pissed at her tomorrow.

"Where to, sir?" Kyle asks from the front.

"Drive around for a while and then to a hotel. Doesn't matter which one."

Kyle glances at me in the rearview mirror. "Everything okay, sir?"

"It'll be fine." I glance out the window as we drive onto the street. "Ellie needs a little space."

TWO

Wyatt

Present Day

I'm sweating. Profusely. It's disgusting. I tug at the collar of my freshly pressed shirt and loosen my tie. I'll tighten it before I go on set.

Leaning forward on the couch, I grab my water from the coffee table. Bottles of alcohol line the bar to the right. A sign encourages everyone to help themselves. There is nothing worse than wanting a drink, being surrounded by alcohol, and not being able to have any. I need to be sober for this interview. Ellie will see it.

I grab some candy off the table and pop it into my mouth, chewing slowly. The greenroom is a weird shade of lime. Whenever I'm in a green waiting area, I'm always disappointed. We're in a creative business—lime isn't creative; it's just hard on my eyes. Jackson Billows, the host of the late-night program, probably thinks the color is hilarious.

I wiggle my back along the too-stiff couch. Maybe I've been doing this whole scene too long. Few things in the entertainment business surprise me anymore. Of course, having this big a stage, a platform for my announcement, is helpful. Surprises may be few and far between for me personally, but I can still deliver a couple.

"You're on in five, Mr. Burgess." A dark-haired man pops his head into the room.

I nod. Say nothing. Check my phone again. The few people who understand my plan are reluctantly on board. A last-minute *Break a leg* text rolls in. I turn off my ringer, readjust my tie and collar. My suit jacket is stifling, but she used to like me suited and booted. Every advantage is necessary. I'm about to blow up her life.

For ten years, Ellie has been coordinating her projects and schedule to avoid me. We've developed an unspoken agreement to keep each other and Isaac, my best friend, out of the press. The weight of his death has remained ours to carry.

Jackson enters from the hidden side door. "You all right, buddy?" He perches on a chair across from me.

"Sweating like a pig."

"It's been ten years, man. This will be great television, don't get me wrong, but Ellie is going to eat your nuts for breakfast tomorrow."

"I picked you for a reason, Jack. Don't let me down." I drain the rest of my water and wish the liquid was something much stronger.

"We could have booked you both on the show. Left you here in the greenroom to sort out your issues in private." Jackson stands.

"She'd have canceled. Whenever she's gotten wind I'm in the area, her cavalry rides to the rescue. I even flew to Bermuda and not one person—not one," I say, holding up a finger, "would tell me where she lived."

"What makes you think she's going to take any notice of you this time?" he asks.

"She'll have no choice." Certainty washes over me, and I point to my phone. "Finally got her address. I'm headed to the airport as soon as we're done."

"Ten years and you're just going to show up on her doorstep? Do you need the public spectacle first?"

He has a point, but if I go without the spectacle, she'll slam the door in my face. "I'm trying to make it impossible for her to say no."

"I hope that doesn't make it hard for her to say yes later." Jack arches his eyebrows.

Truthfully, I haven't thought that far in advance. All I've done is organize Operation Get Her to Talk to Me. The rest will fall into place. A long time ago, I was her kryptonite. God knows she's always been mine.

The doors split as we walk toward the set. Jack heads to the stage and I stand in the wings, waiting to make my entrance.

By midnight tonight, she'll realize I'm done with our unspoken truce.

I'm coming for you, Ellie.

Jackson gives his rambling introduction, then I strut onto the set. The crowd goes wild, and I drop into my seat. I adjust my jacket and wave to the audience as the screams die down.

Jackson's right about one thing: Ellie will not take this well.

THREE

Ellie

Present Day

My Google Alerts tell me Wyatt's on *The Jackson Billows Show* to promote his latest movie. Every time I try to convince myself it's normal to have an alert on for my former boyfriend from ten years ago, I realize I sound crazy. I avoid analyzing it. I don't follow him on social media, so the notifications are it. #Wyllie will never make a return.

While I fold laundry, I flip to the right station and dial my sister. She'll still be awake. As a real estate agent, she keeps the weirdest hours of anyone I know.

Nikki doesn't say hello like a normal person; instead, she says, "I hope you had a good flight. You're not watching *The Jackson Billows Show*. Please tell me you've turned off the TV."

"My flight was fine," I say. "It's idle curiosity." I tuck the phone between my ear and neck. Calling her was a bad idea.

"You call it curiosity, I call it obsession." Nikki's voice is tight with disapproval.

"Tomayto, tomahto. How's Haven?"

"She's sleeping. All okay. Want me to drop her off after school tomorrow?"

"Do you mind?" I finish the last piece of folding. Wyatt struts onto the stage, and I realize my screen needs to be bigger. So much bigger. "Oh," I breathe.

"I'll let you go." Nikki sighs.

Without comment, I hang up and circle the couch to get comfortable. In these moments, when I'm transfixed and hungry for the sight of him, a little voice in my head tells me something isn't quite right. Ten years and just a glimpse of him on a television is enough to scrape off the scab, leaving behind raw, tender skin. His effect on me is a burn that won't heal.

Since I left Wyatt ten years ago, acting is a job now, not a lifestyle. I've built a better, more stable life without him, and seeing him shouldn't cause nostalgia for what once was. We were bad for each other—or maybe he was bad for me . . . but in any event, we didn't work, couldn't work.

He takes his seat and I smother the urge to lean forward. I don't see his movies—I'm not interested in pretend-Wyatt—but I can *never* resist his interviews. If I still did drugs, he'd be crack.

They banter about Wyatt's race-car movie. When Wyatt turns on the charm, he is breathtaking. Jackson shuffles the cue cards on his desk after the brief movie clip plays. A nervous habit. I've been a guest on his show enough times to recognize the pattern. I narrow my eyes. He and Wyatt are genuine friends, so his nerves make no sense.

Wyatt appears sober, which is a delightful change. Sober Wyatt wasn't someone I saw very often, but he'd spent years balancing his moods with drugs before we met. Another ten years since to hone his skills to *appear* sober.

His suit fits him like a glove, and seeing him so together stirs long-buried desires. My eyes travel the length of his body, taking in his dark hair, broad shoulders, and narrow hips. When he gestures to Jackson, his biceps flex under the suit coat. He looks good—too good.

No. No. No. If I saw him in person, I'd run the other way. I've been turning away with military precision for ten years. Sober, witty Wyatt in a nice suit can't change the past, the choices we made.

Jackson squares his shoulders and grins. Wyatt tugs at the neck of his shirt. It's brief, but noticeable. I sit forward. Another nervous habit. There's a vibe between them that I've never seen before.

"Are you single right now?" Jackson's inquiry is a softball. "Anyone special in your life?"

The crowd goes wild, and I cringe. I hate that question—for him, for me.

"You know," Wyatt says, "I've been thinking a lot about old flames still flickering." He winks at the camera.

Jackson laughs. "Old flames. Give us a hint?"

Wyatt opens his jacket and leans against the couch, throwing an arm over the back. Confidence blasts from him like a siren's call. My ship longs to steer toward him.

"Have you got a photo, Jackson? Help a guy out?"

Jackson rotates in his chair and a familiar photograph of the two of us pops up behind him.

There's an explosion in the crowd. My heart threatens to gallop away.

What is he doing?

My phone on the coffee table jumps to life. Nikki's name flashes across the screen. I send her to voicemail. My attention sticks to the screen. When my phone buzzes again, I don't check who it is. I send them to voicemail. Bile rises in my throat, and I swallow it.

Shit. This can't be happening.

The crowd is alive with wolf whistles, catcalls, and screaming. An album of old photos of me and Wyatt flips across the screen.

The memories. Oh, my heart. The memories.

"Ellie Cooper." Wyatt draws out my name like he's licking an ice-cream cone, and his attention is glued to the last photo of us.

Ten years since I've heard my name leave his lips. The genuine animation in him, the love on his face when he stares at the picture, softens me, even as rage builds deep in my gut. He loved me so hard once.

"Have you and Ellie been in touch?" Jackson asks.

I will tear Jackson apart for agreeing to be part of this ridiculous spectacle. He'll never have me on his show again. He's dead to me. I'm half tempted to call my manager right now, but that would mean missing where this is going. Wyatt must realize the storm he's setting off. People still label us #couplegoals. The stories I could tell them . . .

"I'm hoping to be reacquainted with her soon." Wyatt laughs. "Anyone know how I can get in touch with her?" His hopeful bewilderment plays to the crowd. His brazenness is achingly familiar. He wasn't the only one who loved hard.

"Wyllie was huge when you two were together. I think people

even wore T-shirts picking sides when you split. But in the ten years since, neither of you have spoken publicly about what happened."

"Ellie's a classy woman." He holds up a finger. "The best woman. I mean . . ." His expression softens. "That face." He points to another, more recent photo that's appeared behind Jackson. "Brains, beauty, the biggest heart. Our breakup was my fault—completely my fault. I couldn't give up the drugs." He takes a deep breath. "I didn't want to get off them."

"And where are you at now?"

Wyatt or his people approved these questions. Unbelievable. We've never spoken about each other. You ask, you're blacklisted from interviewing me. I assumed Wyatt had the same rule since he's never talked about me either. Our relationship is a void stuffed with public opinion and speculation.

A constant stream of buzzing comes from my phone as calls, texts, and social media notifications flood in. If I ever see Wyatt again, it'll be too soon. I'm ghosting the jackass harder than I've been the last ten years. It might not be possible to intensify our distance any more, considering we haven't shared a room since I left our house, but he's not getting anywhere near me now.

"I've been drug-free for two years now. I'd never tell anyone sobriety is easy, but I'm ready to put the past behind me."

Sure, Wyatt. All talk. He might be sober at *this* moment, but sober for two years? Impossible. His morning routine consisted of popping Vicodin, oxycodone, Percocet, or Adderall and drinking a coffee, often chased with a few shots of Jim Beam or a couple of beers. Lean smoothies of codeine, hard candy, and soda were a favorite snack.

Wyatt, even when he looked sober, was never without

something in his system. His supply was endless and his taste eclectic.

His addictions weren't to be questioned or analyzed, just accepted. One taste. A little buzz to take the edge off. A sharpness that needed to be constantly dulled. For him to be on national television talking about his habits, he must be high.

"I'm sure people battling their demons find a lot of hope in your words." Jackson turns to the audience. "What would it be now? Ten years ago that Isaac Sharma died from an overdose while you and Ellie were with him?"

He's letting Jackson bring up Isaac's death? Talk about a shot to the heart.

"Yeah." Wyatt stares at his hands. "Almost eleven."

There's a deep sadness in Wyatt's voice. Whatever else is going on in this interview, the rawness of his loss remains the same.

"We all expected Isaac's death to be enough motivation for you to get sober."

"It should have been." Wyatt tips his head.

Sometimes I hate myself for watching these interviews. Hearing him talk about Isaac and about me will cause me to spiral into uncertainty for weeks. His movie must be turning into quite a lemon in postproduction if the studio convinced him to get on Jackson's show and talk about the more salacious bits of his life.

"Remind me again where you and Ellie met?" Jackson stares at Wyatt. He knows. Everyone knows. We had the biggest movie in the world the year it came out.

"On the set of *Love Letters from Spain*," Wyatt says. "There was something about Ellie. Right from the start." His eyes bore into the camera, coming through the screen, threatening to burrow into my soul. "I was a fool to let her go, but I'm not a fool anymore."

In a panic, I turn off the TV and stare at the blank screen. Then I flick it back on.

The crowd quiets, and Jackson laughs. "You're going to reignite #Wyllie fans."

He did *not* do that. Another great rush of humming comes from my phone, but I refuse to acknowledge the notifications. People can think what they want. I answer to no one. Besides, I'll have levitated off Bermuda and be landing in New York to commit Jackson's murder soon.

"Maybe they deserve to be reignited." A cocky, playful smile bursts onto his face.

This time when I switch off the TV, I do it with finality. We wouldn't have needed to be reignited if the jackass chose me instead of an eight ball.

Emotions dash through me, hard to identify. Anger, for sure. Fear. But under those is one I don't want to consider because it feels a lot like hope. What could I hope for? He's lying. Wyatt lies. He's not sober. Drugs have been part of his life for as long as he can remember. His constant companions were his prescription pill bottle stuffed with whatever he could get his hands on and a water bottle of codeine, soda, and hard candy mixed together. Lean was his drink of choice.

One of the first memories he told me about was sitting beside his dad and being offered a glass of lean. Those first sips tipped Wyatt and his younger sister, Anna, into a spiral of addiction. Neither of them ever had any desire to climb out. They blamed their parents for their troubles, and I never doubted they were a huge factor in Wyatt and Anna's issues. According to Wyatt, his parents were always desperate for their next fix, and they didn't mind who paid for it or what it cost. But any suggestion of Wyatt or Anna seeking help was met with resistance. They were content to wallow in their dysfunctions. To think Wyatt ditched it all two years ago is impossible for me.

I pray my manager is mobilizing my PR staff, otherwise this stunt could spin out of control. It took years for the swirl surrounding our breakup to die enough for me to be able to spend time in Los Angeles. Any trips there were carefully coordinated to avoid paparazzi. Those damn team T-shirts were everywhere, breaking my heart, mocking my choice.

In a daze, I wander the narrow hall to my bedroom at the rear of my home. Although I can afford a lavish house, I have a small three-bedroom bungalow on an oceanfront lot. Nothing fancy, but it suits my needs. When I have to, I put on the glitz and glamor, but for the most part, I'm hidden away here in Hamilton, Bermuda. The frantic pace of Los Angeles is kept at bay by careful scheduling and an adherence to privacy above all else. The Hollywood pomp and circumstance were never for me; just the right place and people. Wyatt never understood that.

My security intercom buzzes, and I answer the nearest receiver. "Headed to bed, Freddie. What's up?"

"Uh, Ellie, there's a man here who wants to see you."

"It's late. I have jet lag. No one who knows me would come this late."

I've made sure my house is hard to find. Entrances and exits are concealed by overgrown bushes and shrubs. The property is gated and not listed on any documents that are easy to access. Cab drivers and sightseeing tours get a hefty donation at the end of their high season if they haven't used my name or property to advertise their businesses. Extreme privacy has been my companion since I left Wyatt and Los Angeles behind.

"It's Mr. Wyatt Burgess, and he says he isn't leaving until you agree to speak to him."

Ice freezes in my veins and then fire chases it out. Turns out I don't need to levitate off the island to commit murder tonight. "Oh, Freddie. I have a thing or two to say to Mr. Burgess. You can deliver him to the door."

"Yes, ma'am." A grin is evident in his voice. He must have watched *The Jackson Billows Show* too. With the show taped in the late morning, Wyatt had lots of opportunities to hop on a two-hour flight here. Never occurred to me he would.

I check my appearance in the kitchen mirror and then scold myself. I'll open the door only to tell him to go to hell. Using national television to declare his undying love after ten years and a series of bad choices and then expecting me to take him back?! I don't think so. Not happening.

At the side entrance where expected guests are delivered, I swing the door wide.

Immediately, I realize my mistake. He's taller than I remembered, which seems ridiculous. That's not all, though. His dark hair is a little darker, and his blue-green eyes more electric. Without the barrier of the screen, everything jumps at me at once.

My heart does one loud, crushing thump and falls to pieces.

Ten years, gone in a heartbeat.